Scion

Dawn of Midnight

Chellé Luckie

Global Book
Publishing

Scion
Chellé Luckie
©2023 Chellé Luckie. All rights reserved.

ISBN: 978-1-956193-48-0
Book Design & Publishing done by:
Global Book Publishing
www.globalbookpublishing.com

To those who always believed and encouraged me.

Good Morning
Astra

There was no sound, and the image before her eyes was blurry. She felt heavy and sticky with sweat. Astra tried to wake herself from the nightmare. Trying to force the image to stay blurry and far away, she prayed for Haiel to take the horror away. Yet, the more she struggled, the more the image came into focus. Her friend stood in front of her, not quite angry but not happy either. His umber-brown complexion warmed in the sunlight, and he scratched his scalp through his thick dark-brown locs. He raised his gray eyes, and she moved to close the distance between them.

Following a loud bang that sounded like a fire-work, heat warmed her cheek. She frowned, raising her hand to her face, but the flood of red liquid oozing out of her friend stole her breath. She collapsed to the ground in tandem with his body. Panicked movements ensued as she tried to catch him while his wide terrified eyes searched hers for answers she didn't have.

She heard her panicked voice as she strained her vocal cords. "HELP!"

Strong hands gripped her shoulders yanking her from her soaked sheets.

"Malina, open your eyes, sweetheart." Her father's deep voice soothed her, and he combed his fingers through her tangled wavy black hair.

She obeyed, seeing his tired green eyes, which matched her own. His face was weary and his eyes were downcast. "Don't cry," he pleaded.

A moment later, her mother's icy tone chilled the room. "Malina, this cannot continue." The finality of these words made her eyes sting. Her skin was sepia brown, only a shade lighter than her father's. Her reddish-brown hair was braided back from her face. With glacial-blue eyes, her mother surveyed her reaction with cold intensity.

"Elizabeth, not now," her father said, releasing Astra and easing off her bed.

"Then *when*, Victor?" Elizabeth demanded, "when Evaline is failing classes because Malina constantly wakes her through the night with her screaming?"

"Can we at least talk about it downstairs?" Victor asked. A pregnant pause grew between them. Elizabeth looked at Astra's face with disgust and then back to her husband. She pulled her black silk robe closer around her and nodded before turning to leave the room. Victor sighed and looked back to Astra. "I'll make you breakfast, be down at the usual time, okay?"

Astra nodded her response, and her father tapped the door frame before turning away and closing the door behind him. Astra arose, stripping her wet sheets and opening her bedroom window. A slight breeze eased through, fluttering the curtains. The sun had just begun to rise, waking the birds as her parents began their argument downstairs. Feeling defeated and tired, Astra rested her body on her window seat.

Her sister's gentle voice stirred her. "Morning, Azzie."

"Angel," Astra responded, startled, looking at her gentle hazel eyes. She'd gotten their mother's dark-brown complexion. She wore a red sports bra and matching red leggings.

"Heading out already?" Astra asked.

"Yeah, I made the team, so I gotta go to practice," Angel stated, showing off the tracksuit jacket that displayed their school's mascot.

"Right," Astra said softly and turned away to look out the window.

"Astra, you know stopping your life won't bring him back, right?" Angel said callously.

Astra looked back at her, dumbfounded.

"I just mean," Angel began and stopped, searching her brain for her next words. "You weren't his girlfriend."

"Angel," Astra groaned, pinching the bridge of her nose. "He was my friend. He was my best friend's boyfriend. We spent a lot of time together, and he died in front of me. I see him die every night!" Astra shouted, feeling her chest tighten.

Her sister sighed and shifted her feet. "Well, I'm sure if he was still kickin', he wouldn't want you holed up in your room every day," Angel said with an uncomfortable look on her face.

"Don't you have a practice to go to?" Astra asked, running her fingers through her tangled hair.

"Evaline, come on!" their mother called, ending the conversation. Astra looked at her sister and then away to their backyard.

"You know," Angel began again, "you were supposed to be here with me, on the team. I mean—"

"Okay, but I'm not," Astra snapped, rising from the window seat and walking over to her sister. "I'm grieving, I'm having nightmares, and I can't stop shaking!" Astra yelled into her sister's face. Astra watched her sister tremble, and guilt mounted in her already tight chest. "Angel, I'm—"

"Evaline, get to the car," Elizabeth said, the temperature dropping around them. Angel backed away and walked downstairs, past their mother, and out the front door. Astra looked to her mother, whose face was strained from clenching her jaw, holding back what she wanted to say. Astra knew she was upset by how she'd been acting.

"Mom, I—" Astra began and stopped when Elizabeth rose her hand and shook her head. She turned away from Astra and followed Evaline's route out of the house.

Astra walked to her desk, which was covered in neatly stacked books about Hiboria. In the middle of the clutter of loose papers filled with scrawled notes lay a notebook. She picked up the notebook her father had given her a week after Azazel's death and opened to the first page. She wrote down the date and beside it printed, "*Same shit different day.*"

Her eyes traveled up the page to the first entry where she detailed the nightmare and then down the page to entries that were similar to the one she'd written today. She closed the journal with a sigh and gathered her damp sheets.

Upon starting the wash, she heard the sizzle of food cooking. She thought to go sit down and watch her father cook like she had for the past three weeks, but she stopped when she remembered the anguished look on his face. She sighed and decided to shower instead. She grabbed an oversized green shirt and dark denim-blue capris. She waited for the shower water to warm. Then, for the first time in weeks, she looked at herself in the mirror. Her dark-black hair looked matted in certain areas from lack of care. There were dark bags under her green eyes. Unlike her sister, her complexion mirrored her father's earthy hue. Usually, she would be darker, but her seclusion had lightened her to a raw honey hue.

Having showered and dressed, she silently walked downstairs, violently brushing the stubborn knots out of her hair. The sound of another feminine voice broke her concentration only after she made it to the kitchen island, which they also used as a bar. Astra blinked her eyes and looked at her friend, feeling stunned and blindsided.

Tracy was wearing a black hoodie and what looked like sleeping shorts. She had an amber complexion with dirt-brown freckles. Her cloudy green eyes sparkled when she spoke and laughed with Astra's father but dimmed when they fell upon Astra. Tracy's curly ginger hair was tied in a messy bun that sat on top of her head. Sadness and anger filled Tracy's eyes, freezing Astra in the confused unknown. She wasn't sure whether to back to her room or wrap her in a hug.

"Malina," her father said, calling her name and pulling her from her thoughts. "You're late for breakfast," he said lightly, placing a warm plate of scrambled eggs, bacon, and hashbrowns in front of the stool by Tracy.

"I took a shower today," Astra said numbly easing onto the stool.

"Malina?" Tracy said, working the name in her mouth with a sigh. "I haven't heard them call you that since you started high school."

"It's the only thing that brings her back," her dad said quietly, looking at the pills the Shikka had prescribed with distaste.

"I see," Tracy said. Taking a deep breath, she turned and faced Astra. "We're going to school today," Tracy explained.

"What?" Astra asked, dropping a piece of meat from her mouth.

"Tracy," Victor groaned, shaking his head.

"Is mom behind this?" Astra asked, feeling her chest tighten with panic.

"No," Victor said, shaking his head, "your mother wants to send you to the boarding school in Hemlock."

The room grew quiet, and Tracy's mood darkened. "You can't be serious," she protested. Victor looked hopelessly at Astra. "You're refusing the counselor, you're refusing to go to school, and now you're self-isolating," he said.

Astra licked her lips and sighed. "I just need time," she began.

"It's been a month, and you barely leave the room," Victor countered.

"You aren't being fair," Astra said, her voice breaking.

"Sweetie," Victor said in a softer tone, "you refuse to see Gabriel, and Tracy tells me you haven't been returning her calls."

Astra glared at the side of Tracy's stony face.

"Don't you dare snap at her. She loved Azazel too," her father added.

"Fine, then just send me away!" Astra yelled, pushing away from the bar.

"Astra," Tracy said in a strained voice. Astra stilled at her friend's voice, fighting her uneasy nerves. "It's one day at school, and lucky you, it's *Friday*," Tracy said in a high exaggerated voice. "Just one day ... for me?"

Confrontation

A stra agreed after what felt like an hour of silence—at which point her father and Tracy released their breath in unison. As they ate, Astra watched her father breathe easier as though he had just pressed in the last puzzle piece of a giant jigsaw. She hadn't noticed until now, but her father looked slimmer, and the bags under his eyes matched her own.

"Dad?" Astra began and stopped when he met her eyes.

"Yes, sweetheart?" he said, automatically. All the questions she wanted to ask died on her tongue.

"Are you going to work today?" she asked instead. He shook his head and crossed his arms over his chest.

"Let's see how today goes, okay?" he said with a tight smile and moved her empty plate to the sink.

"Thanks for the food, Mr. V," Tracy said, handing him her plate and rising from her stool. "We can still make it on time if we leave now," Tracy urged.

"Okay," Astra mumbled, walked around the bar, and gave her father a hug. "I love you, Daddy," she said into his shoulder. He rubbed her back and kissed the crown of her still wet hair.

"Do you want to take a pill?" he asked before she rounded the corner. She looked at the bottle for a long time and then shook her head.

"I can't focus properly on them," she said— something her father already knew. Then, she followed Tracy out the door, grabbed a pair of shoes she kept outside of the house and slipped them on.

"Why have you been avoiding Gabe?" Tracy asked as soon as they stepped outside.

"I just haven't been feeling like making conversation," Astra said evasively.

Tracy stared at her for a long moment, then shook her head as she walked toward her new car.

"Can't believe your mom is gonna send you away," Tracy said, bursting into a fit of manic laughter. "What am I saying? Of course, the ice queen would do that," Tracy said—more to herself than Astra.

Tracy's father was a car maker. He'd invented all of the vehicles the Shikka used for their covert missions. When he wasn't busy designing vehicles that blended into the night or refracted light by day, he designed safe and ultra-smart cars for the everyday person. And because Tracy was his daughter and he wanted her to remain safe from a distance, he would have her drive the latest model of everything he invented.

The car she was driving today was gray on the outside and built like a box. It was a two-seater, but the back was open with plenty of trunk space. The vehicle appeared to have room for seats in the back, but they'd been removed. Tracy waved her wrist over the driver-side handle, and the doors unlocked for them.

Astra slid inside, and the car system roared to life.

"Welcome back, Tracy. I see—"

"Silence," Tracy snapped, and the automated system obeyed. Tracy tapped in the address to the school.

"Would you like me to drive?" the car asked.

"Yes," Tracy stated and strapped in her seatbelt before the system prompted her to do so.

"That's convenient," Astra marveled. Tracy looked at her for a long time before shrugging and looking away.

Tracy reached under her seat and pulled out a brown paper bag, it was crumbled around an unknown alcohol bottle that sloshed as she swayed.

Tracy's drinking again, Astra thought sadly and looked away from her friend as a chill worked through her body. Tracy tapped her shoulder and extended the bottle to her.

"I'm only seventeen," Astra said, and Tracy scoffed.

"That never stopped you before."

"I don't want to be drunk at school," Astra tried again. Tracy shrugged and tilted her head back with the bottle wincing at the burn as it coursed down her throat. "Do your parents know you started again?" Astra asked.

Tracy scoffed again. "They aren't going to stop me," Tracy shrugged. "We don't all have a Victor for a daddy," Tracy said mournfully, taking another swig.

"Tracy," Astra pleaded and reached for the bottle.

"No!" Tracy snapped, and Astra pulled away. Tracy stared at her and then burst into laughter. "You see, that's all I have to do ..." With that, she shrugged and twisted the top back onto the bottle. "Yell a little, and they all back away, unsure of what to do next."

"You can come stay with me—"

"I don't want to stay with you," Tracy snapped. "You haven't talked to me or anyone since it happened! Like you're the only one affected by his death," Tracy hissed. "Well, I'm affected, too. I may not have seen him die, but I lost him all the same. It *hurts* all the same."

"Tracy, I just don't know what to say," Astra explained, playing with her cold fingers.

"You didn't have to say anything! You could have just sat with me, instead of leaving me alone with no one!"

"You didn't have no one," Astra said.

"My parents couldn't be bothered on a good day, Azzie," Tracy snapped, making Astra flinch.

"If you need to talk about it," Astra said, looking at the side of Tracy's stoic face, "you should."

"Just not with *you*," Tracy said, shifting in her seat.

"I promise to be better," Astra stated, playing with her fingers to relieve her tension. "I know I disappeared after it happened," Astra said, her voice dropping as her discomfort built.

"He died," Tracy said plainly as they came to a stoplight. Tracy looked at Astra straight on, her eyes a dark brown against her pale face. "That's what happened. He died, and the last person to see him alive was you," Tracy said bitterly. Astra swallowed her guilt and looked away from Tracy's prodding eyes.

"Do you think I wanted that to happen?" Astra demanded. The silence stretched between them.

"No, of course not," Tracy said quietly, looking down at the brown bag. "Why did he take you there?"

"What?" Astra asked, confused by the question and the fog pervading her memory of that day.

"He took you to Old Lady Bella, but you didn't have any bags," Tracy explained. "What were you doing there?"

"I don't remember," Astra said honestly.

"You don't remember?" Tracy scoffed and shook her head before taking another swig, "I just don't understand."

"I didn't choose for him to take me there, and everything else gets overshadowed by the fact that he died," Astra explained, shifting in her seat.

"Are you hiding something?" Tracy asked blatantly.

"What! No!" Astra exclaimed. Her heart broke for her friend and the accusation. "I honestly just don't remember anything," she said, her lip trembling. "I told the Carabinieri everything I knew. He was my friend too," Astra said, unable to keep the hurt from her voice as the car came to a halt in the school parking lot. "I want his killer to be brought to justice."

"I know," Tracy said in a sad lonely voice. She nibbled on her fingernail and looked out the window away from Astra. "You were researching Hiboria right?"

"Yeah," Astra said. "Why?"

"Is Hiboria dangerous?"

"Hiboria is a location," Astra explained, "a location, in itself, can't be dangerous ... but hold up. You think I got him killed?" Astra asked, tears brimming in her eyes.

"Why else would the Carabinieri take their time like this?" Tracy asked.

"He was affiliated with the Kipi. Maybe they just want to make sure they're doing everything right," Astra explained.

"Bullshit," Tracy said, her green eyes darkening with specks of brown. "Someone in the Shikka is involved; that's the only reason why the Carabinieri would take their time with an investigation," Tracy raged. "The Shikka have gotten rid of people before!"

"Tracy, you sound crazy," Astra said gently. She eyed the brown bag and sighed. "Lay off the alcohol?"

"Don't tell me what to do!" Tracy snapped. "You know you're the worst!"

"What? That's not true!" Astra protested.

"You know what's not cool?" Tracy hissed, "You! Your mother is the ice queen bitch of the Shikka who has cursed more of the Kipi's children than I can count. Your uncle is the dark prince—a tyrannical investigator who causes most of his victims to commit suicide afterward. And then Gabe—"

"Shut your mouth," Astra warned, unbuckling her seatbelt. "Anyone but him!" Astra snapped, pointing a finger at her face.

"Just get out," Tracy demanded, unlocking Astra's door.

Astra yanked her door open and stepped outside of the car.

"Tracy, I'm sorry," Astra said. "I love you, but you can't lash out at me like this. It's not fair ..." Astra rubbed at her burning eyes and glared at Tracy.

"Fuck you," Tracy snapped, pressing on the gas, revving off after slamming the car door in Astra's face.

Astra placed her hands over her face and crouched down and let out a guttural scream. The school bell ringing behind her caught her attention, so she synched her ragged breathing with the chimes and slowly calmed herself. Astra forced herself to her feet and looked up at the front of her red brick school building. She rubbed at the gooseflesh that covered her arm and crossed her arms over her chest. *I don't want to do this,* was the thought that repeated in her mind. She was cold, tired, and angry from the discussion she just had. She loved Tracy, but hanging out with Kipi members was bad for her.

The Kipi breeds bigots, Astra thought as she walked toward the school. *Well, that's not true; they breed skeptics.*

The Kipi was composed of Gio adults—adults whose megin didn't awaken. Everyone had megin. Most people just didn't have enough for an affinity—or enough to manipulate majik. *If my megin activated, would she hate me too?* Astra thought, climbing the steps. Her mother was a Bahkir with an affinity for Cryokinesis. Her father was a Gio, like herself and Evaline, but they were expected to turn because of how strong their mother and uncle were. *Well, next year is the year of truth. If it doesn't happen then, it won't happen at all ... or at least it usually doesn't.*

"Hey, the bell just rang. Are you coming in?" a random girl asked, holding the door open for her. Astra hadn't realized she had walked up the stairs of Valley High until the girl spoke to her. She walked through the entrance, still holding herself for warmth, when the girl spoke again. "Are you a visitor?" the kind girl asked.

"Hmm. What?" Astra asked dumbly.

"The office is right there," the girl offered and rushed off in the direction of her first class.

Astra sighed and thought about calling her father or just hanging out on the steps until school was over. *But that's definitely condemning myself to Hemlock*, Astra thought mournfully. She took in a deep breath and walked into the front office.

An older woman looked over her glasses to Astra's face and smiled brightly at her. "Ah, Malina, how wonderful to see you in school today," the receptionist said, beaming.

"Yes, ma'am," Astra said. "I go by my middle name, Astra ..."

"Of course you do. What can I help you with?"

"My schedule, please," Astra requested.

Acclamation

Astra stepped out of the main office, looking over her schedule one final time when the tardy bell rang overhead. She placed a hand on the side of her temple and grimaced at the sound.

She regretted not taking the medication as the day dragged on; the side effects scared her, but not feeling anything became more and more appealing as the pain showed up in various ways. She climbed the stairs two at a time and took her time walking the rest of the way to her first class. When she reached her destination, she felt queasy. *Maybe I should just go home*, she thought, feeling herself start to panic.

"You're here?" a semi-deep voice said from behind her.

Astra barely fought off the chill when she turned to face her ex-boyfriend. He was tall with shaggy-brown hair and dirt-brown eyes. His amber complexion was warm and dark from the sun. Her eyes were drawn to his heaving chest where the mist on his skin slid to meet the plain black shirt that clung to his body.

"You're sweaty," Astra said with disdain and opened the door to her class, hoping to put some distance between them.

"Miss Valeno," the female teacher said with an annoyed sigh, "and Mr. Gallen," she added, faking a smile and waving to the back of the classroom. "Please take your seats so I can continue my lecture."

Troy walked past her, grabbing her hand as he led her to the back. Astra eased her hand out of his grasp and took her seat, staring straight into the back of the head of the boy in front of her. The teacher droned on about the importance of something Astra didn't care about. She was too distracted by the waves of color that flooded her eyes. She stretched and rubbed at her eyes, hoping that her fatigue wouldn't make her fall asleep in class. A piece of paper slid onto her desk, causing the hair on her arms to rise.

Astra looked at Troy with annoyance, but he only frowned, awaiting her response. Astra sighed and looked down at the paper to humor him. She didn't sway either way when it came to her feelings for Troy. He wasn't even a means to an end like her previous boyfriends, but he definitely wasn't someone she chose for herself. She scoffed at the fleeting thought. *When have I ever done anything for myself?* She mused as she read his neat writing on the page.

"Are you okay? I've been trying to reach you. Why haven't you answered my calls or texts? The Carabinieri have been questioning me. What did you tell them?"

Astra licked her dry lips and held her hand out looking at him expectantly. He handed her a pencil and tapped his finger impatiently on the top of his desk. Astra twirled the pencil around in her hand as she thought of her response. She took her time thinking because she honestly didn't know where to begin ... and partly because she knew it annoyed Troy to wait. If this had been about anything else, she would have smirked at his discomfort and rolled her eyes at his selfishness. Now, she stilled, looking down at his last question. *"What did you tell them?"*

"I don't know."

She wrote it down without punctuation— leaving it open-ended on purpose although he would think she was being lazy or spiteful. Her pencil hovered over the paper to write more, but she had nothing left in her.

"I don't know," she whispered to herself.

"What?" he asked, leaning out of his seat to get closer to her.

"So impatient," Astra muttered, feeling annoyed by his closeness.

"This is my life, and I deserve to know what you told them," Troy demanded. Astra met his angry brown eyes and remembered the sweat that glistened his skin.

"Why were you late to class?" Astra asked, changing the subject. His thick eyebrow arched up and he leaned back.

"Even if you hadn't dumped me," he began, leaning toward her, glaring, "you ghosted me for the rest of the summer. You don't deserve to know anything about where I spend my time."

Astra sat back in her chair and focused on the soft curls of the boy in front of her. Troy followed suit, tapping a pencil against the desk in tandem with the nervous bounce of his leg. *Monday I'll be on time and sit up front,* Astra promised herself. Then, she released an annoyed sigh and looked in Troy's direction. He lazily turned his head to face her and raised his eyebrow.

"Stop," Astra whispered. Troy stilled and shifted his gaze to the paper in front of her and then back to her face.

When Astra didn't move to write back, his tapping started up again.

Rage boiled inside of her, threatening to blind her completely. She pressed her hands to her desk to keep them from balling into fists.

There's no reason for me to be this angry, Astra thought, panicked, as her breath came quick and shallow. *Troy loves getting under people's skin. I already know this*, she thought, scolding herself for reacting this way.

Suddenly, a warm soft hand touched her elbow, and Astra jumped so violently that she scooted her desk away, causing the teacher to look at her in alarm.

Troy had touched her with his familiar hot hands. She moved away from him and stood up from her desk. She felt disgusted and sweaty with shame. She looked at Troy, confused by his hurt expression ... but more confused by the purple hue that surrounded him.

"Miss Valeno," the teacher said, demanding her attention.

"What is it?" Astra demanded harshly, flinching at her own tone. *What is wrong with me?*

"You can't sleep in my class," the teacher said gently and raised her hand as Astra opened her mouth for a rebuttal. "You were called to room eighty-two."

"Oh," Astra said, tucking a strand of hair behind her ear. "I'll go then," she mumbled, turning away from her teacher and staring at her classmates. When she reached the door, she looked back at her teacher, who was fixing her desk, and Troy, who was looking over the note. "Sorry," Astra said and then left the room.

Astra walked to an empty wall and rested her head against the cool cream-colored brick. Her vision filled with kaleidoscopic colors, and her body chilled more and more with an unexplained coldness. She patted her pockets and sighed when she confirmed that she hadn't brought her phone. *Maybe I can find Evaline at lunch*, Astra thought as she moved through the halls toward the large unused classroom. She wondered if her father had secretly arranged for a therapist to meet with her.

"Tell me, Malina," Astra said mockingly, "which part of the event was the most triggering for you ..." She scoffed to herself and twisted the doorknob to open the door.

The classroom's setup made Astra frown. All of the desks except for one had been shoved to one side of the room and stacked on top of each other to provide more space. In the middle of the room was one student desk and then the teacher's desk. A detective sat on the other end of the teacher's desk, and the female version of Azazel sat on top of the desk, looking pensive and concerned.

"Um," Astra said reflexively to buy her brain time to catch up. "Matoya?" Astra said, drawing the attention of Azazel's sister. The silver eyes from her nightmare bore into her face. Matoya was wearing a red pantsuit and a black top. She straightened, slid off the desk, and walked toward the student desk, tapping the top of it.

"Nice for you to finally join us, Malina ..."

Release the Veil
Gabriel

Gabriel stretched as he walked out of his first class with his new charge taking her time trailing behind him. It amused him how interested she was with the mundane structure of a Gio's life. It bored him to tears. Gios had the luxury of understanding and knowing the details of the life of a Bahkir because the megin would only sometimes activate in their body. Scientists weren't sure if it was a matter of anatomy, genetics, or a stressor that causes the megin to activate. They only knew it to lie within all, and like other genetic traits, it could remain dormant for one generation and grow stronger than ever in the next.

"That was informative," Remilda said behind him as she looked over her notes.

"Sure it was," Gabriel mused slowing his pace so he could walk beside her.

She was always taking notes or looking over the notes she had just taken—and she always took so many. *What a nerd*, Gabriel thought, chuckling thinking about Astra. For the past two years, she'd looked into Hiboria for Juniper. Optimistically, he hoped she would start looking again, but it wasn't the right time to talk to her about it. She was still suffering after what had happened to Azazel, and he couldn't add another tragedy to her shoulders.

"Gabriel!" Remilda shouted right into his ear.

"Ow," he winced and looked down at her apologetically. "Lost in thought," he said with a shrug ... and a smile that made most girls melt. Remilda, however, wasn't like most girls.

Remilda wasn't from Ekocia. She was here on government business as an ambassador. She was smarter and more curious than other girls. *Not Astra, though*, he thought with fondness. *No one is more curious than Astra.*

Remilda had mahogany-colored eyes and tree-bark-brown skin. In her braided hair, there were streaks of green, making Gabriel believe she was more fun than she let on. Since she'd been under his watch, all she did was go to school, to the library, or to the local herbal store for research.

"You're always doing that," she complained. "I asked you a question," Remilda said in her thick native accent.

"And what was it?" Gabriel asked, smiling when she sighed and rolled her eyes.

"Your friend that you mentioned once before," Remilda, said jogging his memory. "Will you take me to meet her?"

"Meet *her*," Gabriel repeated. "Do you mean Astra?"

Remilda nodded slowly, coming to a hault she placed her notes in her binder.

"You said I would," Remilda said with an expression that was supposed to make her look stern, but her full round face was full of cute impatience.

Gabriel often traveled to Serinytas to retrieve their ambassador in Dante's stead. On the latest trip, he had expected Juniper but found Remilda. And she was breathtaking.

She'd looked at him with those beautiful browner-than-red eyes—eyes almost like his own— and he wondered if Serinytas was where his own family had come from.

The first thing she'd asked him was if he knew her mother. Then: "Do you know someone named

Malina? And if you do could you arrange a meeting? I have urgent questions to ask her."

"What do you want with her?" Gabriel had demanded.

"Answers. She was the last person to see my mother alive," Remilda said with a determined expression.

"Well, princess," he'd replied with equal determination, "you'll see her, but only on my terms."

"Gabriel!" Remilda snapped, at her wit's end, pulling him back to the present, "we spent two months together. Are you telling me you still don't trust me?" she asked, exasperated.

"No, that's not what I'm saying," he said, running his fingers through his short curly hair.

"Gabe!" Troy's familiar voice broke into their conversation.

Gabriel turned to the boy and gave him a handshake that turned into a quick embrace. Pulling back, he saw the pained expression on his face that he disguised with a bright smile.

"You saw her today?" Gabriel asked, surprised.

"Her who?" Remilda demanded. "Malina?" Remilda stated, staring back and forth between the two boys in front of her.

"Y-yeah," Troy stuttered, looking at Remilda for the first time. "No one but her family calls her that, though," Troy replied.

"When did you see her? Is she in school?" Gabriel asked.

"Yeah," Troy said, reluctantly taking his eyes off Remilda, "she got pulled out of class to talk to the Carabinieri detectives," he said and then looked back to Remilda. "My friend is dense ..." He smiled, sticking his hand out to Remilda. "My name is Troy Gallen."

"I don't care," Remilda said and shoved past Troy to race after Gabriel.

Gabriel felt rage build in his chest as he used his long stride to race toward where he knew Astra to be. He hadn't talked to her since he returned from Serinytas. As soon as he'd stepped onto Ekocia soil, he was ambushed with the news of his best friend dying. He went to the Kaine household to give his condolences but was met with shock and egregious accusations. Dante was able to get him out of their home before they were able to do anything, but he was still rattled.

"Dante, they think I killed Azazel," he lamented. "He was my best friend and—"

"Stop," Dante said, grabbing him by his shoulders. "Pull yourself together, and don't come back to this town," he ordered. "We have the best Bahkir on the case. We *will* get to the bottom of this, but in the meantime, maintain your composure and only grieve in private."

Gabriel did exactly as Dante said, focusing on Remilda, determined to figure her out. Last week, he'd decided she was someone worthy of trust and reached out to Astra. She didn't pick up or text back, so he reached out to Tracy, and she told him Astra wasn't talking to anyone.

"Azazel was shot right in front of her," Tracy said softly. Gabriel heard liquid sloshing followed by a loud gulp.

He sighed her name. "Trace ..."

"It's not considered a lapse if you're grieving," Tracy joked dryly.

Gabriel made time to see Tracy, spending the afternoons with her when he wasn't with Remilda. He'd tried going to Malina's house, but her father either shook his head or Elizabeth would glare him down. Gabriel knew they didn't hate him, but they also made it very clear they didn't approve of the closeness they had for each other. Gabriel was trained to submit to their authority and never broke their rules, but he planned to do that today. *Thank Haiel I don't have to. Ending up a human popsicle wouldn't be great for anyone.*

"The Carabinieri are here interrogating Malina," he said into his phone as soon as his mentor and guardian answered. There was a long sigh, and then Dante's dark voice came through his speaker.

"Stop the investigation, I'm sending Vic over to handle the rest."

Gabriel grabbed the door handle and shoved the door open, locking eyes with a determined Matoya and an uninterested Carabinieri detective. The detective looked up to Gabriel with a sigh and started gathering up his paperwork, but Matoya placed a hand on top of the mess, forcing the detective to stop. Astra slowly turned in her seat to face him.

She looks like shit, Gabriel thought and would have laughed at her if the situation wasn't so damn unfunny. Astra's complexion was pale like she hadn't received any sunlight for a month. Acceptable for the winter but not the summer—not when she was the kind of girl that loved to hike, sunbathe, and swim. Her face was sullen with bags under her usually bright eyes. She looked burnt out, uncomfortable, and cold. *Why is she shivering?* Gabriel pondered as she fought off a chill and goosebumps rose on the flesh of her forearms. Never missing a beat, he slipped off his jacket and draped it over her shoulders.

"Get the fuck out," he said, shooting daggers with his eyes at Matoya.

"This is an open investigation," Matoya stated, standing her ground. "We have every right to re-question a witness if we see fit."

"You don't have any jurisdiction in Meirth," Gabriel growled, glaring at the detective. "You should know that since it's *your* job."

"Matoya, let's go," the detective said with a sigh.

"No," Matoya said calmly. "Gabriel, you killed my brother and you aren't—"

"Shut up!" Astra bellowed. "Stop saying that!"

The hair on Gabriel's arms rose, and his stomach churned with anxiety. He looked behind him, expecting to see Dante, but he wasn't there. Remilda stood at the entrance, wide-eyed and confused. He looked back to Astra, who wasn't breathing properly, and her hand was on her chest like it was hurting her. The detective had risen with all of his evidence packed in his suitcase except for one picture that lay on the desk between them. A black and white picture of someone who looked like him walking away from a crumbled building with a time stamp of that day.

Khalan? Gabriel thought.

"I won't stop until—d" Matoya began, but Astra was out of her seat, her eyes glowing white as the air cooled dramatically around them.

"I said shut up!" Astra said in a voice that didn't belong to her.

Gabriel felt her veil before it happened. He was trained to anticipate a veil so he could arm himself against it thanks to Dante. A veil was an overwhelming burst of megin shoved at someone's psyche ... and if that person was weak or unprepared, they could crumble. Gabriel looked at the detective, who had fallen to the floor, eyes staring at the ceiling. Matoya fell to her knees, shaking her head and frowning at the fog that seemed to be overtaking her mind.

"I f-felt, it was y—" Matoya said, wide-eyed looking at Astra before her eyes rolled back and she dropped to the floor.

Gabriel felt another wave of energy radiate off of Astra as she glared at Matoya. Gabriel's mouth was dry and his heartbeat fast. *It's too similar to Dante's. Can she do what he does?* Gabriel thought, proceeding to push the thoughts aside when he glanced at Remilda who was on her knees, one hand on the door handle to keep her body from falling to the ground. Gabriel closed the distance between himself and Astra. He grabbed her biceps, giving them a light squeeze despite the burning pain the raw megin oozing out of her and into the atmosphere caused him. "Astra, calm down."

"Don't tell me to calm down!" she barked, despite the easing of her veil and the tears flooding down her cheeks.

He lifted a hand to wipe the tears from her face, using his knuckles, but she flinched, pulling away upon contact. "Haiel, what did I do?" she asked, panic causing the veil to grow even stronger.

Gabriel sat her down in the seat and pulled the jacket back around her shoulders and knelt in front of her. "Look at me and breathe when I do," he urged. He clasped his hands around hers and breathed in deeply with his nose and out dramatically with his mouth.

Astra followed his instructions, and the veil slowly returned to her, but the panic was still evident on her face. She looked around, saw the damage she had caused, and slowly closed her eyes, dropping her head to his shoulder.

Ordeal
Victor

Victor climbed the steps and rushed into the evacuated building, hoping another student had set off the megin attack alarms but aware, deep down, that Astra was involved. He felt so stupid for shoving her off to school, but his wife had demanded a change in their daughter. *How was I supposed to know that her megin was activated?* Victor thought in anguish. He hadn't been sleeping well. He spent his nights on the floor outside of Astra's room, and it had been giving him back problems. *It was selfish to push her into going to school today. I should have just put my foot down about the therapist.* He continued to mentally chastise himself as he rounded the corner and was met with a metal wall.

He grimaced at the door and shook his head. *If the neophyte's megin is strong enough, this metal door will mean nothing to them.* He thought about Elizabeth and her Cryo affinity. *Well, maybe it would stop her,* he thought, trying his best to stay positive as he punched in the code that allowed him to move under the metal door. As he crossed the threshold, the door dropped back down. He walked through and felt the uneasy tension in the air. He followed that feeling until his stomach was twisted in knots and he saw a hallway filled with five collapsed students.

Victor carefully stepped over their bodies, pulled out a dart gun, and loaded the nonlethal sleeping darts. He came across an open door and frowned. *Protocol is supposed to shut all doors. What's going on?* He pressed his back to the wall and slowly eased down the hall, gun raised, at last poking his head into the room. Looking down, he found that a young girl had fallen into the threshold, preventing the metal door from slamming down. He looked up from the girl and saw Gabriel cradling Malina in his arms, rubbing her shaking back. Victor pulled back, released a sigh of relief, aimed his gun, and pulled the trigger.

The effects were swift. Malina's limp body fell into Gabriel's embrace. Then, Victor walked into the room, surprised by the girl in the doorway stirring and struggling to stand. Before she could look up and see him, he shot her too. She dropped back to the ground.

"Victor, that was the ambassador," Gabriel scolded.

Victor looked to Gabriel, unphased and unamused by the situation at hand. Gabriel held Malina like she was the most precious person in the world to him. Her head rested in the crook of his neck, her back rested against his bent knee, and she sat on the knee he rested on. He plucked the dart out of her neck and fearlessly glared at Victor.

"Give me my daughter," Victor commanded.

Victor watched Gabriel's anger flare as his red eyes flamed. The vein in his throat bulged as he clenched his jaw. Gabriel looked down at Malina's sleeping face and brought his ochre-brown hand to her brown face, brushing away a strand of hair that fell over her eye and lips off her face. Gabriel took his time and rose to his feet, carrying Malina to Victor. Victor reached out to take her and then stopped when he saw a faint glow coming from her chest.

"Wait, what's that?" Victor asked, causing Gabriel to frown as he looked down at Malina.

"What are you talking about?" Gabriel asked, "I don't see anything."

"Lay her on the table," Victor ordered, walking to where her head would lie.

Gabriel followed the orders immediately, and once she was on the table, Victor tugged at the collar of her shirt, revealing a glowing sigil on her chest. Its intricate shapes were carefully drawn out inside of the glowing white circle.

"How could you allow Elizabeth to do that?" Gabriel criticized. "This is her daughter."

"Gabriel shut up," Victor commanded and picked Malina up off the table. "Watch after the girl you were assigned and leave Malina alone," Victor demanded, heading out of the room.

"Just let her stay with Dante and me," Gabriel pleaded, walking after Victor.

"She's fine where she is," Victor said, walking down the hall, but Gabriel rushed and grabbed his arm to stop him.

"Vic, Elizabeth cursed her daughter. Astra is *not* fine," Gabriel said. "You have to know what that curse has done—"

"Gabriel, I'm her parent. I know what's best for her, and I know my *wife* didn't do this," Victor said with finality and walked out of the school through a side door.

Malina's body painfully chilled his arms, making him wonder how Gabriel was able to withstand the torture. Victor placed Malina on the ground beside his car as he fumbled with the keys, fighting to steady his tremulous hands. *How could Elizabeth do this?* he thought, shaking his head. *Maybe it wasn't her, but the possibility of it being her is too high. She's the one that invented the sigil, and she's the only one who had access to Malina. She's the only one who could have done it.* He placed Malina into the backseat, climbed into the driver seat, and sat down, thinking about what to do next. He placed a call to Elizabeth and waited for her to answer.

"What did the girl do now?" she asked resentfully.

"It's more like what the fuck did *you* do, Elizabeth?" Victor snarled.

"Wh-what?" she asked.

"You hexed her!" he shouted into the mic. "Why the hell did you do that?"

"I didn't," she responded coldly. "I promised I would never touch her, and I kept my word."

"I'm your husband. You really think I wouldn't recognize your sigil?" Victor responded, anger still bubbling in his chest.

"I'm telling you, I. Did. Not. Touch. Her," she said slowly and clearly.

"Who else would—"

"Send me a picture," Elizabeth snapped.

"What?"

"Send me a fucking picture of what you saw," Elizabeth hissed.

"Fine," Victor responded. He turned and reached back to Malina, moving her shirt and turning on his flash to get a shot of the megin sigil. As the light flashed on the sigil, it altered. Victor sucked in his breath and looked at the image and sigil.

"I'm waiting," Elizabeth said impatiently.

"I sent it," Victor said, shining a light on Malina's chest, watching the sigil alter, cementing his gut feeling. *My sister did this.*

"Got it," Elizabeth responded quietly. "It's not mine, but it *is* a good replica," she commented. "I understand why you were confused, but you should trust me more. I didn't do this."

"I believe you," Victor stated, leaning his head back against his headrest. *What the fuck am I going to do now?*

"Victor!" Elizabeth snapped, pulling him from his thoughts.

"What?" Victor groaned.

"I asked you what changed your mind."

"Well," Victor said, buying himself some time. "You get especially cold when you're accused of something you didn't do." Victor hoped the truth was enough to deter her from prying.

"I see," Elizabeth said coolly.

"She's breathing," Victor commented, watching the rise and fall of her chest. "Will the sigil cause her harm?" Victor asked, and Elizabeth sighed.

"The sigil is close enough to mine that it won't," Elizabeth said distantly. "I don't know the user's intent, though. A sigil only works as well as the intent and focus of the person who placed it," Elizabeth explained. "You should bring the girl here so we can check on her and make sure she's okay. That way, we'll get an idea of the person who did this ..." Victor clenched his jaw at the thought of them looking at the sigil and seeing Jade's megin as he had. "Do you know what triggered the sigil?"

"From what I can tell, it was triggered after she released her veil," Victor stated.

"She had a veil surge?" Elizabeth asked quickly.

"Yeah," Victor said with a sigh. "I didn't even know her megin was activated."

"Did you take her off her medication?" Elizabeth demanded.

"Are you implying the drugs that you've been feeding our seventeen-year-old child were to suppress the gift Haiel gave her?" Victor bit out.

"The medication suppresses her memories and kept her appetite up," Elizabeth said with a sigh. "The suppression of her megin was a plus."

"That's not your fucking right, Elizabeth," Victor growled.

"Are we really—"

"Yes!" Victor yelled. "Because that's what you do when you're in a partnership. You discuss the best course of action for your child together," he raged.

"Mmm, I wish you were this passionate about *our* child, too," Elizabeth said snidely.

"For Haiel's sake, Elizabeth, they're both *our* children!" Victor shouted.

Elizabeth sighed and muttered something indistinguishable.

"What did you say?" Victor demanded.

"If that's all," Elizabeth said loud and clear, "I have important things—"

"What's more important than helping your daughter Elizabeth?"

"Evaline is in trouble?" she asked in a way that told Victor she was smiling at her own joke.

"Haiel, why did you give me this woman?" Victor groaned to himself. "How do I break—"

"You don't," Elizabeth said, all humor draining from her voice.

"What?"

"My sigil is created with the intent for the bearer to never be able to use their megin, and only I will be able to remove it. If that sigil is anything like mine, it will be the same. I don't know for sure, though, so you should just bring—"

"No," Victor said abruptly and hung up the phone.

Victor sat quietly and then yelled, punching the steering wheel repeatedly to release his built-up anger. After he calmed down, he looked up into his rearview mirror and saw Malina's face twisted in pain as she breathed out a cloud of air. *A sigil only works as well as the intent and focus of the person placing the sigil. That's what Elizabeth said*, Victor thought. Then, he reached back and touched his daughter's cool skin. It still hurt him to touch her. She was so cold, she was hot. *Would she freeze to death? Is that what Jade wanted? But why?* Victor turned back to the front and placed his finger on his fingerprint scanner to start the car.

Victor pulled out of his parking spot, turning the wheel slowly as he considered where he ought to go. As he started to press on the gas to leave the school grounds, he saw his daughter walking away from the campus. Evaline was wearing leggings and a workout top. Her duffle bag strap was resting on her shoulder, trapping some of her voluminous hair. He pulled up beside her, rolling down the passenger window to glare at her. Evaline froze, her brown face flushing as her eyes grew wide with surprise. *I don't have time for this*, Victor thought with a frown.

"Daddy," she said weakly, her eyes dashing to the side, looking around for an excuse.

"Get in," he demanded. Evaline flushed and looked down at her feet.

"But Dad—"

"I don't care. Get in," Victor stated and waited for her to obey. Evaline sighed and walked over to his car, sliding in and reaching to place her bag in the back when she saw Malina.

"Is she okay?" Evaline asked with genuine concern her eyes wide and fearful when she looked up at him.

"She will be," Victor promised and began driving again. "Were you meeting up with a boy?" he asked directly, making Evaline flush.

"No, Daddy," Evaline said sweetly, looking him directly in the eyes.

"Of course not," Victor grumbled, shaking his head with disappointment. *How can two children be raised in the same house and grow up so differently?* he thought, looking in the rearview mirror at Malina, who reminded him so much of his sister. "Evaline, give me your phone."

"But Dad!" she whined.

"I don't have time for this. Give it here," he ordered, and she obeyed. "I'm not taking you home, but where I'm going to take you, you can't leave the car."

The joyful humor in his daughter's face faded.

"Do you understand?"

"Yes, Daddy," she grumbled and glared out the window as they sped off.

Kore's Palace

Victor stopped outside of a brick mansion that was known as the nightclub Kore's Palace. The parking lot was empty except for a black van, a red sports car, and an older vehicle that he knew belonged to the owner's ward. Victor looked at the time clock on the dashboard that read 4:00 and knew that the club had three more hours before it would open for business and the first few patrons would begin showing up. He looked to his right and found Evaline frowning at their destination. Her mischievous hazel eyes sparkled with curiosity and interest for more information.

"Daddy, why are we here?" Evaline asked with a tilt of her head.

"We're here because I can't trust you to be at home by yourself," Victor said flatly and then looked back to Malina.

His heart plummeted, and he rushed out of his seat and around the car to her side. He opened the door, and she fell out like she was already dead. Malina's lips were blue, and her pallor was decreasing by the second. Her chest was barely moving, so Victor placed two fingers on her throat to make sure she still had a pulse. *Why did I waste so much time?* Victor thought in despair. Evaline screamed, falling to the ground beside him. Tears filled her eyes, and she shook violently. *I should have just left her to her own devices*, Victor thought harshly and then shook the thought away when Evaline's shaky voice called to him.

"Dad—"

"Hush, Evaline," Victor demanded. "Malina's all right," he said clumsily.

"All right? She's blue!" Evaline yelled. "Why is she blue?"

"Because," Victor began and then shook his head. "Too long to explain, and she needs your help now."

Evaline looked queasy like she might vomit.

"Evaline, your sister isn't dead, but she *will* be if you don't help her ..."

This caught Evaline's attention, giving her focus. "What can I do for her? She's never depended on me for anything," Evaline said in a bewildered tone.

"I need you to watch her," Victor explained. "Keep her warm; she's really cold," he added, picking Malina up and placing her in the passenger seat Evaline had ridden in not long ago. "Just stay here and watch her," Victor reiterated, turning on the car and turning up the heat. On his way out, he grabbed and pocketed Evaline's phone.

Evaline's frazzled body shook, but she nodded her head. "Wait," she said, walking away from Malina to follow him. Victor grabbed her by the shoulders and walked her back to Malina's side.

"Don't move, Evaline. Stay right here."

"I'm scared," Evaline complained.

"Damn it, Evaline. I don't ask you to do much," he snapped, breathing out a rugged breath at his frustration. "Just look after your sister this one time," he pleaded. He watched her face fall, her bottom lip tremble, and her eyes begin to water. "Dry your face and watch after your sister," he demanded mercilessly. Evaline nodded, her body still trembling, but it was the best he could ask for. "If it's easier, sit in the car and watch your sister," Victor stated, and Evaline nodded, climbing inside his vehicle.

Breathing out a loud sigh, he rushed toward the mansion and pushed through the double doors. On the bottom floor of the building, the space was cleared out for the dance floor and an ice bar. In the four corners, there were stages with poles for the owner's special dancers. He stepped onto the dance floor and heard the clacking of high heels approaching. He looked up to his left and saw the infamous owner in all of her glory. She wore a black bra with a white button-up flannel she left open, along with a black pen skirt with a slit up the thigh. Her nails were almond-shaped and painted purple to compliment her violet eyes. She smirked at the sight of him, and her catlike eyes sparkled with interest.

"Vicky, darling," she said in a sultry voice, stopping in front of him with both of her hands on her hips. Her long curly hair was twisted and clipped to the back of her head but her long black hair still fell just beneath her ear. "To what do I owe the pleasure?" she teased.

"Is Carina around?" Victor asked. She narrowed her eyes and, with a sigh, shifted her expression again. "There was an incident at the school. They could use her medical expertise," he explained.

"That's not all you want, though, is it, Vicky?" she all but sang.

"Rita," Victor sighed feeling churned up inside, "you don't have to—"

"Why do you feel guilty?" she asked, all sweetness and humor leaving her face.

"I'll tell you everything, but Carina—"

Just then, the door opened behind him, and goosebumps covered his back due to the cold. He turned his head to grant him a side view of the scene behind him. Carina had placed a jacket on Malina and dragged her into the mansion. He panicked partly because he didn't see Evaline until she slowly made her way inside. Victor took a step toward Carina, but Rita blocked his way with a disappointed expression.

Rita clacked her way to a stage Carina dragged her to and placed her on, and Victor slowly walked toward them, watching a ring of fire circle the stage. Rita frowned upon his approach but didn't move to stop him. Carina was nineteen—only slightly older than Malina—and the same age as Gabriel. Unlike his children, Carina hadn't been forced into public education. She studied and was mentored under Rita's supervision. The rumors say she was born with her megin already activated and Rita saw that and groomed her to her advantage.

Victor knew about the sexual deviance that happened at the club, and the way she dressed herself and her girls was always suggestive, but he hadn't believed the rumors. Victor knew her before her world darkened and she fell into the flames that would help to mold her glassy sharp edges.

Carina looked over her shoulder at Victor. She had piercing blue eyes and a round babyface that made her disappointed countenance look cuter than menacing.

Carina was a smart girl, but she was angry with the world. She dyed the naturally dark-brown hair—now returning at the roots—blond and cut it at an angle down to her chin, layering it short in the back. She had seven piercings in her ear and one in her perfectly groomed eyebrow. She never wore makeup, as her natural beauty didn't require it. She wore biker boots, fishnet stockings, leather shorts, and a white crop-top that said Kore's Palace. She donned a large black jacket that only allowed the tips of her fingers to peek through.

Victor saw the blisters and blue hue of her flesh from carrying Malina inside. "You should have just left her where she was," he said, stopping the conversation she was having with Margherita.

Carina squared off with him, wearing a frown on her face. She pointed at him and then, with both hands raised, clawed the open air between them as she pulled her hands back to her chest. She pointed at Malina and raised both of her hands again. Her left hand was palm down and her right was palm up. She flipped them and then placed both hands on her hips and glared at him.

Rita walked over and stood by Carina's side, placing a hand on her shoulder. Carina shrugged her off and was about to resume their conversation, but Rita raised her hand and shook her head.

"You know me, Care," Rita said, pinching Carina's chin gently. "Victor, didn't you have something for Carina to do?" Rita said, not taking her eyes off Carina.

"People were hurt at the school," Victor explained. Carina glared at him, pressing her mouth into a tight line. Victor grabbed his wallet out of his back pocket and Carina held her hand up and shook her head. She stormed out of the building without another attempt at communication. "What did she say to me earlier?" Victor asked, pulling out $400 dollars and handing it to Rita.

"She asked if you wanted Malina to die," Rita sighed with a pouty frown.

"No!" Victor snapped. "That's why I brought her here."

"Then why did you have her in the car without at least the heat on?" Rita asked incredulously.

"I did turn—"

"I turned it off," Evaline's frail voice said.

"What?" Victor asked. "Why?"

"I got hot," Evaline complained, tears welling up in her eyes as sweat beaded her forehead.

"I see," Rita said with a frown on her face.

"Evaline," Victor snapped, stepping toward her.

Rita strode over to stand between them and stared into Victor's eyes.

"Do I need to calm you down or are you in control?" she asked with an amused expression.

Victor breathed in deeply and turned away from them to walk toward Malina. "Do you have homework or something you need to do?" Rita asked Evaline. She nodded her head, and Rita led her to a table off to the side of the dance floor. Then, returning to Victor with a sad smile on her face, she said, "I see you're the type to be mesmerized by fire." With that, she handed him a glass filled to the rim with a strong liquor. The rim was covered in sugar and a slice of lime, and the glass itself was cold so she didn't add any ice.

"What is it?" Victor asked with a frown.

"Medicine," she said with a smile. "For your nerves." She took a sip from her own cup as she walked closer to the fire to peer at Malina. "Elizabeth didn't do this," she added, looking at him over her shoulder.

"How did you know?" Victor asked, fascinated, taking a swig from his cup, satisfied by the contents. "This is probably the best Margarita I've ever had," he muttered, smiling at a distant memory.

"Well, that's how I got the name," Rita teased, "but back on topic, she's crystalizing too fast. When was the sigil placed?"

"That's the thing. I'm not sure."

"Why did you bring her here and not take her to base?" Rita asked, crossing her arms.

"I need your help, not theirs," Victor explained, and Rita frowned at that. "I need your discretion."

Rita looked back at the sigil and then to Victor.

"So her *mother* did this," Rita concluded, her eyes shifting to a red hue.

"The megin matches," Victor said softly.

"Why are you protecting her? She's caused so much harm," Rita said with a disappointed frown.

"And as you personally know, she's helped a lot, too."

Rita looked away and pursed her lips.

"Rita, will you help Malina?" Victor asked.

"The child will not pay for your mistakes," Rita said with a sigh and drained the rest of her drink. "I'll meet you there, and this time, you keep her warm," Rita insisted. "Don't leave her in the hands of your Angel," Rita added with a hateful smile.

"Right," he said, understanding that he had to hold the burden of his choice as well as Evaline's.

"I have to pick some things up if I want to break the sigil," Rita said, walking upstairs and into one of the rooms. Victor waited for her to come back down to continue the conversation. She held a blanket and her purse as she descended the stairs.

"I thought the sigil couldn't be broken," Victor said incredulously.

"*Anything* can be broken," Rita said with a wink and cheeky smile. "You really think I would allow my people to be burdened with a curse?"

Victor opened his mouth to speak but then closed it. "No, I suppose not," he finally responded.

"You suppose *right*," Rita said and flipped a switch on the stage, turning off the ring of fire.

Malina had her warm brown complexion back, and Victor scooped her up, holding her to his chest.

Rita draped a warm fuzzy blanket over her body and ran a hand through her hair, a sad expression crossing her face, shifting her irises back to a violet shade.

"Where are we going?" Victor asked, pulling Rita out of her thoughts.

"You're going to the place you first met me," Rita said, walking him to the door. "And bring Angel along with you."

"I was thinking of just leaving her at home ..."

"So, she can tell your wife everything?" Rita prodded with a raised eyebrow.

"I have her phone," Victor rebutted and looked back at Evaline as she neared.

"Do what you feel is best. I should be there within two hours ..."

The Kipi
Margherita

She sat in her sports car, letting the roof fold back, and watched Victor leave with his two girls. She shook her head at Malina's freezing body with sad shame. It is true that Elizabeth didn't place the sigil, but Jade didn't do it either. Margherita pulled out her phone and dialed her old friend and co-leader of a group she physically left months ago. The phone rang twice before a familiar voice answered with a panic she wasn't prepared for.

"Is she alright?" Tirany demanded.

"Tirany, I don't know what you're talking about," Margherita said with calm that didn't match the speed her heart raced at.

"Mary, it's my baby girl," Tirany sobbed, "they got her."

"Was she at Valley High?" Margherita asked.

"Yes," she answered quickly.

"Carina headed there not to long ago, I don't believe it's as bad as you think, of course, I don't know that for sure," Margherita said quickly, knowing Tirany's quick-witted thinking. "But Carina will inform me if anything is beyond her expertise."

"Okay," Tirany said with a sigh.

"I'm coming to see you," Margherita said with gentle authority.

"Mary, Lionel is here," Tirany warned. A pregnant pause built between them.

"That never stopped me before," Margherita said with a grimace, "I'll see you soon," she said and hung up the phone. She sent out a quick text to Carina and placed the car in reverse when she received a text back.

CB : Matoya is coming out of it now, veil coma.

Veil coma, huh? Margherita thought as she drove into Macden. *A veil doesn't even activate until a person is in their twenties. Hell, most people can't even control their megin enough to use its raw power as an attack. Malina was able to do it at seventeen?* Margherita thought, troubled by the progression. *She had two sigils placed on her, one to trap her megin inside and another to crystalize her if she used it at all. When were they placed on her?* Margherita wondered, believing that could be the answer to the activation of a veil. But she was jarred out of her thoughts when she hit the roads of Macden.

These roads weren't nicely paved. They were pothole-riddled, gravel-covered, and in some places no more than dirt paths. The sidewalks were cracked from the weather with new patches of grass growing through. Margherita frowned, driving by old abandoned houses with smashed windows and mold growing on their outer wood panels. *Why hasn't the Kipi done something about this? If I was the leader—*

Margherita bit the inside of her cheek as soon as the thought tried to show itself. *I left this life for a reason,* she reminded herself, thinking of Carina as she pulled into the grassy yard of her friend's property.

She grabbed her phone and sent out a message to Carina:

"Update?"

CB: *"She's more than fine raising hell as I send this to you."*

Margherita smiled at the thought and placed her phone in her purse. She stood by her car as the roof unfolded itself, eyeing the youth, who watched her carefully. As she walked up the path she spotted a gray Macel—a new model she hadn't seen advertised before. *Tracy must be here*, she mused as she walked up to the front steps of the house and saw Tirany's baby daddy.

A statuesque black man stood with a disapproving scowl on his face. His hair was cut short, but Margherita could tell that if he allowed it to grow, it would have a wool-like curl. He wasn't wearing a shirt today, which allowed the permanent artwork that covered his chest and arms to be seen. It displayed skulls, pinups with smoking guns, roses, blood, and the birthdays of both of his children. There was a bandage over his bicep where the birthdays lay, and she knew he'd added on to that particular piece. Margherita frowned at the thick purple smoke that surrounded him.

"Lonnie," Margherita said curtly.

"We don't want you around here, Mare," he said, bristling with anger.

"I called first," she said with a smile that didn't last long. *I don't have time for the back and forth*, she reminded herself. "Lionel, I need to talk to Tirany," she said, staring into his soft brown eyes.

He quickly looked away. "Don't come here using that devil majik on me," Lionel growled.

Margherita sighed and reached into her purse and put on her sunglasses and then her gloves. "I tell you this every time. That's not how it works, but look," she said, sliding on her gloves. "Truce," she snapped. She watched the distrust ease from his body as he nodded and turned his head to the side.

"T, she's here," Lionel said and sat back down on the steps. Margherita bit the inside of her cheek with frustration.

I could have just announced myself like that, she thought and began to pace. Tirany stepped out slowly, and her puffy gray eyes looked at Margherita hopefully.

Margherita removed the glasses and placed them on top of her head. Then, she opened her arms to her friend, who slowly walked down the steps before rushing into her embrace. Margherita looked at Lionel's disapproving face as she rubbed Tirany's back. Tirany pulled back, drying her face, and looked into Margherita's eyes.

"Has Carina said anything?" she asked, and Margherita nodded.

"Matoya is fine raising Kaine apparently," Margherita said with a smile alluding to their family's last name. Tirany chuckled as Lionel breathed out a sigh of relief.

"Are they going to let her go?" Lionel asked.

"They can't hold her," Tirany added, looking between Lionel and Margherita.

"Carina will make sure she makes it back," Margherita said reassuringly. "How did you know she was affected?" Margherita asked, crossing her arms.

"Affected by what? She was supposed to be home an hour ago. She found out that Valeno girl was at the school and convinced the detective to ask some follow-up questions," Tirany said.

"You shouldn't tell a Bahkir everything so loosely like that," Lionel cautioned.

"She was and will always be a Kipi," Tirany snapped, ignoring Lionel's shaking head.

"What was she infected with?" Lionel asked Margherita but refused to meet her gaze.

"I said affected not infected," Margherita replied, shifting her weight. "Malina released her veil ..."

"Veil?" Lionel asked, his purple smoke cloud turning a red hue. "Matoya has been infected with that devil majik," he said.

"Lonnie, that's not how it works," Tirany said soothingly.

"Here's a drink, Lonnie," Tracy said, stepping out with a sweaty clear glass of what appeared to be lemonade. Accepting, Lonnie gratefully drained it.

"That *is* how it works," he snapped as placed the glass on the wooden steps. "Our baby girl is one of them now," he growled, nodding his head at Margherita.

"Matoya is fine," Margherita said, "and if I find out you did anything to her—"

"Mare, stop," Tirany said, immediately raising a hand between them. She walked Margherita a little way down the path and hushed her voice so Lionel couldn't overhear. "You know you can't talk to him like that," Tirany said.

"How long has he been back?" Margherita asked with a frown.

"Two months," Tirany said, looking back at him and then meeting Margherita's gaze. "Just before the incident. He's better."

Margherita gagged at the words, but with Lionel in the picture, things made more sense. "That's bullshit and we both know it," Margherita said, shaking her head. "Wait," she added with wide eyes. "Has he been staying with you all this time?" Now, the pieces were starting to fit together in her mind.

"It's not that simple," Tirany said and Margherita shook her head, biting the inside of her cheek. "They listen to him—"

"They voted for you," Margherita snapped. "They want to listen to you," she insisted and then shook her head to shut down anything Tirany might be thinking to say. "Malina had a sigil placed on her," Margherita continued, watching Tirany's fluid violet aura shift to an orange hue. "Do you know anything about that?" she asked, knowing the answer as a smug smile appeared on the fact of Lionel, who was approaching.

"I know about that," Lionel said proudly.

"Lonnie you *didn't*," Tirany said, clenching her hands into fists. "Are you trying to start a civil war?" she yelled.

"Matoya getting hurt today is your fault," Margherita shot back, walking away with all the information she needed.

"Wait!" Lionel shouted, chasing after her. Margherita didn't wait, though. She just kept walking.

"Bit—"

Margherita stood still and without facing him or touching him honed her megin and lashed her veil out at Lionel. Feeling smug, she turned to face him.

His irises shifted colors as she pushed him to the brink of madness by forcing him to feel the fullest extent of competing emotions before draining them away. Lionel shuddered before her, tears rolling down his face, his heartbeat thudding in his throat as fear gripped him.

"Margherita, please," Tirany cried, rushing to his side.

Margherita gritted her teeth and pulled back. Lionel dropped to his knees as Margherita returned her glasses to her face.

"You're no better than him," Tirany said.

"Explain," Margherita demanded, looking down at the man as he took deep breaths to regulate the torment he'd just endured. She watched his black stormy aura slowly fade into an orange hue as he glared at her.

"Lashing out at someone because you heard something you didn't like—"

"Ah, so he hasn't actually changed," Margherita challenged.

Tirany paused and shook her head. "That's not—"

"I have other places to be," Margherita said, opening her car door. "Oh, and send Tracy home," Margherita demanded, "two addicts in the same household isn't wise," Margherita said disdainfully. Tirany walked to Margherita's door and held it open.

"Will Malina," Tirany began, but let it trail off, uncertain of her next words.

"I'm going to help her," Margherita said confidently tapping her finger on her steering wheel as her frustration grew, "T, you're better than this. You're so smart."

"I know," Tirany said with a nod, looking back at Lionel, "Azazel—"

"Can't help you anymore," Margherita said coolly, "and you knew better. You know what to do when you're ready to be done. Just try not to drag the Kipi down with you," Margherita stated. She looked at Tirany, who stepped away from the vehicle.

Then, closing the door, Margherita peeled off and drove toward the fields of Belladonna.

Fields of Belladonna

Margherita parked on the side of the store with bated breath and stared up at the stormy sky. She stepped out, eyes still fixed on the front of the store. The wooden trellis hosted the belladonnas that the store was known for. The store's roof-to-floor glass windows were intact, and the open sign glowed to let patrons know it was open. The roof was filled with flowers and butterflies. *The store looks normal enough*, Margherita mused, realizing she didn't know exactly what to expect.

Margherita walked around to the front door and noticed that on the cement was an irregular red stain, and crime scene tape flew haphazardly in the wind, enraging Margherita's temper. *They could have taken the tape with them*, Margherita thought with a frown, walking over, snatching at the tape, and balling it up in her fist. She placed it in her purse and walked back to the red stain and crouched down, placing the tips of her fingers on the cement.

"Mary ..."

Margherita looked up upon hearing the faded voice.

The woman stood before her with a gnarled wooden cane. She wore a gray netted shawl that fell over her shoulders, which sagged with weariness—as did her skin. Her usually well-kempt loc'd hair lay loose and frizzed over her shoulders. Her gray eyes were dull, and the bright smile she was known for was absent from her face.

"Old Lady Bella," Margherita said with a nod and a small smile.

"I'm closed," she said, frowning at the cement that Margherita's fingertips still touched.

"Your sign says differently," Margherita challenged, rising to her full height and walking toward the woman.

The woman raised a shaky hand and with a stern face shook her head once. Margherita didn't need her affinity to tell her the woman was devastated. "Please," Margherita said gently, "there's a child that needs my help."

The silence stretched between them, and for a moment Margherita thought she just hit a dead end, but the woman stepped to the side. Margherita walked through the front door quickly before Bella could change her mind, proceeding to expertly gather and handle the herbs and crystals with care. Margherita smiled, recalling the early years of her life in the shop, and chuckled at the moments she spent apprenticing with Bella.

"Care to share the memory?" Bella asked, softly walking to the stool and taking a seat.

"I just remembered the time you fired me," Margherita mused, scooping mugwort into a bag.

"Which time?" Bella asked with a sparkle in her eye.

"The time I sold Arnica to a man as a special enhancement," Margherita said with a sly smile and wink as she walked to the counter with her goods. Bella sighed and shook her head.

"He could have died," Bella chided.

"He was beating his wife," Margherita said, just like she had the day Bella stopped the transaction. "*She* could have died."

"There was no way for you to know that he wouldn't have fed it to her," Bella said with a sigh. "Are you thinking of attempting the stunt again?" Bella asked, raising the bag of Arnica from the rest.

"No, I'm gonna be on my knees a lot this afternoon—"

"All right," Bella said with a surprised chuckle, cutting Margherita off mid-sentence and slicing through the tension.

"*There* it is," Margherita said gently. Bella brought her old wrinkled hand to her mouth. "It's okay to smile Bella," Margherita soothed, gently tugging her hand away from her mouth. Bella's other hand went up to cover her eyes as tears ran down her face. Margherita rounded the counter between them and pulled her into an embrace. Bella cried, and Margherita rubbed her back until she calmed down.

"Thank you, sweet girl," she crooned, pulling back from Margherita.

"Sweet?" Margherita said, shaking her head. "No, no. I did that so I can get this for free." With that, she smiled and winked.

Bella shook her head as her eyes looked over the material gathered and mentally calculated the total.

"Two fifty," Bella said with an outstretched hand.

Margherita slapped her hand over her chest and gasped.

Bella shrugged and smirked.

"Okay, okay," Margherita conceded and

dramatically rolled her eyes as she walked back around the corner. Shuffling through her purse for her wallet she noticed Bella gliding her eyes over her items. "Trying to figure out what I'm up to?" Margherita asked, and handed over three hundred-dollar bills.

"You said you needed to help someone," Bella said thoughtfully, opening her cash register.

"Don't I always, though?" Margherita said, gently bagging her own merchandise. "Keep the change. I'm about to make it back tonight," Margherita said with a shrug.

"Is it *that* girl?" Bella asked, closing the register.

"My clientele is confidential—just like yours," Margherita said, leaving no room for negotiation. Bella's eyebrows rose and Margherita sighed. "Yeah, it's her."

Bella nodded, looking over the items. Touching a crystal briefly, she gasped. Her eyes widened and brightened as megin thunder boomed overhead and rain poured down outside.

Margherita's heart thudded with shock, but Bella's eyes dimmed just as quickly as everything had happened. Bella briskly walked into her back room through her beaded curtain, returning with a wooden box that had a peculiar symbol carved into it.

"What's this for?" Margherita demanded. "What did you see?"

"You know I can't tell you that," Bella said with a weary expression. "When you perform the extraction, place the contents of this box beside her."

"Wh-what? What's in the box?" Margherita asked, feeling fear for the first time in years.

"Promise me you will do this," Bella said urgently, placing the box in Margherita's hand and then closing her own around it. "Mary, please."

"Will it harm the girl?" Margherita asked.

Bella shook her head and blinked away her tears.

Margherita sighed and placed her hand on top of Bella's. "Then I'll do it."

Bella released a sigh and pulled away her hands. Soon after, she walked Margherita to her car and waved as she drove off.

Margherita occasionally glanced down at the mysterious box and tried to remember where she'd seen the symbol before. Unable to place it, she forced herself to rely on the faith she had in Bella. *Bella would never hurt a kid. I just have to trust in that*, Margherita thought as she drove toward her childhood home and the place where she'd first met Victor.

9

Endurance
Carina

Carina sighed and stretched out the kinks in her neck after draining the megin from the detective, the five students that were affected, and Matoya. Carina eyed Matoya curiously with a smirk on her face. Matoya was frowning and narrowed her eyes at Carina when she caught her looking. Carina raised her eyebrows as she gathered her supplies to move on to the next room. Matoya walked to the door and closed it gently before turning back to Carina.

"Are you sure you want to close the door?" Carina signed with a smirk on her face.

Matoya flushed and narrowed her eyes again.

Carina laughed and continued to pack her things. "Make it quick. I have someone else I have to see," she signed and turned, ready for the girl to lunge at her, but Matoya didn't. She remained still and defeated by the door.

"You're just mute right?" Matoya asked, searching Carina's face for an answer.

Carina rolled her eyes, shrugged, and nodded.

"I'm not ready to be like you," Matoya whispered. "I'm not ready to be known as a Bahkir."

"I didn't come here to out you," Carina signed. "That's not what Rita and I do."

"I know, I know," Matoya grumbled, her heart rate increasing, "but my dad," Matoya said and trailed off.

"He's back?" Carina asked, pinching her eyebrows together and stepping closer.

"Yes, but it's not—" Matoya started but soon stopped, watching Carina's face, which was full of expression. "Don't look at me like that," she snapped. A knock came at the door and Carina turned her back to Matoya.

"Everything good in here?" Gabriel asked.

Taking a deep breath, Carina looked back expectantly at Matoya. Matoya nodded and hurriedly walked pass Gabriel and the other Shikka guards. "I can't believe her of all people is doing this to me," he commented sadly.

Carina picked up her bag and walked to Gabriel's side. She made sure to keep some distance between them, but she offered him a friendly smile.

Gabriel smiled back at her and pointed with his head in the direction they were walking next. Then, he pulled back the curtain and revealed a sleeping girl with a gentle face.

Carina activated the megin in her eyes to look at her megin levels and saw that everything was perfectly normal. Carina looked at Gabriel and frowned. She raised her hands to sign, but the orange state of his aura gave her pause. *That's not your problem*, she reminded herself stubbornly.

"Everything is okay here. Why did you bring me to her?" Carina signed.

"Victor did this," Gabriel signed back.

"Oh," Carina mouthed and then nodded. She placed her bag on a chair and opened a drawer beside the bed and snapped an ammonia packet and waved it under the girl's nose.

The girl groaned and pushed Carina's hand away.

"I suppose I could have done that," Gabriel signed, rubbing the back of his neck sheepishly.

Carina smiled and nodded, walking over to her bag, which she slung over her shoulder, prepared to leave.

"Carina, wait," Gabriel said, causing Carina to freeze.

She looked at him and watched him struggle with the phrasing of his next words. *Just leave. Get out of here, Carina. He's not your problem*, she reminded herself.

Gabriel frowned, licked his lips, and looked up at her with his striking red eyes. He lifted his hand, touched it to his chin, and brought it forward slightly.

Thank you? Carina thought, feeling her anger boil. She pursed her lips and tightened her grip on her bag's strap.

"Thank you?" she said aloud, unable to contain it any longer.

"Y-yeah, thanks for doing all of this," Gabriel responded calmly. "You're gonna be a great doctor," he said genuinely.

"That's not what you wanted to say though," she hissed. "Is it Astra? Do you want to know where she is?" Carina asked, crossing her arms over her chest.

"I do," Dante said, raising his eyebrows expectantly.

Dante stood six feet tall in the Shikka uniform— a plain black shirt and tactical black pants. Around his neck, he wore a silver chain with a pendant of two overlapping curved blades. He had umber brown skin and pitch-black eyes that unnerved Carina.

"What happened to her?" Dante asked, looking directly at Gabriel.

"Astra's veil knocked her out," Gabriel explained.

Dante narrowed his eyes, scanning Carina's face. "Is that true?" he asked.

"I checked her levels, and she's fine now," Carina said, calmly adjusting the straps of her bag on her shoulder. "I'm done here, so I'm going to go now," Carina said and attempted to walk by Dante.

But Dante grabbed her upper arm to stop her. Gabriel wrapped his arm around her middle and pulled her away from Dante and then placed himself between them.

"Don't touch her," Gabriel said sternly.

"You telling me what to do now?" Dante challenged.

"You want to hurt her," Gabriel stated. "I'm not letting that happen."

Carina tightened her fist in the material of Gabriel's shirt.

"Don't lie to me then," Dante demanded.

"What's going on?" the sleeping girl slurred, breathing deeply as she tried to pull her foggy mind from her dreams. She gripped her head as though it pained her to speak.

"Remilda, do you remember what happened?" Dante asked, walking over to her. Carina slowly eased by Dante to stand on the other side of Gabriel. Gabriel gripped her hand tightly and shook his head when she attempted to leave.

"We found Astra being questioned. She released her za ..."—she paused and corrected herself—"megin, and everyone fell to the floor except Gabriel ..." Remilda looked around and frowned. "Where am I?"

"The nurse wing of the school," Gabriel replied.

"Where is *she*?" Remilda asked, looking back and forth between Gabriel and Dante.

"She's with her father," Gabriel stated, and Dante looked from Gabriel to Carina.

"Gabriel, take Remilda home so she can rest," Dante said, walking away from them.

"Gabriel," Carina said, pulling at his hand.

Gabriel turned to block Carina from Remilda. "I can't take Dante to Astra, I don't know where they are," she signed, panic constricting her vocal cords.

"I'll take care of it," he said, rubbing her goosebump-covered biceps. Then, he walked out of the room after Dante to continue a conversation.

Carina stood, trembling and angry. Dante terrified her, and being in the same room as him made her want to vomit. Dante's veil touched her once before—only for a second, but it was enough to haunt her. She knew it was an accident and that he wouldn't hurt her, but she still couldn't shake away the damage he'd left her with.

"Hey," Remilda said gently as she placed a hand on Carina's arm.

Carina jumped and thrust her palm at Remilda.

Remilda caught the blow before it hit her chest. "Whoa," she said gently, "I didn't mean to scare you."

"Carina," Gabriel said, voice laced with regret. Then, he paused at the sight before him. "Remilda are we making friends?" he asked with light humor.

"I hope," Remilda responded, directly a kind smile at Carina.

"Well, Dante is taking her home," Gabriel announced to Carina's horror.

"Why?" Carina signed quickly. "I drove myself here."

"Tell him where she is and you won't have to go," Gabriel offered with a frown.

"That's the best you could do?" Carina frowned as her breathing picked up.

"That's all he wants," Gabriel said apologetically.

Carina shook violently, and Remilda gently touched her.

Carina shrugged her off, and she stepped away from both of them.

Gabriel looked at her with sad distant eyes, and she shook her head at him. She walked out of the nurse wing, passed all of the Shikka, and made her way out the front of the school. Dante stood before her, resting against the railing for the stairs. He looked at her with little interest but straightened at her approach.

With both hands, he slowly and carefully crossed his middle finger over his index finger and waved them to the side twice.

Ready? Carina thought to herself. *No, I'm not.* Carina sighed and nodded her head. Dante tried to sign something else and Carina shook her head and walked toward him.

"I'm not deaf," Carina signed by pointing to herself, shaking her head, and tapping her earlobe to her chin.

"You can hear me," Dante said with a sigh of relief. "I need to find Astra. If you tell me where she is, you don't have to come with me."

Carina began to sign and watched Dante frown. "Do you know sign?" Carina asked, pointing at him, and then touched the side of her forehead with her fingertips. Bringing her hands in front of her, she pointed her index fingers at each other and circled them. Dante shook his head and pulled out his phone, pointing at it. Carina chuckled. *Why do people always do that? Just because I have trouble talking doesn't mean you have to stop talking too.*

Carina took his phone and noticed his notepad was already open.

"*I don't know where she is*," Carina typed and showed the phone screen to Dante, who reached for the phone, causing Carina to pull it back. Pointing at him, she opened and closed her hand, imitating a talking mouth.

"Right," he said clearing his throat. "You must have an idea of where she is if you saw her last," Dante stated.

"She was with Victor. I last saw them at the club talking," Carina offered with a shrug, showing him the screen. She knew that Margherita never did business at the club so the ritual location would be unknown—except to those involved.

Dante tapped his chin as he thought and then nodded. He took his phone back and started down the stairs, pausing on the bottom step to look back up at Carina. "Thank you for your help, and I apologize for our previous unfavorable encounter," he offered and then continued walking away.

Carina watched him leave, hugging herself against the cold. The nighttime atmosphere was quiet, except for the storm brewing further south. The doors opened behind her, and she felt Gabriel's energy before she heard his deep baritone.

He stopped talking when he saw her, and she felt his eyes trail over her. Carina looked back at him, watching his wavy aura shift from a blue to orange hue. Gabriel walked to her side with Remilda trailing behind him. He turned to face her and placed his keys in her upturned palm.

"I'm sorry about Dante," Gabriel offered.

"I'd rather you be sorry about *you*," Carina said softly.

"What?"

"You gave me up to Dante," Carina said.

"I didn't."

"You did because it involved Astra's safety," Carina explained. "She can't love you, you know."

"That's not how love is supposed to work," Gabriel said defensively.

"No," Carina said with a sigh, feeling empty and cold. "I suppose love *doesn't* work like that."

"Do you need a ride?" Gabriel asked, walking down the steps to follow her.

"Not this time," Carina said, heading for her car.

Remembrance
Astra

The last thing Astra felt and remembered was Gabriel's warm breath—his distinct scent of sandalwood and cinnamon that embraced her with warmth. Her heart pounded fiercely with fear and uncertainty as she was forced to question every past conception of who and what her best friend was. *Gabriel wouldn't have killed Azazel,* Astra thought with certainty. Astra felt a pinch in her neck, and she lost the strength in her limbs. She leaned into her best friend and tried to erase the image Matoya had shown.

For what seemed like forever, her mind was submerged in darkness which brought her great comfort. *This is the most rest I've gotten since Azazel died,* she fleetingly thought with instant regret. Then, a fuzzy image began to paint itself in her mind's eye. The sky was a vibrant blue color, and the cirrus clouds reminded her of a cotton ball that had been pulled into thin strands. The blades of grass beneath her feet were bright green and rough, clinging to her skin when she rubbed her toes against them. Slowly, the soothing sound of water flowing over rocks filled her ears. Astra walked through the stream and toward the roar of a waterfall. At the base, she found a woman holding a golden chalice with jewels embedded in the mold.

The woman had wavy black hair that was cut short—almost to her scalp. Her brown skin was soft and smooth, and her green eyes reminded Astra of the grass she walked on. She wore a silk red and white gown with a makeshift twine belt wrapped around her waist to hold the fabric closed. She smiled at Astra and held the chalice out to her. Astra took the cup, eyeing it cautiously, and the water shimmered and glowed surrounded by the gold metal. Astra brought the vessel to her lips and tasted what she could only describe as ... power.

Suddenly, the vision changed. The sky was dark with angry gray clouds, and the rain that beat down on her face felt like needles. The woman stood between two men. One man appeared to be her twin, and the other looked older than them with golden hair and a beard. He had amber skin and wore a bright joyous smile. The man spoke so loudly that Astra couldn't hear anything outside of the vibrations that shook her whole body. Looking over her shoulder, Astra saw the god that her family prayed to.

Haiel stood stoically, his blue face dripping with the blood of the innocents he had slain to get this far. Fire roared behind him as the forest crackled and broke under the pressure of the flames. Despite the rain, the fire raged, and the woman dropped to the ground, burying her hands in the moist dirt, her green eyes brightening as roots lunged up from the ground and wrapped around Haiel's body. Her twin ran toward him with a hilt that held no blade—or so Astra thought. He swung his hilt at Haiel's neck, and Haiel broke free from the roots to grasp the open air. Blood broke free from Haiel's hand, covering the invisible blade.

The bearded man jumped the gap between himself and Haiel, the hammer he held aglow with lighting. As he landed, he swung the hammer down at Haiel, who looked at the weapon with unflinching curiosity—even as it approached his face. When the hammer made contact, the earth shook, and lighting struck. However, as the men and Astra were focused on one enemy, another enemy struck. The woman gasped, drawing Astra's attention. A glowing blade poked through her chest, taking on a green hue as the woman's eyes dimmed. The woman holding the blade smirked, her red eyes sparkling with satisfaction as she placed a boot on the dark-skinned beauty's shoulder and kicked her off her weapon.

The grass beneath Astra's feet immediately shriveled and died despite the rain pounding the ground. Turning away from Haiel, the remaining twin released a wail. Yet, the redhead sunk her glowing green blade into the earth, and roots sprung up, stabbing through the twin, killing him, and promptly stopping the rainfall. Astra shook violently, closing her eyes to a massacre and the hidden truth of the god her people worshipped.

Astra felt a hand shake her body, and she blinked open her eyes, met with gray eyes staring back at her. Azazel's dark-brown face was weary with worry and distant with distrust. He was mad at her, but he was worried about her, too. She looked past him to the older woman crumpled on the ground; her shoulder looked dislocated. Astra looked down at her hands, and guilt swelled in her chest.

"Az, I'm sorry. I didn't mean to," she heard herself stammer.

"Get out of here," said Azazel said, turning his back to her. "I knew this was a bad idea."

Astra gathered her coat and looked at the open book on the table, which was open to the picture of the woman she'd seen in her vision. *That's right*, Astra thought. *This was right before the accident. Azazel took me to see Old Lady Bella, his grandmother. We talked about Hiboria, and she got me to drink an herbal tea that showed me what happened to the gods back then. Freya, her twin Frey, and their older brother, Thor. But was it true or a lucid dream?*

Astra walked out of the store and felt panic while taking the inevitable next steps. *No, I can't do this again. Not now. Not again!* She thought with short shallow breaths. *Wake up, wake up, WAKE UP!* She mentally screamed, and to her surprise, it worked this time. She opened her eyes, and finding herself underwater, she lurched forward, gasping for air. As water splashed out of the tin bath she was in, she breathed in deeply and held the air in her lungs, forcing herself to calm down, all the while grabbing the metal edges tightly, focusing on how the cool metal felt. Then, at last, she exhaled.

Astra looked around the room she was in and noted that it smelled old. The floorboards looked warped from water damage. Astra looked up and was able to see the night sky due to a massive roof light—or was it simply a hole? She carefully worked her way to her feet but found that her jeans and oversized shirt were drenched, clinging heavily to her thin body. She stepped out of the tin tub and cringed at the sound and the feeling of the fabric rubbing together.

"Malina?" Angel exclaimed, surprised. She sat in a corner with earbuds in while she read a book. "How long have you been standing there?" she asked with a frightened expression.

"Not long," Astra said and chuckled. "Dad told you to watch me, but you got bored, huh?"

"All you did was sink and float," Angel said with a shrug and closed her book, carefully removing her earbuds.

Sink and float? Astra thought, confused. *Well, I was at the bottom of the tub, but wasn't she worried?* Astra watched Angel walk over to a two-shelf bookshelf and grab a towel. Fingering the threads, Angel walked over and handed it to her, clearly lost in her own thoughts.

"How are you feeling?" Angel asked with sincere curiosity.

"Wet," Astra answered dryly. Astra looked like her twin, but she didn't have a caring bone in her body. Astra remembered the battle and the way Frey was fearlessly going to avenge Freya. Then, she looked at Angel's disinterested face. *Couldn't be her.*

"I'm gonna go get Dad," Angel said, walking carefully to the door, only to stop and double back with a dress in hand. "Here, put this on," Angel said.

"For what?" Astra asked. "Where are we?"

"Oh you're awake," a gorgeous woman said, peeking into the room, and Astra's father was close behind.

"Angel," Victor began.

"She just woke up, I was coming to get you!" Angel said in a rush.

"Dad, what's going on?" Astra asked.

"Can you give us the room?" Victor asked the woman, who nodded in response.

"Come on Angel," she called and Angel left out with her.

Astra continued to dry off the best she could while still wearing wet clothes. Her father watched the woman and her sister leave before partly closing the door. He looked at Astra, and there was a glimmer of disappointment in his eyes. *What's going on?* she wondered as she fought off a cold chill. She parted her lips to say something but sneezed instead.

"Bless you," her father said automatically.

"Thanks," she said with a chuckle and a sniff.

"Are you still cold?" he asked.

"Um, yeah," she said with a raised eyebrow. "I'm still wearing wet clothes."

This drew a chuckle that broke the tension—or at least cracked it.

"Right," Victor said with a smile. "I'm going to let you change, but we need to talk about what's about to happen."

"Okay," Astra said drawing out the word, feeling nervous about his distant demeanor. "What's about to happen? Why was I in a tub of water? And why are you looking at me like I'm a stranger?"

"I'm sorry, sweetheart," he said, immediately closing the distance between them and hugging her.

Astra didn't realize she needed that until his warm embrace was gone. When he pulled back, she tightened her hold for another embrace.

"Okay," said Victor, tapping her back and prompting her to let go. Then, he walked her over to the corner Angel sat in and sat her down. He turned his back to her, and she began to change out of her wet clothes into the ones provided for her. She now wore a plain white linen dress that resembled a night gown.

When she was done, she cleared her throat and sat back down. "Okay, dad, what's going on?"

"Do you remember awakening your megin the night Azazel died?" Victor asked bluntly.

"N—" she began and winced as a pang in her brain stopped her from accessing the memory. The pain of losing Azazel and watching him die in her arms had broken something open inside her, and when she'd screamed for help, something had broken lose. "Yes actually," she said distantly with a frown. "I didn't before," she added defensively.

"I know," her father soothed. "I need you to tell me what happened."

"I don't want to remember," Astra said, shaking her head and picking at the loose skin on her fingers.

"You have to," Victor urged. "You know better than anyone that suppressing emotion and memories won't help you survive. It's time for you to face this."

"I went to school—"

"Malina!" he snapped. "You almost killed eight people today!"

Hearing this, Astra shut her mouth, processing this information as her ears burned with embarrassment.

"I know you didn't mean to, but if you had faced this sooner, that wouldn't have happened today. Haiel gifted you ..."

Victor's words trailed off at the mention of their god, and Astra's mind traveled back to the battle. *Haiel killed innocent people. Was that because he wanted to? Or was that a matter of unresolved trauma? Is that the gift he gave me and my mother? Will I be like her from now on?* Astra pondered. *Focus on that night, Astra!* she told herself. Her father was still talking, but she had missed what he said. Luckily, he hadn't noticed she was zoning out.

"Just try to remember. We're trying to help you," Victor urged, kneeling down in front of her.

"I remember yelling and feeling something burst out of my chest," Astra explained, and her father nodded eagerly.

"What happened after that? Did someone approach you?"

"Ye—" Astra began and stopped when an image of Gabriel flashed in her mind. "No," she said, quickly correcting herself and shaking her head.

"Yes or no, Malina?" he said sternly.

"I don't know. I don't remember," she said and began chewing on her fingernail.

"Malina, you've been marked," Victor said with exhaustion, pulling her hand from her face. "If we don't remove the marks in the right order you *will* die."

Malina quieted, thinking back to the day. "I don't want to die," she admitted, and her hand squirmed in her father's embrace. She suddenly felt claustrophobic in the corner where he'd placed her.

"You have to remain calm or you'll hurt me," he said calmly.

"You trapped me here on purpose," Astra said with a frown, voicing her revelation.

"Think back to that night, Malina."

"I want to stand," Astra said, moving to do so, but Victor placed a hand on her shoulder, holding her down. "Dad please," she begged.

"I need you to focus. We have to do this tonight ... and *soon* or you're going to die. Who was there with you?"

"I told the Carabinieri everything I know," she said evasively, looking away.

"Not everything."

"Daddy," Astra whined.

"Do you want to die?" he asked incredulously.

"No," she replied.

"Then what happened? Did someone do something to you?"

"No! I don't know. I can't remember," Astra said snatching her hand away from him and nibbling on her finger.

"Was it Gabriel? Did you see Gabriel?" Victor asked quickly.

"He wasn't there," Astra said vehemently. "It wasn't him," she added, picturing him crouching down, his face before her. His eyes were brown, and his hair was long, falling past his ears. *It wasn't him. Couldn't have been him.*

"Is that why you refused to see him when he *came back*?" he asked incredulously.

"Daddy, stop it! It wasn't him," Astra said fervently. "That's impossible. He wasn't here!"

"He was the first person you saw though, right?" Victor asked, searching Astra's face. Suddenly, he rose, and Astra watched him with surprise.

"Dad?"

"We have to start the ritual now," he said. "You're getting cold, which means the sigils are fighting each other again."

Astra looked down at her fingernails and found that they were turning blue. She shivered and blew out a cloud of air. *Why me?* she wondered as her shivering knees knocked together. She watched her father as he walked away. *I don't want to die,* Astra thought again. Struggling to her feet, she followed after him into the hallway, hoping with all of her heart that he'd believe her.

"Dad," Astra began, stopping at the top of the stairs he was already descending.

"What is it, Malina?" he said, stopping and turning to look her in the eyes.

"You have to believe me," she prefaced. "The young man I saw wasn't Gabriel."

Victor looked at her for a time before he nodded his head. "He just looked like him?"

Astra nodded solemnly. "He drew something on my chest ... and he was also wearing a rope necklace with a pendant. Daddy, it wasn't Gabriel," Astra repeated.

"I believe you," he said with conviction that gave Astra pause.

Why does he believe me so certainly? she wondered, watching him descend the rest of the stairs before following him down.

The Ritual
Margherita

Margherita looked over the steps she'd written down and planned to follow while carrying out the planned ritual. She had broken many sigils in the past but never two, back to back, within the same person. Margherita prayed to her goddess Yemaya for balance and guidance. She knew Yemaya was present and helping her when Malina awoke from her chrysalis with greater clarity regarding the events of that day. Margherita looked down at the two symbols Malina had drawn for Victor. One was a simple sigil, but the first was a rune. Margherita felt her hands tremble. *I never had to deal with a rune before.* Margherita chewed the inside of her cheek with frustration and ground down the herbs some more.

Margherita was awash with both skepticism and curiosity. She looked over her shoulder and found Victor watching her from a distance. Margherita's breath caught in her throat the same way it had when she was a little girl. *Something about this house has me feeling nervous*, she thought, ignoring Victor and filling the thirteenth bottle that she needed with the herbal powder. Victor stepped closer to her, and Margherita smelled the unique fragrance of rosewood and vanilla, which filled her mind with visions of yore.

"I didn't think you would remember this place," Margherita said, sealing the tops of the bottles.

"This place wasn't so bad," he remarked with a small smile.

"No, I suppose it wasn't," Margherita said, looking into his green eyes.

"Thank you for helping," he said softly.

"You know *me*," Margherita said with a smile. "Helping is what I do."

"I do know you," Victor said with a smile, "and I know it's *not*—not *always*."

"Well, you caught me on a good day," Margherita said, grabbing the bottles.

Victor placed a hand over hers. "Why are you really doing this?" he asked, bending his head to try and look at her.

"Just know, I have more reason to help you than hurt you," Margherita said, meeting his eyes and licking her lips. "Grab the rest of those bottles. We don't have time to waste," she said and turned her back to him.

She stepped into the sun room, which she already illuminated with candles. Malina was sitting in the corner near the heater and under an electric blanket Margherita. With Victor's help, Margherita placed the bottles in a half-moon shape on the floor. Then, she helped Malina to the floor—right in the center of the crescent. At the last moment, she remember the box Old Lady Bella had given her for the ritual. The old woman's words echoed in her mind as she lifted the lid. *Handle all things with gloves.* After grabbing a pair, she lifted the lid, revealing a satin ribbon ... on which sat a moonstone that bore a carving. Margherita clasped the necklace around Malina's neck and then grabbed a large crystal and placed it in Malina's hands.

"Hold this tight," Margherita urged, placing the girl's hands over her torso.

Malina nodded and kept her hands where they'd been placed.

"It's glowing," Victor commented.

"That means it's working," Margherita said. "I need her megin weak so it won't hinder the process," she explained. Victor nodded with a frown, and Margherita offered him a smile in return. "She'll make it through this. Don't worry."

"I'm ready," Malina said with heavy eyes, and Margherita nodded.

"Rita?" Victor said with uncertain hues coloring his aura.

"Hurry and take the crystal so that I can begin," Margherita ordered.

Victor obeyed, and Margherita began, opening the vials and setting the herbs inside on fire. As she did this, she prayed and chanted in Yemaya's name. She asked Yemaya for strength, balance, and healing. She envisioned the goddess in her mind as she knelt before the crescent and prayed to the moon above. The rain began to pour, filling Margherita with peace—with confidence the ritual would go smoothly. She activated her megin with hands stretched toward the crescent she focused on, contemplating the tangled aura. Malina's aura was twisted into the same sigil that was placed on her chest. Skillfully Margherita focused her megin to calmly unravel the knot. However, she knew that any wrong move—even a simple jolt of emotion— could cause lasting damage to both of their psyches.

"Dad, what is this?" Angel whispered.

"Angel, put it back." Margherita looked at Angel, who held the box Old Lady Bella gave her. Margherita looked to Malina's chest, where the stone necklace was glowing, illuminating its snowflake-like shape.

Suddenly, Dante's voice boomed in the small space. "What's going on in here?"

Margherita stood, easing away from Malina and toward Victor's side. Angel moved back toward her sister away from the drama that was about to be unleashed.

"How did you know where we were?" Victor asked.

"Carina," Dante said in a bored tone, looking over their heads to Malina.

"What did you threaten her with?" Margherita demanded.

"A ride home," he said innocently with a smirk that pulled into a frown. "What the ... fuck?"

Margherita and Victor followed Dante's gaze. Angel was kneeling in front of the crescent; the pendant's glow was almost blinding, and Margherita couldn't help but think that something was off. Thunder boomed, and lightning shot across the sky. The stone lifted off Malina's chest, and her body slowly began to follow. Dante walked forward past

Margherita and Victor, stopping where Angel knelt. Margherita noticed Dante reach for Malina, and she sprung forward, grabbing his arm. He pulled away from her, and before she could say anything, his hand wrapped around her throat.

"Dante, stop!" Victor demanded.

Thunder rattled the building, and lighting shattered through the glass and struck Malina's floating body. The lightning illuminated her convulsing frame, and Angel screamed, beginning to cry as blood dripped from Malina's mouth. Somewhere in the distance, a loud boom sounded. Dante released Margherita's throat and tried to rush to Malina's damaged body, but the border Margherita set in place with her bottle of herbs threw him back.

"What the fuck have you done?" Dante demanded, slowly rising to his feet.

"That wasn't me!" Margherita snapped, stepping away from Dante in shock, pulling her megin around herself to mitigate further damage. *I'm lucky he didn't just activate his veil in the beginning*, Margherita thought with a frown, though she still hated the position she was currently in. *I'm not making it out of here alive.*

"Killing you would be a service to the world," Dante snapped.

Victor stepped between them, shielding Margherita.

"I'm not hurting her," Margherita said with finality.

"Guys!" Angel yelled.

Everyone turned their eyes to Malina. She was now floating an inch off the floor, head drooped to the side with blood dripping from her ears and nose. Rain poured into the building through the shattered window, but where Malina was concerned, the rain fell around the barrier. Margherita's heart was going like a jackhammer, and she impulsively took a step back. *If the barrier is protecting her from the rain, why didn't it protect her from the lightning?* she thought calmly despite her panic.

"Help me, Sister," Malina said in a strangled voice. As she looked at Angel, a streak of her hair began to grey.

"Victor, don't let her," Margherita demanded.

Victor looked back at her and nodded, making his way to Angel. But Dante stood in his way. "Move," Victor demanded, and Dante shook his head.

"How?" Angel asked Malina.

"Angel that's not your sister," Margherita shouted.

Angel looked back at her with a frown.

Malina stooped to be level with Angel's ear and whispered something in it.

Angel's face flashed with anger and something else.

Margherita pulled her megin to her eyes to look at the aura surrounding Angel. Specks of orange and blue ... but it was mostly green. *Green? What did that entity say to make her feel important?* Margherita pondered. "Angel, get away from her!"

"My sister needs me," she declared with a wide smile. "I'm going to help her!"

Margherita frowned. *Fuck it*, she thought and channeled her megin at Angel, enhancing her fear as she reached toward the barrier.

Dante must have sensed the attack and released his veil full-force because Margherita dropped to her knees, feeling light-headed and weak. She released control of her veil, pulling control of her megin back around her body. Through the pounding in her head, she heard the sharp shatter of glass vials. When she looked up, Angel's hand was wrapped around the necklace's pendant. Malina dropped to her knees, her arms cradled around Angel's unconscious form. Margherita looked to where Victor once stood and found him slumped on the floor she pushed herself to her feet and stumbled toward the girls.

Dante gripped her by her neck and slammed her to the ground. "What did you do?" he growled.

Margherita clawed at the man's hand around her throat. "I removed a sigil—that's all," she wheezed, scratching the skin of his hand, which began to bleed. Swiping her finger into his blood she tasted it. Dante lifted her by her throat to slam it down again, but she tapped into his emotions directly, using the blood ingested. "You forgive me," she declared, and he released her at once.

Margherita felt his disgust directly, but she didn't care. The forbidden majik she was practicing was going to save the girls' lives. She tapped into his fear and saw the images of losing Malina. She implanted her mental image of hospitalized Malina in his mind, creating yellow hues in his aura.

"Let's get the girls into the car," she suggested, wiping away her nosebleed. *I'm at my limit*, she noted, following Dante's lead.

Dante gathered Malina's body in his arms and yanked her away from Angel. Margherita dove to catch her before she hit the ground. She glared at Dante as he walked away; then, she looked down at Angel's peaceful face. Using all of the strength she had left in her body, she rose, carrying her off. As she walked by Victor's slumped form, she kicked him awake. Groggily, he blinked his eyes open, and Margherita waited patiently as he fought the lightheadedness and rose to his feet.

"What?" he asked in a daze.

"Carry your daughter, please," Margherita said.

Victor nodded and took Angel into his arms. Then, they slowly made it outside where Malina sat beside the car. Dante was nowhere to be found. "Will you please drive?" Margherita asked.

"Yeah, just … Rita!" Victor yelled as Margherita's world went black.

Bound
Astra

Astra was awakened by raindrops striking her face. Opening her eyes, she found herself in the grass. Her body felt light and well-rested as she pushed herself to her feet. There were no buildings around her—no sounds of cars or people. There was only the crickets' song. She started to walk toward the forest to give herself protection against the rain that slowly became heavier. In the forest, she heard the trickle of water, reminding her of the stream she'd seen in her vision of Hiboria what felt like hours before.

Perhaps I'm dead and Hiboria is the place of the dead, she concluded morbidly. She remembered the weakness she felt, which put her into a dreamlike state when the ritual began. *Maybe the ritual killed me after all*, she thought as she put one foot in front of the other. She stopped walking when she reached the edge of the forest. In the clearing were a stream and a girl around her age, seeming to kiss the water.

"He-hello," Astra stammered, suddenly afraid.

The girl before Astra was a darker shade of brown, and some of her hair was loc'd while other parts were braided or bone straight—like she couldn't fully commit to a look. When the girl looked up at her, Astra was struck by how oddly beautiful she was ... and the gray streak in her otherwise black hair. Astra swallowed nervously and then winced from the soreness in her throat. *Well, I can't be dead if I'm feeling pain*, she thought with slight relief.

"You're stronger than I expected," the girl before her said. She stood in an animal-skin tube top and linen skirt. On the right side of her face was a scar that ran through her right eyebrow and down her right cheek. Her hazel eyes were so striking that Astra had a hard time maintaining eye contact.

"Where am I?" Astra asked.

The girl thought for a moment before answering. "You're in Limbus."

"Where is *that*?" Astra asked with a frown, "I've never heard of Limbus before."

"Well, that's because most that enter here are dead," the girl said.

"Malina!"

Astra chilled at the sound of her sister's voice distantly behind her.

"Evaline!" Astra called back. "Did you do this?" she asked, turning back to face the girl, only to find that she was gone.

Astra walked into the clearing and felt strangely calm near the stream.

Evaline tore into the clearing, her face full of panic that soon turned into relief. Evaline rushed toward her, arms wide, ready for a hug, but passed right through her.

Astra looked down at herself, confused, and noticed for the first time that she was wearing a white dress that had droplets of blood on it. She looked back at Evaline's face, which was twisted with confusion and sadness.

"Evaline it's okay," Astra said.

"Okay?" said Evaline, scoffing. "You're the one bleeding out of your face, and you're telling me it's okay?" Evaline snapped with tears building in her eyes.

"What?" Malina said, again confused, and looked into the stream, which reflected the truth. Her heart thudded hard in her chest as fear seized her. She cupped the cool water and rubbed it against her face, but the blood refused to leave her skin. The whites of her eyes were bloodshot, and the dried blood wouldn't come off tear ducts, lips, cheeks, or ears.

"Evaline, dear, I'm so glad you could join us," the girl from before said with a knowing smile.

Malina hadn't seen her return.

"It was you," Evaline said, marveling at the girl before them. "Yemaya?"

The woman said nothing and gave them a slight bow.

"Who is *Yemaya*?" Astra asked with a frown, racking her brain, trying to remember a goddess by that name from the old world.

"No one you would know," she said with a slight frown. "My people died long before your great grandparents came to exist," she explained, kneeling before the stream.

"Very sad," Evaline said, crossing her arms and walking over to stand next to Astra. "You said you needed me to help Malina ..." She uncrossed her arms and held them open wide. "Well, I'm here, so what do we do next?"

"Are you that eager to die?" Yemaya asked.

Alarm bells went off in Astra's body, and she started to shake her head vehemently, thinking of the way Frey had run toward Freya's dying body.

"No," Evaline responded weakly to the woman's question, making her chuckle.

"Is Evaline dead? Did you kill her?" Astra demanded.

"No, nothing like that," Yemaya said with a serious expression, her hazel eyes taking on a yellow shade. "I watch over rituals performed under the gaze of the moon," she explained.

"That woman was praying to you when she was performing the ritual. Did she do something wrong? Isn't that why you brought me here, so that I can help you fix it?"

Astra looked from Evaline's trusting face to Yemaya's careful expression and sweet smile.

"Yes," Yemaya said. "When the ritual went wrong, I jumped into your body," Yemaya explained, locking eyes with Astra. "Unfortunately, my megin was too much for your body to handle ... and it's killing you," she said and waved a hand over the stream bringing into focus an image of their father driving while Evaline and Astra lay in the back seat.

Astra saw the color of her skin fade as more blood dripped from her body. "Then leave my body!" Astra said.

"It's not that simple," Yemaya replied, regretfully waving her hand over the stream again and standing.

"What do I have to do?" Evaline said, stepping forward.

"All you need to do, sweet Angel, is take Malina's megin."

"What?" the girls said in unison.

"Follow me," Yemaya beckoned and walked away.

Evaline followed the woman blindly, putting Astra on high alert. She walked behind her sister, looking around the space for any sign of the truth. In the next clearing, there stood two doors, and Astra frowned. She knew the trick was right in front of her, but she couldn't tell what it was. *This is too simple. Too easy*, Astra thought.

"If you keep frowning like that, you'll wrinkle faster," Evaline teased with a straight face.

"Evaline, this is all too convenient," Astra began.

"Convenient?" Evaline said, feigning shock. "You were dying in front of me! Dante's veil knocked me out, and now I'm here feeling nauseous with every step I take. This is anything but convenient," she snapped.

"Evaline, I didn't force you to come here," Astra said with a frown.

"No, but I'm here because *you* need me," Evaline said with a smile. "I'm helping you in a way that only a twin can," Evaline said and walked toward Yemaya.

"Right," Astra said, bitterly rolling her eyes. *And as the older sister, I have to protect you, dumbass*, she thought, clenching her jaw.

Yemaya stood in front of the doors, wearing a smile. She held a ribbon in her hand and stood waiting patiently for Astra to walk toward them. Taking her time, Astra obliged, standing in front of the woman and beside her sister. She immediately understood what the ritual was, having seen it before. It was a megin bond performed between a Bahkir and a Gio that was often applied to Shikka pairings prior to dangerous missions. *She wants me and Angel to do this?*

"This is to bond you two together through megin. A bonding of souls will bring you two closer together while she uses your megin."

"We're twins," Evaline proclaimed proudly. "There's nothing closer than that! We shared the womb with each other," she said with a chuckle.

"Evaline," Astra groaned, "what if I die? Will Evaline die too?"

"Malina," Evaline chastised, "I'm here you aren't going to."

"And what if I *do*?" Astra demanded, refusing to back down. "I don't want Evaline to get hurt."

"Let me help *you*!" Evaline snapped. "Just because you're older doesn't mean you get to be heroic all the time. I can help you, too! Trust me ..."

Astra thought about Frey and Freya, briefly wondering who the older sibling was. And then, she wondered if it mattered because they were both dead. She looked at Evaline and felt the love they shared between them. *I'm willing to die for her. I just never believed she felt the same*, Astra thought with a slight smile. *She thinks I'm heroic?* With a sigh and chuckle, she raised her arm. "Okay, fine," Astra said, caving under the pressure of Evaline's pouty face. "Let's do it."

Trauma
Victor

Victor paced in the lobby of the ICU. Occasionally, he sat in a chair and rested his head in his hands as his nerves began to overtake him. Every time he closed his eyes, he was ten years old again. Smelling burnt flesh and tasting the metallic iron of blood in his mouth. He held the cold hand of his little sister, who was eight years old and as calm as a domestic cat. Their mother was dying in the next room, and the nurse was working frantically to try to save her. A doctor had already alerted them that their father had passed, but their mother ... she stood a chance.

"Jade, don't worry," he said more for himself than her, "Mom is going to pull through."

"I hope she *doesn't*," Jade whispered coldly.

Victor stilled, unable to take his next breath.

"What?" he asked, taking her into the lobby and away from potential eavesdroppers. "Why would you say that?" he asked, kneeling in front of her.

"Because she watched while he hurt us," she explained calmly. "You shouldn't have saved her," she said with a frown. "I couldn't pull it back in once it got out. It could have gotten to you, too," she said, touching his cheek with her small hand and then wrapping her arms around his neck as she cried at the thought of losing him.

Victor stood and started to pace again. He did so as if to outrace his demons, but no matter how much he moved, the past still played out in his mind. He remembered the stress of going into the system and watching his sister like a hawk to make sure she didn't lash out again. He remembered going to the hospital every other day, hoping for any good news about his mother's condition.

"It looks like they're going to pull through," Rita said with a gentle smile, offering him a bottle of water.

"What?" Victor asked in a haze as he envisioned her younger self standing in the same spot, speaking the words more than thirty years ago.

Rita's smile disappeared, and she waved for him to follow her. "Let's get some fresh air," she offered, and he hesitantly followed her to the roof.

As they climbed the steps, he registered the tape on the inside of her elbow—where an IV once was—and the medical bracelet. *Is she really okay?* He thought as his anxiety grew. She looked back momentarily, stopping, something unreadable crossing her face before she pushed the door open. The fresh air hit Victor's face, and he sighed, feeling a great weight lift from his shoulders. Rita handed him the bottle again, and this time he gladly took it. He drained half of its contents, feeling better than he had in months. He looked back to find Rita rising from propping the door open and noticed her glowing eyes. He smiled and released a soft chuckle.

"And here I thought fresh air and a bottle of water was the cure to my worries," he said with a smile.

Rita smiled back and sighed as she walked to the edge of the roof and leaned against the protective wall. He wanted to be angry with her, but the proper feelings wouldn't come. He walked to the edge to stand beside her, breathing in her rosy scent, and a forgotten memory suddenly came to him.

He'd wept in frustration until he had a headache, and Rita eventually found him on the roof. She silently sat beside him and offered him water when he calmed. She had no judgment in her eyes and even offered him a gentle smile.

"I thought you'd be happy about your mom," she said casually, her light blue eyes studying him.

"I am," he said defensively.

She smiled and looked away. "Then why are you afraid?" she asked, facing the door.

"Jade," he said, studying the water bottle. "She might finish what she started." He wasn't afraid to be open with her. She knew their whole story and never shied away from them. She'd even fought for them to stay at the halfway house.

"What if she doesn't?" she said, leaning her head against the cement wall and flattening her ponytail.

"I don't think I can take that chance," he said quietly.

"So, what will you do?" she asked, genuinely curious.

"I'm not sure," he stated.

"Victor," Rita said, pulling him from the past. Victor looked at her, and she stared at him with undistracted interest.

"Did you ask me something?" he asked apologetically.

She released a small chuckle and shook her head. "No," she said gently, "but how are you feeling?"

"Nostalgic," he said with a heavy sigh.

"I see," she said and looked out into the parking lot. "Elizabeth should be here soon."

"How do you know?" he asked.

"Jezabel called her for us," Rita said matter-of-factly.

"I see," said Victor. "She told 'em they should pull through, right?"

"Yeah," Rita said firmly. "I don't understand what happened with Malina, but I know it's not good," she said with a frown. "I have some leads, and I'll look into them shortly."

"Who are your leads?"

"I can't," she said, firmly shaking her head. She met his eyes, and her irises were a vibrant violet hue. "I'll follow up when I have something," she said, then turned away from the roof's edge.

"Rita, I asked you before why you decided to help," he said carefully, turning to face her, but the rest of his question dried in his throat when he saw Dante blocking her exit.

"Please keep going," Dante taunted. "Don't stop on my account." With that, he stepped forward and kicked away the prop that held the door ajar.

"Don't," Rita said, trying to reach past him for the door, but Dante grabbed it before it shut and, he raised an eyebrow at Victor.

"*Blood majik?*" Dante growled.

Rita flinched away. "You gave me no other choice," she said standing firm, "the girls were dying."

"Victor, if she has leads, we aren't going to let her walk away."

"Information is my trade," Rita countered. "I won't give up my contacts."

"Oh," Dante said with narrowed eyes, slamming the door behind him. "So, why should I let you go?"

"Dante," Victor said, pushing off the wall, "just let her go. She's *helping* us."

"Helping us by putting children in the hospital with amateur rituals?"

"*You* put them here when you unleashed your veil," Rita hissed.

"I'm getting real tired of your mouth," Dante said, closing the narrow distance between them.

Once again, Victor walked up and pulled Rita behind him.

"I said, let her go," Victor said in a deep, authoritative voice. "She's always been better to us alive."

"Her usefulness expired a long time ago," Dante growled. "Malina had to receive blood transfusions because of your little mishap."

"That wasn't my fault," Rita insisted.

"No, it just happened under *your* watch during *your* ritual," he said.

Just then, a feminine voice came from behind Dante. "Funny ... that's what *I* was about to say."

Turning, Dante found Elizabeth glaring at him. He stepped in front of her, and Elizabeth's jaw clenched.

Victor felt a chill that wasn't caused by the nighttime air.

"Vic, what the hell were you thinking?" Elizabeth demanded. "Why did you hire a novice to perform a complex ritual? We have trained people in the Shikka to deal with these things."

"Rita's no novice," Victor said.

Elizabeth moved her brother to the side and walked forward to stand in front of Victor. Rita backed away, and Dante walked forward to block Rita. She released an aggravated sigh when the rooftop door clicked shut.

"Perfect," Rita said sarcastically.

"Victor, explain yourself!" Elizabeth shouted. "Why didn't you—"

"It's because Jade did it," Rita lied. Elizabeth quieted, and Dante stilled, not allowing his expression to reveal anything.

"Jade did *what*?" Elizabeth demanded.

"I'm not telling you shit until someone opens that door," Rita snarled.

Elizabeth frowned, her glacial green eyes glowing as she lifted her hand, around which a white cloud formed. "I'm confident I can change your mind," she hissed.

"What makes you believe I'll cave to pain?" Rita said with a smirk. "You might get the wrong response," she added with a wink. Elizabeth stepped forward, and Dante moved forward to stop her.

"How much do you know?" Dante demanded.

"I'll know more if you let me go," Rita said, staring into his stormy eyes. "And I'll make sure you're the first to know my next move."

He clenched his jaw and walked to the door, gripping the knob with all of his strength and twisting it until they heard a snap.

"Go," Dante demanded, and Rita walked toward him without hesitation. "Elizabeth, don't," said Dante when Elizabeth moved to stop her.

Then, Rita raced down the stairs and out of Victor's sight.

"Dante, care to explain?" said Elizabeth, lowering her hand and pulling back her megin.

"She's back," Dante said, placing his hand on his waist and slamming the door shut.

Control
Elizabeth

Elizabeth shook with anger at the mention of the infamous Jade. *How does she always manage to blow up my life?* Elizabeth pondered. She looked at the man she'd been forced to marry and replayed their conversation that morning. *"Because that's what you do when you're in a partnership. You discuss the best course of action for your child together ..."* *The fucking hypocrite*, she thought, seething. Elizabeth glared at her husband and fought the angry tears she wanted to shed. She controlled her breathing and looked to the heavens for strength before turning back to the man in front of her.

She walked over to the men who were talking in hushed voices. *You've got to be fucking kidding*, she thought, storming over to them. Dante looked at her with dark irises as a warning.

"What are you talking about with *my* husband," she hissed.

"We don't have time for your high emotions Elizabeth," Dante said, turning his head away from her.

Victor refused to meet her eyes.

"If it's about Jade. I deserve to know," Elizabeth retorted, not backing down.

"Elizabeth," Victor pleaded.

"Shut your fucking mouth," Elizabeth snapped. "*You* don't have a right to talk to me about anything right now," she said, pointing an icy finger at him.

"Look at you," Dante snapped, grabbing her hand, which she quickly snatched away. "You can't even control your emotions! You're of no use to me," he snapped, and Elizabeth's heart hurt as it often did when Dante belittled her that way.

"Don't talk to her like that," Victor said with a frown.

Elizabeth looked at her husband, and at that moment, all of her anger melted away.

"I'm the only one that can reign in my sister when she's like this," Dante said, "so don't tell me how to handle her."

"She's my *wife*, and megin-enhanced or not, you don't belittle her like that in my presence," Victor said, moving forward until he was only inches from Dante's face.

Dante chuckled and stepped back, shrugging, and waved a hand to Elizabeth. "Then tell her and see how she handles it," Dante challenged.

Victor's forest-green eyes looked at Elizabeth.

She breathed deeply, forcing her anger to melt away. She felt her hands warm as she focused on the green eyes before her. The eyes that never looked at her with contempt or disinterest. Even on the days, she was especially hateful—even though she ordered him not to talk to her moments before. Those eyes looked at her with trust and understanding.

"Did Jade place the sigil on her daughter?" Elizabeth asked.

"No," Victor said, shaking his head. "That was your old partner."

Elizabeth frowned at that. "Why would he do that?" she demanded. "He's been lying low since he left the Shikka."

"Apparently, he joined the Kipi and did it at the request of Azazel's father," Dante said, shaking his head and looking at Elizabeth's hands.

Elizabeth bit the inside of her cheek and focused on her breath. "Who gave you that information?" she demanded. "Was it, Margherita?"

"No," Victor replied. "Rita doesn't give up information that's irrelevant to the trade."

"Trade?" Elizabeth asked in a nasty tone, "and what exactly did you trade away for this botched ritual?" she demanded.

"Nothing," Victor said, meeting Elizabeth's gaze. "She just said Malina wouldn't pay for the sins of her parents."

"She knows," Elizabeth said, shocked.

"She deals in information. It's not that surprising," Victor said with a shrug.

"Sins of her parents," Elizabeth repeated. "So, what exactly did you do, Dante?"

Before Dante could answer, the rooftop door opened. Gabriel stood at the entrance, and his red eyes held a deep-rooted pain, but he forced a smile that appeared to be more of a grimace. The more Elizabeth stared at him, the more it looked like he wanted to cry or lash out.

"Evaline is awake," he forced out.

"What about Malina," Dante asked immediately. Gabriel shook his head and glared at Elizabeth before looking somewhere over her head. That hateful glance made Elizabeth bristle with anger. *I'm not a horrible guardian to that girl*, Elizabeth thought self-righteously.

"If that's all, we have a conversation to finish—one that you interrupted," Elizabeth said to Gabriel, who looked once at Dante and then left.

"Did you have that boy do what the Kipi believe he did?" Elizabeth asked.

"What?" Dante scoffed aggressively. "What do you think, Elizabeth?" he asked in a dangerous tone.

"I think whatever sins you and Jade have committed are now infecting Malina, and I will *not* allow that shit in my house," Elizabeth stated.

"What are you saying?" Victor asked, walking toward her with concern in his eyes.

"Victor, we're taking *our* daughter home," Elizabeth said with finality.

"They're both—" Victor began.

"No," Elizabeth said, shaking her head and ignoring the warning gaze of her husband, and plunged forward. "I think it's time Malina is raised by her father."

"I'm—"

"You aren't and it's better for our family that we stop cleaning up our siblings' mess," Elizabeth explained. She closed the distance between herself and her husband. "She's your niece, Vic, and you almost killed your daughter for her," she said gently.

"That's not what happened!"

"Elizabeth, are you sure—" Dante began and stopped as his face softened and hardened once again. "Don't take what you're saying lightly."

"When she wakes up, she's fully your responsibility,"

"Elizabeth, I don't consent—"

"You don't have a say," Elizabeth snapped, interrupting Victor. "You're the one that went to that *whore* for help, and she's the one that placed her in a coma. If you had just brought her to base like I asked ... if we'd made the decision together like the *team* you want us to be ... this conversation would have gone differently."

"I apologize for that, but you don't—"

"I *do*," Elizabeth shot back.

"I won't let you do this to her," Victor said, shaking his head.

"I won't allow my daughter to die for your pride," Elizabeth said and left the rooftop.

15

Hope
Gabriel

Gabriel raced down the stairs, heart pounding with the information he had just overheard. *Malina isn't Elizabeth's* daughter, he thought, considering the implications. The disinterest and disconnect that never made sense to him finally computed in his mind. Dante treated him the same way, holding him at arm's length, never comforting him—always bending to the will of Malina. If it wasn't for Malina begging him, Gabriel wouldn't have had a home; he would have been lost on the streets of Anicha. It wasn't a bad place to be at seven—he was already a skilled fisherman like his father—but that wasn't good enough for Malina.

He stood outside her door as the nurses wheeled out a cart of empty blood bags, and the head nurse gave him a gentle smile, patting his shoulder. Jezabel was always kind to him; in the early weeks, after his father disappeared and his mother went into a coma, he spent a lot of time at the hospital. Watching his mother sleep. *Sleep but never wake up*, he thought grimly as he walked into Malina's room and sat in the chair they arranged by her bed.

He sat down in the chair and grabbed her hand like he had his mother's a thousand times. It hurt him deeply to be in the same position, knowing that the last moments together had been spent arguing and the last time he saw her, she'd had fear in her eyes. He brought her hand to his forehead and tried to breathe through his pain, but it was all too familiar.

"I'm sorry to interrupt," Remilda said from behind him.

"What is it?" he asked.

"I talked to the nurse who told me—"

"She's in a coma," said Gabriel, running his thumb across the back of her hand. "But she's strong. She *will* wake up from this."

Malina's complexion had returned to its regular pallor. When he first came to the hospital, she'd looked like a ghost. They'd cleaned the blood from her face, but even so, he knew he'd have nightmares about it.

"Well, what I was going to say was that it sounds like she's suffering from an advanced case of Heka sickness," Remilda said gently.

"Are you implying that the medical staff could be doing something more?" Gabriel asked.

"Yes," Remilda replied.

Gabriel felt hopeful but skeptical. "What is it?"

"In Serinytas, they would check her zawadi," Remilda stated.

"Za what?" Gabriel asked, finally turning his head away from Malina to look at Remilda.

She was staring at Malina with a frown that made Gabriel believe there was something seriously wrong. Her mahogany eyes shimmered, and she gave him a reassuring smile. She walked to a chair and pulled it up next to him.

"Za-wha-di," she said, pronouncing the word slowly. "It's the part of the soul that carries the megin."

"How would you check someone's soul?" Gabriel asked incredulously.

"In an advanced ritual," Remilda stated. "Well advanced for Ekocia, but second nature for Serinytas."

"Do you know how to do that?" Gabriel asked, but before he was finished asking the question, Remilda was frowning and shaking her head.

"I'm sorry, but no," she said. "In most cases, the zawadi heals on its own," Remilda said hopefully.

"In others?" Gabriel asked, feeling a fist tighten around his heart.

"Let's just hope Ma ... *Astra* wakes up soon," Remilda said, patting his hand.

They sat in comfortable silence, Remilda looking through the notes she had taken at school while Gabriel watched the news. He put the subtitles on so he didn't feel the need to turn the volume up until they mentioned Macden. When the time came, he grabbed the remote sitting on the end table and unmuted the TV.

"*The outage could last for at least three weeks due to their grid running independently from ... Oh wait, what is this*?" the news anchor said, pausing and turning around to see the flicker of light come back on. "*What a surprising turn of events. It looks like, despite the blown transformer, light has found a way back into these peoples' lives—*"

Gabriel muted the tv again and frowned.

"What did she mean by their grid running independently?" Remilda asked.

"Macden is a city that's full of citizens that oppose the government and how they run things. They're Gios that hate the Bahkir and other Gios that live among us. They chose to live separately from society, so we allow them to suffer and die on their own sword," Elizabeth said coldly, scowling at the TV. "They're a bunch of hypocrites."

"What makes you believe that?" Remilda asked with a scowl of her own.

"They have one transformer for their city. No electrician would go out in a storm to fix it. A skilled Bahkir is powering that city right now," said Elizabeth with a look of disgust. "Evaline, hurry. I have work in a few hours, and you need to rest in your own bed," Elizabeth said, stepping to the side and crossing her arms over her chest.

Evaline stepped into the room, wearing a bewildered expression. She walked toward her sister, stopping on the side that wasn't occupied by Gabriel. She grabbed Malina's hand with her own bandaged hand and squeezed it. She looked to the monitors, to Gabriel, and then back to Malina's face. She shook her head, and when tears flowed down her cheeks, Elizabeth stepped forward, alarmed.

"You'll hurt her by holding so tight," Gabriel cautioned, reaching over Malina toward Evaline.

"You don't understand. She's supposed to be awake!" Evaline snapped.

"What makes you say that?" Gabriel asked with a frown.

"Well, because *I'm* awake," Evaline explained simply.

"Astra was exposed to more Heka—"

"What?" Evaline interrupted Remilda, "I don't know what that is or what you're talking about. I bonded with her, and she—"

"That woman forced a bond on you!" Elizabeth hissed, alarmed by the news. The temperature in the room dropped, making Remilda shiver.

"I wasn't forced!" Evaline snapped. "Yemaya said it would help—"

"Yemaya," Remilda repeated, shaking her head, "you must be mistaken."

"I'm not! I was helping my sister! With the bond, when I awoke, she was supposed to, too," Evaline explained, glaring at the disbelieving eyes and then looking back at her sister, "but she didn't."

"Who is Yemaya?" Elizabeth pried. "Was she with Margherita during this"—Elizabeth waved her hand over Malina's body, exasperated, while she searched in her mind for the right word—"performance?"

"Yemaya is a goddess," Remilda said, but Elizabeth glared at her. Remilda shivered and looked away.

"Evaline," Elizabeth prompted.

"I-I don't know," Evaline stammered, rubbing her sister's hand nervously.

"What *do* you know?" Elizabeth urged. "What happened tonight?"

"Mal was floating and bleeding, but then she saw me and asked *me* for help. I reached out to her and ..." Her voice trailed off, and she held her bandaged hand up to her face. "My head," she said absentmindedly, holding the back of her head with a bandaged hand. "When I woke up, I was in this big meadow. I ran through the forest and found Mal with Yemaya. She told me if I bonded with Malina and returned home, Malina would follow and we would be awake together," Evaline explained with a nod of her head.

"It was a dream," Elizabeth said, shaking her head.

Gabriel watched Remilda's body tense as Evaline told her story. Gabriel raised his eyebrow at her, and Remilda placed a finger to her lips, her eyes wide with wonder. *There is more to it than that*, Gabriel concluded. Evaline was shaking her head, and hot angry tears flooded her eyes and ran down her cheeks.

"No," Evaline said, glaring at her mother.

"What?" Elizabeth said, stepping toward her daughter.

"I'm not leaving my sister's side!" Evaline snapped, gripping Malina's hand tighter. Gabriel saw a shine of megin glimmered in Evaline's eyes as the heart rate monitor's beeping increased. Gabriel breathed in deep and smelled the hint of dewy rainfall emanating from Evaline.

"You both need to leave," Gabriel said in a level tone.

"I said—" Evaline started with a snarky attitude but stopped when she saw the look he gave her.

"Malina was attacked by megin," Gabriel snapped, making her flinch. "We all know how Elizabeth can get," Gabriel said, glaring at the party in question. "You purposely provoking her is only hurting Malina. Is that what you want?" Gabriel demanded.

"Wh-n-no," Evaline stammered, touching her face and wincing as her head pounded. "I was—"

"Leaving," Victor said, walking into the room. "Visiting hours are over, and we all need our rest."

Remilda was the first to walk out, with Elizabeth following behind her, but she lingered beside her husband, placing a hesitant hand on his bicep. Victor covered her hand with his own and then held a hand out to Evaline. She hesitated, looked down at her sister one last time, and then went to her father. Gabriel found himself sitting alone in the room with Malina once again. In the quiet, he found his center and blew out his frustration. He scrubbed the bottom of the chair back as he stood and stretched.

"I'll be back tomorrow," he said quietly and bent down to kiss her on the forehead. He found Remilda not quite waiting on him outside the room, but she stood nearby as she spoke to Dante. "Hey," Gabriel said in a level voice.

"Remilda tells me Evaline recanted quite a story," Dante responded.

"Oh, yeah," Gabriel said with a shrug and frown that couldn't hide the hope in his voice. "I think there's more to it, though."

"Hmm," Dante grunted.

"We deal with similar cases in Serinytas all the time," Remilda interjected.

"How often do patients come out of it?" Gabriel asked.

"Often. If we get Malina to Serinytas, the pharaoh will be more than happy to help a friend of the throne," Remilda added—like sugar and cream to a bitter drink.

Dante grunted again and looked at Gabriel.

"What do you think about this?" Dante asked.

"I—" Gabriel started and then stopped to lick his lips and think over his response. "If there's a higher chance *Astra* will come out of this, we should try," he said, looking pointedly at Remilda before returning his gaze to Dante.

Dante nodded, lost in thought while looking back to the room. "How is she?" Dante asked with a softness only reserved for her.

"They cleaned her up," Gabriel said with a nod. "She doesn't have her megin," Gabriel stated.

Dante's eye twitched at that, his mouth set in a firm line. "Remilda mentioned that Evaline said they had bonded."

"I saw and felt a trickle of her megin in Evaline; what she said was true," Gabriel confirmed.

Dante remained silent but nodded. "I'll talk to the Yakim tomorrow and start on the proper paperwork," Dante said and walked away.

Shadow
Margherita

Margherita was in the depths of Macden when the lights flickered back on, and the cheering from the residents began. Margherita felt herself smile briefly at their relief and happiness, but her inside still churned, leaving her queasy. She drove back to the halfway home she grew up in and gathered the evidence of the ritual she had performed hours before. On her way out to the car, her phone buzzed, alerting her to a text message.

Margherita placed the box of her things in the car and stepped back to pull out her phone when she felt something hard beneath the tennis shoes she'd changed into. Stepping away, she bent down and picked up the necklace she'd placed on Malina by the lace ribbon. She touched the pendant gently to trace the carving in stone, but as soon as her finger touched the etched line, it crumbled and blew away in the wind.

Margherita wanted to scream in frustration but knew that would only add to the trouble she found herself facing. *It was only supposed to be a simple removal*, she thought in a foul mood, yanking out her phone as it vibrated again.

CB: Dante is on his way.

CB: Did he find you?

CB: Aunt Jez said you were admitted but you left against doc orders where are you?

CB: ANSWER ME!

Three dots bubbled up, and Margherita texted back quickly.

M: I'll be back later tonight.

CB: Where are you?

M: See you later.

Margherita pocketed her phone and drove toward Belladonna's fields. As she cruised along, Carina called her twice, and on the third attempt, she answered with a sigh.

"Care, please ..."

"You can't leave me like that. We're supposed to be a team. Isn't that what you told me?" Carina's voice was shrill with emotion.

"Carina you can't work with me on this one," Margherita said calmly.

Carina's heavy breathing filled the speaker. "Why not? Is it because I told Dante—"

"No," Margherita said, quickly cutting off Carina, "No, that's not it."

"Did he hurt you?"

"Carina, don't do this to yourself," Margherita pleaded, "listen I'll be back tonight, and we can talk about everything then. This isn't simple, and I don't want you hurt. That's all there is to it. I promise."

Margherita opened her mouth to speak again, but the line went dead. "Shit," she muttered.

Margherita sat in her car thinking about how she was going to confront Old Lady Bella when she felt an aura she hadn't experienced in a long time. She stepped out, grabbing the spare key to the shop—the one she had never turned in. She grabbed the handle and pulled, testing her theory. The door gave, and with bated breath, Margherita stepped inside.

As soon as she stepped in, she was almost blinded by the brightness of the aura that emanated from the room below. Vibrant red light filled her vision in tandem with the rage that boiled her blood. She gripped the handle in her hand so tightly that the pain pulled her from her shaken head space. Margherita opened her eyes and forced her megin to protect her from being overwhelmed again.

"Oh, look at that," a voice from the corner hummed.

"What?" Margherita barked at the woman without delay.

Jade widened her gaze and smirked with surprise. Then, she pushed away from the wall she braced herself against and straightened her relaxed posture. Jade was wearing a breathable black shirt with decorative belladonnas on it. Her bottoms were white, bearing an image of a mortar and pestle. If the situation wasn't so dire, Margherita would have laughed at Jade's attire. Her hair was wet and hung loose in her pixie cut.

"It looks like your discipline has improved since last I saw you," she said with admiration in her green gaze.

"And it looks like you've aged," Margherita retorted, drawing a scoff. "Why are you here?"

"Trying to find the loose ends," Jade said cryptically.

"You sound like her, you know?" Margherita said, walking toward the back of the store. She was aware of Jade following her and stopped when she reached the door.

"You caused the blackout didn't you?" Margherita asked, hand on the knob of the door.

"Something traumatic happened to me," Jade said with a shrug, "but you and her know all about that don't you?" Jade said in an accusatory tone.

"What are you talking about?" Margherita demanded, standing in front of the door that Bella never bothered to lock. "What happened to you," Margherita asked with a frown as she scrutinized Jade's stoic face. "What did you do to her?" Margherita demanded, realizing Jade had already made herself comfortable in the store.

Margherita opened the door and ran downstairs she rushed through the basement sized home in search of Bella. With her chest heaving, she walked back into the living room area and glared at Jade's bored face. She had made a pot of tea and poured herself a cup while Margherita searched the home.

"She's not here," Margherita declared violently shaking.

"Good observation skills," Jade said sardonically.

"What did you do to her," Margherita demanded.

Jade huffed at Margherita's resolve. "Nothing yet, because I haven't had the luxury of finding her."

"What did she do to you?" Margherita inquired, walking into the kitchen.

"Would you believe she slighted me first if I told you the truth?" Jade asked with genuine curiosity. She hoisted herself up on the counter sipping on her cup of tea as she waited for Margherita's answer.

"Why are you here?" Margherita asked in a sigh.

"She used you to *take* something important from me," Jade alluded. Margherita frowned at the accusation and looked around the home. "She left knowing I was here and I would look for her after she did what she did," Jade mournfully lost and thought. "She left perhaps three hours ago," Jade muttered.

Margherita wanted to argue with her, but it was rare for Jade to be wrong and calm. The calmness was making Margherita anxious. *Why would Bella leave? Where did she go?* Margherita thought to herself as she left the kitchen and walked into the living room. To no surprise, the old woman's home smelled of herbs and spices. She channeled her megin and frowned at the complete absence of Bella's presence from the home. Even on the pictures of Bella with her family and Azael, Bella's unique aura was exhumed.

"Did you come to kill her?" Margherita inquired, turning to face Jade's deceitfully innocent face.

"Before I tell you anything," Jade began, her brown skin and green eyes reminding Margherita of Victor in the lighting, "tell me why you performed the ritual." As she spoke, she stared at Margherita, eyes burning.

"What?" Margherita asked, pinching her eyebrows together in confusion.

"You heard me. Why did you do it?" Jade repeated. "You don't—"

"You told me to before you left," Margherita stated, walking toward her but stopping at the arm of the couch. "You came by Kore's Palace after dropping off the girl and asked me to look after her."

"Well you didn't, did you? Because—"

"I know, you don't understand the lifestyle of parenthood, but a huge part of it is allowing them to make mistakes on their own. Also, what happened to her wasn't completely her fault, you should know. You're the one who cursed her," Margherita baited.

"What?" Jade asked incredulously.

"I've seen your rune work before," Margherita clarified.

"Mmm," Jade hummed. She walked into the living room and took a seat on the loveseat. "Have you now?"

"The delay rune on top of the hex mark was killing her," Margherita explained, taking a seat by Jade. "I did it to save her life."

Margherita watched Jade carefully and as usual she gave nothing away. Joining the Shikka only helped amplify her poker face among other skills, as they sent her on covert missions. Margherita couldn't tell what Jade was feeling and she didn't have enough strength to open up her mind to see Jade's aura.

With a sigh, Margherita took a seat by Jade. "Why are you here now?" Margherita asked. "I told you why I helped. So, tell me why you're here."

Before
Jade

Jade stood at the entrance of the forbidden forest smirking at the annoyance Lunis would feel about the situation. However, the longer he made her wait, the more annoyed she felt. *It's only right to make him feel my pain*, her sadistic mind told her as she stepped into the forest. She removed her mask as she walked through the brush. The forest was rich with untapped heka, causing her skin to bubble with goosebumps as she neared streaming water.

A strong hand slammed down on her shoulder, gripping her hard. Jade's hand slammed down on top of his, and she immediately twisted his wrist as she turned her body. He ignored the pain she knew she had caused, and he slammed his hand into her throat. She released her hold on him; her hands instinctively went to her throat as the trauma forced her to clamp shut.

The man grabbed her wrist uncomfortably tight as his golden-brown eyes brightened. Jade's head swam with vertigo as he used his megin to transport them out of the forest. On solid ground, he released her to allow her to self-regulate. His hair had been shaved around the sides, revealing a faded tattoo she couldn't make out. His tightly kinked hair was styled back into two-strand twist braids. His sepia brown skin glowed as the use of his megin subsided.

"Why can't you just wait for me?" Lunis complained in his baritone voice.

"I did," Jade said with a chuckle to cover up the pain she felt in her throat. "You were late."

"I'm *always* on time," Lunis said, shaking his head and frowning. "You're an hour early."

"What alarm systems do you have in there that alert you to any—"

"Why are you here?" he growled, and Jade found herself smirking again.

"For a subordinate, you're very aggressive with me," she mused, arching an eyebrow. Lunis crossed his arms and said nothing else. Jade sighed and pulled out a contract, which she handed to him.

"You know the process," he said, taking the paper and holding out a hand for the bag of gold.

"You aren't even gonna read over the contract?" she asked with a raised eyebrow.

"Why are you in such a good mood today?" he asked with a frown. Jade shrugged and began to walk around Lunis, irking him further. "Stop moving," he said, casting her a sober look.

"Open the contract and I will," she bargained.

Lunis sighed and broke the seal of the contract to read over the details. "I can't take this," he said with a scowl. "This puts me out of Hiboria. I'm needed here!" Lunis said, crumpling up the parchment.

"What you were assigned to do here is already done," Jade said with a shrug, tossing him a bag of coins. "Next assignment."

"No," Lunis said, shaking his head but pocketing the coins. "King Alrick is dead, but the ruler in his place—"

"Was never supposed to be your concern," Jade said levelly. Silence mounted between them as his anger churned and boiled. "Assigning you in Hiboria was a courtesy don't forget that," Jade muttered and began to walk toward the forest. "I have no one but myself to blame for your insolence," she said, shrugging. When she turned, he was close to her back. "You're taking the payment and you're doing the job," she said with finality.

"Or what?" Lunis growled.

"I'll add to your debt," she said with another shrug. "This could be your last job or—"

"This is my last job?" Lunis said, taking a step back.

"And to think I was so happy for you," she said with a pout.

"Jade don't fuck—"

"Oh Lunis," she groaned, shoving him away. "You're such a whiner. Honestly, I'm happy to be rid of you ..."

"When do you need it done?" Lunis asked, and with her back to him, she smirked and pulled on her mask.

"Your eagerness is what I'll miss," she teased, looking back at his stony face. "You could do it *now*," she suggested.

"Are you headed to Ekocia?" Lunis asked.

"Trying to hitch a ride?" Jade mused, channeling her megin to the tip of her finger.

"Are you or not?"

"Yes, yes," Jade said, waving away his impatience. She drew a home rune into the bark of a tree at the entrance of the forbidden forest and smiled Lunis' grunt of disapproval.

The tree split, soon crumbling under the pressure of the megin that was channeled into it. Lunis grabbed her hand and shielded his eyes from the blinding light that illuminated their position. Jade jumped, quickly pulling Lunis through with her. On the other side, thunder boomed, and rain chilled her body. *Why am I here?* She pondered, staring at the molded wooden structure of the halfway house she grew up in.

"I need your release," Lunis said, tapping her with the contract. She turned to face him, taking in his loose linen cream shirt and brown cotton pants.

"You're going in *that*?" Jade said incredulously.

"This is—"

"If you're caught," Jade said in her rehearsed no-nonsense voice, "you'll owe me your life or the equivalent," Jade warned. "Did you enjoy taking the lives of five hundred men that much?"

"I won't be caught," Lunis said and held the paper out to her.

She looked down at the parchment and illuminated the return sigil that would be used after the kill was made. Lunis clenched his jaw and walked away from her. She turned her head slightly enjoying the view of him walking away.

"*You could meddle and make him owe you more lives,*" said the melodic voice in her head, tempting her. She smiled at the thought of his anger. He was the only one in the web that had tried to kill her and had almost succeeded ... twice.

"I'll keep my word and let him go," Jade said to the voice and looked up at the sky. The heka in the air unnerved her. Something about the way it was pulling at her megin didn't sit right.

"*You should leave,*" the voice warned.

"What aren't you telling me?" Jade asked, pausing at the edge of the building in the back.

"*You're about to see her again, and she isn't happy about what you did,*" The voice warned.

Jade's mind flashed to seventeen years ago. She was in the mysterious land of Hiboria. Ekocian leaders were skeptical of it's existence and were looking for leads. A favor to a friend. *It may be there; it may not. All that matters is that you try.* Ralceo was urgent in her request. With the debt Jade felt she owed to the old woman she was eager to help. Too eager.

Following Ralceo's directions Jade found herself in the forbidden forest in front of a cave. She felt heka (what she thought back then was a veil) pulling at her in a cave. She followed it and found the golden chalice that she'd been seeking for over a month. She was low on food, water, and megin, and the combination left her vulnerable and weak to any attack.

Lunis had appeared young and angry even back then, and for a week they fought everyday until she was exhausted. He should have killed her but Lunis held back, seeing that she was already in a weak state, and he offered her an out on the seventh day. "Leave and never return ..."

It was a bluff that Jade called him out on.

"If I were a man, would you treat me this way?" Jade challenged.

"Men don't get pregnant," he said with a frown and turned his back on her.

Jade ignored him. There was no way she could get pregnant, so he was mistaken about that. She ran past him to the chalice, but Lunis used his megin to appear before her. She dropped to slide between his legs, reaching out and claiming the prize, Lunis managed to grab her cramping leg. Jade placed the stem of the chalice between her teeth to keep it within her grasp, but she didn't know that was all it took. Contact with the mouth anywhere on the chalice activated its majik.

Whoever thought of that was an idiot, she thought, rolling her eyes. *He is an idiot*, Jade thought with a frown. Recalling his explanation, he was clever for a seventeen-year-old who had the stress of the world on his shoulders.

"*She's stronger than you,*" the voice marveled with melodic joy.

"Who are you talking about?" Jade asked, stilling herself in the present.

Jade rounded the building, making her way to the back where she expected to find the person or thing responsible for the heka pulling at her megin. Thunder boomed overhead, and lighting struck in front of her like it had that day all those years ago. The lighting formed into a man, and he stuck his hand through her chest. She felt the extra megin she had since that day drain out of her, but there was no pain.

"*It's been fun,*" the voice said, chilling Jade to the bone. The lighting disappeared from her, glass shattered, and light filled the room she knelt outside of.

All at once the pain hit her, Jade's head snapped back, and she felt the megin rip away from her. Her heart pounded painfully in her chest as a nosebleed poured down her face. The pain slowly subsided as her residual megin combed through her body to heal her from the trauma.

"Help me, Sister ..."

The voice was familiar yet foreign.

The heka left me and found its way into another host. Jade understood, easing down to the ground with a hand over her chest as her megin healed the discomfort she felt.

"Victor, don't let her," Margherita demanded.

"Move," her brother's voice found her ears and unexplained emotion choked her throat.

"Angel, that's not your sister," Margherita shouted. "Angel, get away from her!"

"My sister needs me! I'm going to help her!" a younger voice announced.

That must be my niece, Jade thought as she moved back to her feet. She dropped to the ground, feeling her will drain completely from her. *I didn't even sense his presence,* Jade thought, paralyzed with fear. *Dante can't find me here...*

Yet, a moment later, his veil pulled back and his deep voice boomed through the open window.

"What did you do?" he growled.

"I removed a sigil, that's all," Margherita said in a strained whispered.

Margherita performed the ritual, Jade thought, pushing herself to her feet as she moved back to the front of the building. She spotted Margherita's bright red sports car and crouched down beside the building. She watched Dante carry Malina's slumped body outside and carefully set her down beside Margherita's car.

"Are you going to say something?" Dante asked the air around him. Jade stood and walked toward them.

"Wasn't planning on it," Jade admitted.

"Why now?" Dante asked but refused to turn and face her.

Good. It's better this way, she thought, not wanting to fight Dante. "The girl," Jade answered, nearing so she could see the face of the child she'd abandoned.

"Did you have something to do with this?" Dante demanded, looking over his shoulder.

Dante frowned and turned to face her fully. His face twisted with rage, and he lunged toward her. Jade jumped back and grabbed her smoke pellets. She tossed them on the ground and released her megin to change the smoke into fire. Dante stumbled back, blocking his face from the fire, and then ran forward. Jade had already moved away and began to run down the path she'd used in her youth.

They ran through abandoned backyards and abandoned buildings. She jumped through a second-story window to a nearby rooftop, then stopped for a second to catch her breath, but Dante was never the type to shy away from danger. He rolled to a stop right in front of her, lunging at her feet. Jade jumped up, running over his back, and she dropped the fire escape to the ground and ran like her life depended on it because where Dante was concerned, it was.

"If you stop running we could talk about this," Dante beckoned, not even slightly out of breath.

"How are you not tired?" Jade mumbled and turned too soon, stopping at a dead-end. She turned back and saw his body blocking the exit.

"Ready to talk?" he taunted.

"Nope," Jade said and backed up further toward the wooden fence.

"So be it," Dante said and ran toward her.

Jade turned and ran toward the fence, but before she made it, his hand was on her shoulder, turning her to face him. With a blade in her hand, she sliced up to cut him at the wrist of the hand that had grabbed her. He dropped his hold and threw a punch with his other hand. Jade dipped down, dodging the blow, but moved his momentum along by brushing his throwing arm further into the attack. He plunged his fist through the wooden fence that blocked their way. Jade channeled her megin into her speed and agilely moved up Dante's back, proceeding to jump up the window's ledge.

Dante jumped up, grabbed her ankle, and yanked her to the ground. Jade bounced on the ground from the force, wheezing as the air left her body. She rolled to her stomach and moved to her knees, but Dante kicked her arms out from under her. Then, he kicked her over, placing his foot on her chest to keep her in place.

"Really. Let's talk."

Present

"Well, what did you two talk about?" Margherita demanded, drinking down the tea with eager, thirsty eyes.

Jade couldn't help but smile. She did miss her friend's nosey nature. "He wanted to know why I was working with the Mahavidya," Jade said with a shrug.

"But you don't work *for* them," Margherita said with a frown. "*They* work for *you* ..."

"You're too clever," said Jade, frowning as she took a sip from her own cup.

The room was quiet and thoughtful now that Jade's story was done. Jade reached into her back pocket and pulled out six golden coins, which she placed on the table by her cup. Margherita's eyes snapped toward the money, and she reached out, picking one up. In her eyes was a sheen of recognition that told Jade everything she needed to know.

"Is that all you two talked about? I highly doubt he would just let you go after that," Margherita said with a frown.

"That's all I care to share with someone who meddled with objects she didn't understand," Jade retorted, snatching the coin from Margherita's hand.

"Well, when you put it like that, it sounds like I was being reckless," Margherita said in a sardonic tone. "I only use objects I buy from Bella. Everything was supposed to be safe. What is the origin of those coins?"

"The carvings are Hiborian in origin. Like the coins—and my runes," Jade explained. "And what you did was remove a curse from me and place it on a child. Just the way that old hag wanted."

"Malina is fine. I removed the curse that was placed on her. What you're talking about doesn't make sense," Margherita stated. "You would have had to be in the protective circle—"

"Don't sell me that bullshit," Jade hissed. "I was there. Think about it. If pure heka was used to form that circle, there's nothing there to stop pure heka from getting in."

"I don't know what you're talking about," Margherita said slowly and calmly.

"Well, aren't you the perfect pawn," Jade sneered with disgust. "Practicing shit you don't understand," Jade said, shaking her head.

Silence built between them as Margherita processed Jade's hurtful words. "Bella wouldn't curse a child ..." Margherita said with uncertainty.

"She cursed me all those years ago," Jade lamented, "and if you don't believe that," Jade said quickly holding her hands up to stop Margherita from talking. "Where is she now? Why isn't she here? I know you two were close ... you always come here after a big ritual, where is she Margherita?" Jade inquired.

"You know I don't know," Margherita said shaking her head as she thought about what would cause Bella to attack at all. "Wait ... did you kill Azazel?" Margherita asked recalling Bella's accusation a week after his death.

"Not me personally," Jade said, her face smoothing over and becoming unreadable. "I hired someone for the task," she said not meeting Margherita's eyes and breaking her heart.

"Why would you do that?" Margherita asked, breathless.

"Because," Jade said, laughing as she mocked Margherita's breathing, "*Bella* had the boy nosing around where he had no business. He had to go."

"He didn't."

"He didn't," Jade repeated, placing her hand to her heart and then one up to the heavens. "I wrote the job and offered it up. That person chose to go this route."

"Was it Lunis?" Margherita asked in a whisper.

"No," Jade said in a mocking tone and laughed, "the man has morals too," she said, rolling her eyes. "No woman, no children, only corrupt officials ..." she mocked in a deep voice. "Almost reminds me of you," Jade said, looking at Margherita for a long time before tilting her head to the side. "What's wrong Mare, Mare? Confused about what to do next?" Jade said with manic humor shining in her eyes.

"I can't be a part of this," Margherita said, shaking her head and rising from the couch.

"Oh no, no, no," Jade shot back, pulling Margherita back down to the couch, "if you leave, you'll have blood on your hands," Jade said.

"I'm not one of your killers," Margherita said coldly. "Killing innocent children—"

"Azazel had just turned eighteen," Jade said, raising a finger and smiling. "Just for clarification. But please continue."

"He hadn't even had a chance to live!" Margherita yelled.

Jade's humor fell and she yawned. "I don't care," she said with a vacant stare, "but let me tell you something I know *you'll* care about. I will reveal the location of every person and creature you smuggled out of Ekocia," Jade said stoically, "if you don't save Malina's life."

"Wh-"—Margherita's heart pounded—"Why would you do that? Malina is fine ..."

"Ah, but she's not," Jade said, smiling. "She's cursed, and as long as she's cursed, she's dead," her smile faded, "and as a mother, I can't have that."

"Where is Lunis?" Margherita hissed.

"Why? Are you going to interrupt another mission?" Jade said with a glare.

"I don't know—" Margherita began.

"So, he was the one to kill Adonis?" Jade prodded.

"He was the one assigned to do it, wasn't he?" Margherita said evasively, displaying a poker face that Jade was almost impressed by. "Listen, I ..." she breathed out a frustrated breath. "I will help Malina, but you can't expose those people."

"Hmm sounds like a contract to me," Jade sang. Her smile fell and a long annoyed sigh followed her change of mood. "You see, unlike me and *Bella*," she said the old woman's name in air quotes. "You believe you have these *morals*. Proper home training some would say. You want to help people. Laudable though that is, it makes you vulnerable to manipulation— as *you* personally know ..." The sparkle of humor dulled, leaving her irises a cloudy green hue.

"The contract," Margherita said in a cold tone.

"Right here," Jade said reaching for a piece of paper that sat on the coffee table all the while staring at Margherita with a loathing so potent you could feel it in the air.

"Bella can't die," Margherita stated with finality. Jade rolled her eyes and sighed.

"I'm aware of the attachment you have to her," Jade said, pushing away from the couch and walking out of the living room without another glance or word.

Margherita followed Jade into the kitchen. "Bella was hurt because of Azazel, Malina is alive and will pull through, can't you just let this be water under the bridge?"

Jade said, sliding the parchment over to her. "Read and sign the fucking contract," Jade growled.

So, Margherita grabbed the paper and looked it over.

I (insert name here) agree to restore Malina Astra Valeno to a healthy state. I will do this in a timely manner with the knowledge that every day, a person I saved will be placed in imminent danger starting at daybreak of the following day.

"Jade!" Margherita shouted feeling flushed.

"What?" Jade asked, looking up from the fingernail she was cleaning with her blade. "What's the problem?"

"Malina's not in danger," Margherita repeated, feeling drained by the argument.

"If that's true, you should be able to pull her out of the coma *you* placed her in without issue tomorrow," Jade said without blinking. Margherita breathed out a frustrated breath and continued to read the rest of the contract.

I (insert name here) agree to do this for free. I will not ask Jade for help regarding this matter. I am fully aware this is my fault and will fix it within the week or offer my life in exchange for the life I took.

Margherita looked up from the parchment to find Jade holding a pen for her to take. Margherita signed her name in the necessary spots and handed the pen back to Jade. Jade grabbed Margherita's hand

and sliced opened her palm. Margherita yelped and attempted to pull out of Jade's grasp, but she slammed it down on the page. Jade drew out a symbol with the blood Margherita shed and then handed her the parchment.

"What is this? What does this mean," Margherita snapped. Jade laced her hands in front of her and gave her a nasty smile.

"If you asked those same questions this morning, perhaps you wouldn't be in the mess you're in now," Jade said with a shrug. "Go on now," Jade said, sitting on the stool and waving toward the door, "the contract says you don't get to ask me any questions, and I have beauty sleep to catch up on."

Begrudgingly, Margherita walked out of the store and to her car. Releasing her megin from around her mind, she allowed its healing effects to move to her hand. She placed the contract beside her and then noticed an old book that had Hiboria etched into it. She opened it up and found a slip of paper inside. She picked it up and recognized the old woman's handwriting.

Sorry.

"That's all you got?" she growled, punching the steering wheel and releasing a loud guttural scream.

19

The Next Day
Dante

The Shikka base stirred with excited energy with the new recruits being accepted into the corps. Dante walked passed the youth with a raised head as they stood at attention. The youths here were more open than those of his generation, and he frowned with distaste, considering the future that would result from the world being handed down to these *snowflakes*. Turning the corner, he spotted his apprentice walking out of the library with a bored expression. Suddenly, he thought of Gabriel's family.

His family had come to Ekocia under suspicious circumstances and disappeared in a way that made Dante uneasy. In the afternoon, he was assigned to investigate the family alongside Malina. She was a lovely added touch who got the family to open up to them more than he could have on his own.

At the time, they met the family, Gabriel was nine and undeniably his father's son. Two years later, an uncertain tragedy befell the family.

Malina had made it her personal mission to befriend Gabriel and in doing so had enlisted the help of Victor and himself to visit their family's shop every week. It was Dante's week with Malina, and she had crafted him a gift of friendship, which made him cautious of the boy that had captured her attention.

"What did you make for your friend?" Dante asked her while they rode in the car, his eyes falling to the small box with a bow in her lap.

"I braided together strips of leather with a fish pendant I bought last week, see," she said matter-of-factly with a self-satisfied smile as she opened the box to show him.

"Very nice," he said—the generic response—after taking his eyes off the road for a moment to glance at the artwork and then her bright face. "What made you make that for him?" Dante inquired, making her frown.

"Because it's his birthday. That's what you do for your friends on their birthday."

"Oh," Dante said, slightly relieved. *As long as it remains innocent.* Dante had switched on his turn signal to turn onto the street his family lived on.

"No, no," Malina said.

"What's wrong?"

"Gabriel wants to meet at the shop."

"Why?"

"He didn't tell me why?" Malina said with a frown. "Uncle, if we go to his house he won't be there."

"Okay, okay," he conceded and patted her head.

Gabriel was sitting in the parking lot, distress evident on his face although he forced a smile when the car pulled up. Malina jumped out as soon as the car was parked. Dante took his time getting out of the car, noting the lack of other vehicles and Gabriel's father's missing boat. Malina wore a nervous smile as she handed Gabriel the gift.

"What are your parents doing for your special day?" Dante asked.

Gabriel looked up from the unopened box in his hands, defiance glimmering in his eyes as he looked at Dante.

"Gabriel?" Malina asked, worry creasing her brows. Gabriel looked out to the ocean, his shaking hands crumbling the box in his hands.

"Did they leave you here?" Dante asked bluntly.

"They wouldn't do that!" Gabriel snapped, crushing the box.

"Gabriel, your present," Malina cried.

"You both should go," Gabriel insisted, turning away.

"Take me to your parents," Dante insisted.

"They aren't here," Gabriel retorted.

"I can wait," Dante said.

Gabriel frowned at the resolve as he opened the gift, pausing to marvel at it before carefully putting on the bracelet.

"Thank you for this," Gabriel said, looking at Malina's sad conflicted face. "You two can go now." He looked away from them to the ocean as his fingers played with the woven leather.

"We'll wait for your parents," Dante said, crossing his arms.

And they *did* wait, Dante recalled with an inward chuckle. *That boy made me wait three hours*, Dante thought in amazement. He'd never before and never since met a person that wasn't afraid of him. *Well except her*, Dante thought and then gruffly pushed the image of Jade from his mind. Gabriel's mother had been poisoned. She was a former alcoholic, and

Gabriel believed she had relapsed and was sleeping off a bender. Gabriel's father had left the night before and hadn't returned. Dante knew that Gabriel still struggled with that reality to this day.

When it was all said and done, Dante had placed Gabriel's mother in Hygieia Hospital. The doctors worked hard, but the poison had been in her system so long that she had to be left in a coma. Gabriel was placed in the system for a week until Malina stormed into his office and demanded a better home for him. So, at eleven, Gabriel was made an apprentice and a Mozo for the Shikka. Gabriel flourished as a warrior and magnificent spy under his tutelage. Next year would mark the end of his servitude, and he'd be able to live his life as he pleased. Dante wondered if he would want a life outside of the Shikka or if he would be the next Yeoman like himself and Elizabeth.

No matter his choice, Gabriel has a future in the Shikka. Dante thought, bringing himself to the present as Gabriel approached him. Remilda stood beside him timidly but with evident curiosity in her eyes as she carried an armload of books in front of her. Gabriel must have noticed the displeasure in his face because he laughed.

"It's not what it looks like," Gabriel said halfheartedly. "The independent princess demands to carry her own things."

"I'm not a princess, you brute," Remilda said. Her eyes lifted to Dante's face doubtfully before resolution shifted over her face as she stepped forward. "The pharaoh is ready for Malina. We're prepared for—"

"What are those books?" Dante asked, interrupting her.

She blinked confused and shocked. "Wh-well. These are books on Hiboria and Limbus. Personal studies," she said, frowning. "Are you not—"

"Malina studied Hiboria briefly," and Dante said, "is that why you're so eager to help her?"

Remilda looked at Gabriel briefly and shook her head, annoyed. "Yes and no. I want to help her because she needs it. I do plan to talk to her because she worked closely with my mother on the subject," she said, glaring at Gabriel. "Even if we already talked, I would have helped her."

"I see," Dante said. "I'm headed to the Yakim now."

"Are you starting your shift?" Gabriel asked.

"Yeah, it's Saturday. You should show her the sites," Dante suggested and walked off waving a hand and ending their conversation.

"Why does he always suggest that? I'm not here for leisure," Remilda grumbled.

"That may be true, but what we do for leisure is a part of our culture," said Gabriel.

Dante rounded the corner cutting off the rest of their conversation. Ascending the steps—four flights—he checked the windows on each floor to make sure they were secure. On the fifth floor, he noticed one of the windows was cracked open. He shut it firmly and locked the latch with a frown.

"Double your security for tonight's ceremony," a robotic voice said. Dante ascended the steps to reach the sixth floor where Kaleen was studying the Yakim's reaction to what she said. Kaleen appeared to be a young teenager, but she was actually seventy-eight years old and a siren. She had cocoa-brown skin and cloudy white irises with hints of gray. Her dark gray hair was pulled into a tight bun via the Shikka dress code.

"Kaleen, per usual, you're overreacting. The people love me and more guards would make them think I don't trust them," the Yakim stated.

"I don't know what this is about," Dante stated, climbing the stairs, "but I'm inclined to trust that Kaleen is acting within your best interest."

"Thank you," signed Kaleen, exasperation declining with the extra support. She quickly typed away on her phone, and then had the robot read out her message: "The threat on your life is still present. We still haven't found the individual that planned the attack last night."

"Okay, fine, fine," Yakim said, caving. "Just make sure these new people understand the protocols," he added and left to go inside his office.

Kaleen frowned at his back and rolled her eyes.

"Fill me in," Dante demanded, and Kaleen obliged with a pre-typed-out summary of the events. "Someone broke in during the blackout, and no one thought to check the windows on the perimeter?" Dante asked in disbelief.

"The break-in happened at his house. Finish reading before insulting other peoples' intelligence," Kaleen retorted in sign language.

"I don't have to finish reading this to know whether or not you operated by the book," Dante explained, typing on his phone. "Walking up these stairs, I saw a cracked window. Someone could have gotten in here, and the house could have been a distraction."

"I'm telling the techs to check the cameras now," she signed to Dante to keep him in the loop. "Elizabeth was on duty at base, and her report said nothing was amiss."

Dante nodded.

"Of course, I trust my sister's judgment," Dante said. Kaleen's face fell as she frowned.

"She was distracted," Kaleen signed.

"She's always distracted. She's raising teenage girls," Dante said defensively.

"Of course," Kaleen signed, smirking. "How could I forget?" she rolled her eyes and then looked down at her phone with disapproval, showing him the screen.

TG: Power was out for five minutes backup generators blew.

"I'll meet you down there," Dante said with a frown. "I need to talk to the Yakim about an important matter first."

"Of course," Kaleen signed with a disapproving once over and then left.

Dante watched her walk away before stepping into the Yakim's office. The office was octagonal with pictures of the progression of the country decorating the walls. Soft shag white carpet was placed in the middle of the oakwood floor. An oak coffee table sat in the middle of two burgundy sofas, and a bottle of whiskey with two cups sat on the coffee table. Dante stopped at the edge of the carpet and stood at attention as the Yakim stared out of the body-length bulletproof window.

"You would think I'm doing something diabolical," the Yakim muttered.

"What do you mean, sir?" Dante asked out of courtesy.

"I've been the Yakim for the past decade," he said, turning away from the window to look at Dante.

Dante met his lavender eyes and nodded.

The Yakim combed his hand through his white hair and sighed as a handful of hair fell to the floor. "A decade is the longest a Yakim has lasted in my position, and this is how they treat me in my last year? By breaking into my home and threatening my life?"

"The report said they barely made it past your front gate," Dante corrected. "Was there information withheld?" Dante asked.

"No," the Yakim said, walking toward him and waving away the correction. He picked up a glass to pour himself a glass of whiskey. "Would you like a glass?"

"No," Dante answered curtly. Dante hated exaggerations. *The fact they got past the gate is problematic enough*, he thought, clenching his jaw.

"You and Kaleen make the same serious face," the Yakim said, plopping down on the couch and draining his glass. "Too serious," he said thoughtfully as he poured himself another glass. "Destroying the city and rebuilding Macden is the right thing for this country," he said with uncertainty in his voice. He looked up to Dante. "Right?"

"You're going to allow rowdy children to sway your resolve?" Dante asked with a frown.

The Yakim chuckled. "My boy is their age," he stated, looking at the amber liquid in his glass. "Your people killed them with relentless precision."

"If that were true, they wouldn't have made it as far as they did," Dante said coldly.

"I see," the Yakim said, looking Dante in the eyes without speaking. He drained his cup again, clearing the burn from his throat with a small roar. "Why are you in my office?" the Yakim asked, standing to his feet.

"I need to leave town with my niece," Dante said.

"Why?"

"She was exposed to mishandled majik, and she's in a coma," Dante explained.

The Yakim's face fell as he grew thoughtful. "Must be Malina," he said. "Elizabeth would be the one in here if it was Evaline."

"Yes."

"Where will you be taking her?"

"Serinytas. Remilda—"

"Ah Remilda, the replacement ambassador for Juniper," the Yakim said with a fond smile. "She talked less."

"She was deaf," Dante said with a frown.

"More women should be," the Yakim said, turning away from Dante. "You can't go, but your niece can," he said as he walked to his desk.

"I need someone to be with her in another country," said Dante, bristling.

"Send Remilda," the Yakim insisted. "You can't leave me guarded by two women," he said with a frown.

"Kaleen and Elizabeth are the best Yeoman the Shikka has," Dante said in a level tone. "Kaleen is the reason you and your family were protected last night."

"Even you implied they were soft on the intruders," the Yakim said. "I don't need someone soft protecting me. Your niece can go. I want her to be in full health, and I need to discuss a private matter with her regardless."

"What matter is that?" Dante asked with a frown.

"She dumped my son," the Yakim lamented. "Can you believe that?"

"Not in a million years," Dante said levelly, "I'll send—"

"Gabriel," the Yakim suggested.

"I was going to say Taka. Gabriel is guarding Remilda."

"I'm aware," the Yakim said with a nod. "While he's there, he can drop Remilda off. She's not needed here," the Yakim said with a satisfied smile. "When you're done delivering this news and making preparations, return here to go over the security plans. I want you by my side tonight. No more women," he said with a shake of his head and then waved Dante out of his office.

Family
Gabriel

Gabriel pulled up in front of Remilda's temporary home and parked the car. Then, he walked around to her side of the car and opened her door. He grabbed the books from her so she would have an easier time getting out of the car. Once out, she tried to take the books back, but he smirked and pulled back pointing to the door with his head.

"I don't have the keys to your house, Princess," he teased.

An "Oh yeah" look crossed her face before she covered it with an eye roll. She walked up the steps to her condo, unlocking the door as she waved him inside.

He walked inside and carelessly placed the books on the couch as he ogled the decor. There was a space on the wall devoid of furniture and pictures. Strange markings on the wall that seemed both foreign and familiar to him were drawn in an arch. The smell that emanated from that area was rich earthy majik. He moved his eyes around the living room until his eyes landed on a picture that was framed on the nightstand. He picked it up, frowning at the image: Remilda standing beside Juniper, who had a softer complexion, though it didn't take away from her beauty. She had a soft round face and hair shaved low to her head. Her eyes were a honey-brown shade almost mirroring the blonde strands sprouting from her scalp. Beside them stood a man that resembled his father.

Remilda gently took the picture from him and placed it back on the end table.

"It's impolite to touch things that don't belong to you," she said curtly, turning her back to him.

"When was this taken? You look so young," Gabriel asked, clearing his throat unnerved by the man standing beside Juniper.

"Probably when I was twelve," Remilda said, shrugging, and walked into her kitchen.

Gabriel walked around the house, entering each room and checking the doors and windows for tampering or foul play before joining her in the kitchen. "Glass of water?" she asked.

"Sure, thanks," Gabriel said, tapping his fingers against the marble counter. "That pendant the guard was wearing."

"What about it?" Remilda asked, handing him the glass and then leaning against the counter.

"Do all the guards wear it?" Gabriel asked.

Remilda stared at him for a time and then shook her head. "No, the pendant he's wearing is called the Eye of Ra. A cousin to the gods that I worship," Remilda said. "Why don't you ask what you really want to know?"

"Who is he to you?" Gabriel asked, attempting to ignore the butterflies in his stomach.

"A nuisance," Remilda said, grimacing. "Kalair, grew up with my mother. My father died, and my mother apparently never truly loved him. At least not the way she loved *him*," she said in a bitter tone.

"Is he looking for her like you?" Gabriel asked, releasing the tension he held.

"Maybe," said Remilda with a shrug, pouring the rest of her water into the sink and heading for the living room. "He went missing when she did."

"How are you—" Gabriel started.

"We don't have to do this," she said with a frown.

Gabriel was about to talk when a hissing noise pierced his ears. He grabbed Remilda by the wrist and pulled her to stay behind him, backing her into a corner.

"What the hell are you doing?"

"Did you schedule a visit today," he asked gruffly.

On the far wall the markings began to glow making the heady majik scent stronger in the air around them. Gabriel moved forward, sliding brass knuckles over his fingers he settled into his fighting stance.

"You gonna tell me who it is or am I gonna swing and find out answers the hard way?" Gabriel asked.

"That's most likely my Vizier," Remilda said, standing at his side and placing a calm hand on his forearm.

A woman with burgundy hair and dark-brown skin stepped through the portal. She had red eyes with specks of yellow, and her scowl deepened as she stepped into the temporary home. She looked Gabriel up and down and then turned, reaching back through when her arms came back through the portal closed and she was holding a young girl in her arms. Remilda stiffened and then stepped forward the small girl wiggled out of the Vizier's arms and ran to Remilda's legs causing her to stumble. Gabriel quickly grabbed Remilda's shoulders to steady her.

The young girl at Remilda's legs had a warm-brown complexion with dark-brown eyes. She had thick black hair and a smile that looked more deviant than innocent. She vaguely reminded him of the man in the picture as she cast Gabriel an uncertain look.

"Are you supposed to keep my sister safe?" the little girl asked, looking at him with curious recognition. "You look like my daddy?" she asked, suddenly twisting Gabriel's gut in knots.

"Hush now," Remilda scolded, pulling the little girl to the side, she glanced back unable to disguise the recognition and weariness in her face.

"Who's the kid?" Gabriel asked in a calm tone he'd refined over the years.

"That's princess Shivanya," the Vizier stated, addressing him like a solider would address someone they didn't quite trust yet.

"Why are you two here?" Gabriel demanded.

"Gabriel," Remilda scolded.

"No, we just talked about this in the car," Gabriel stated. "You have to treat my country with the same respect you would expect from an outsider visiting your country. You may be young, but you're still representing Serinytas."

"I'm aware of who I'm representing!" she snapped, offended.

"Are you aware of your responsibilities?" Gabriel inquired.

"Of course I am," Remilda declared, standing to her full height and shielding her sister behind her.

"Then I'm certain you're aware that your safety is paramount," Gabriel stated, causing Remilda to roll her eyes. "You're rolling your eyes, but because these guidelines weren't followed in the east, your mother is missing," Gabriel said coldly. The room quieted and suddenly became claustrophobic with tension.

"You leave—"

"I won't. I've allowed some of your disrespectful behavior to pass because you're young. But this," Gabriel said, motioning around the room to the Vizier and the young girl, "is unacceptable."

"My Vizier and sister—"

"Have scheduled days and times to visit through proper channels," Gabriel growled, pointing at the symbols on the wall. "So, what was so important that you broke protocol?" Gabriel demanded, looking at the Vizier's smirking face.

"Rana," Remilda prompted as their staring contest dragged on.

"The girl is refusing to eat," Rana said, refusing to break eye contact.

"Why?" Remilda demanded in a hushed tone.

"Your name is Rana," Gabriel stated and pulled his megin to his eyes and nose to memorize her scent and aura signature.

"Yes, and what you're doing is something that should have happened before," Rana scolded.

Yet, Gabriel noticed the way her eyes glowed in response. "She's sneakier than I predicted," Gabriel said nodding at his miscalculation. "I wanted her to have privacy."

"She signed that right away," Rana reminded him in a serious tone.

"If you two are done talking about me," Remilda snapped, gripping her sister's hand and leading her to the portal entrance, "she's ready to go and eat."

"Are you sure you want to end your visitation time?" Gabriel asked with a raised eyebrow. "You have four hours and fifty-five minutes left," he said and caught the smirk on Rana's face.

"Gabriel, can I have a word?" Remilda asked through clenched teeth.

"Well," Gabriel started and stopped when there was a knock at the door. "Expecting more company?" he asked sardonically.

Taka's deep voice carried through the door. "Gabe, it's Taka. We've been lifted to code blue. Heidi and I are here to relieve you."

Remilda's face paled, and Rana rushed Shivanya through the portal, closing it behind them as Gabriel walked to the door to open it.

"Hey," Gabriel said, coolly stepping back with the door in hand to allow the two Askari into Remilda's home to check the perimeter per protocol.

"Anything we need to know about?" Heidi asked.

"No," Gabriel said, meeting Heidi's pierced face. "The bookworm said she just wanted to remain in for the night."

"Okay," Heidi said, relieved, and then addressed Remilda.

Gabriel left, walking toward his car, and Taka rushed out to stop him. Gabriel turned to face the burly young adult.

Taka was twenty and grew up in Macden. Gabriel knew him from basic training. He was a former Kipi member but traded in that life for the life of an Askari.

"What's up Taka?" Gabriel said casually.

"There' portal scarring on the wall you didn't tell us about," Taka said.

"Her little sister came through," Gabriel explained, shrugging. "She's seven and missed her big sister. I just finished talking to Remilda about it. I didn't want to rehash the subject."

"I see," Taka said a frown sat on his face.

"Anything else?" Gabriel asked.

"I heard Matoya came by Valley High," Taka said. "I heard she was knocked out after interrogating your girl."

"Are you trying to start something you can't finish, Taka?" Gabriel said, balling his hands into fists.

"What happened?" Taka demanded.

"I'll tell you what's about to happen if you don't stay focused on your job," Gabriel threatened.

"Taka, are you ... what's going on?" Heidi called with a frown.

"Nothing," Taka said and backed away from Gabriel.

Gabriel grabbed Taka's bicep and whispered in a hush tone, "Remember you work for the Shikka, not the Kipi." Taka snatched away and walked toward Heidi.

Gabriel got into his car and called Dante as he drove to the house they shared. Dante didn't answer and Gabriel silently cursed. He was in the dark about too much, and it was making the back of his skull itch. He knew Matoya was fine, but her passing out after interrogating Malina made him look more guilty. Malina had been his best friend since he was eleven, and back then, she was his only friend. It had never been a secret that he cared about her and would do anything for her. He never believed that would be a determent to him until now.

Azazel is dead, and somehow that's my fault because there's a rumor they may have been more than friends. Gabriel scoffed at the idea. Malina was a beautiful girl. There was no denying that. As soon as she went through puberty, boys and grown men tried to talk to her. It annoyed him and made him more protective of her, but she was her own person. Even so, Dante made sure she knew how to protect herself. She dated and often complained to him about her little boyfriends. He never once laid a finger on them. *Maybe if I had, the rumor wouldn't exist*, Gabriel thought grimly, stopping at a red light as he considered where to go.

Who was that? Gabriel thought, thinking back to the picture that Matoya brought to the investigation. *It does look like me, and when I showed it to Dante, he just became stoic*, Gabriel thought with a frown as he turned left to go to the hospital. *Code Blue means they'll have two Askari on guard today,* He thought, suddenly feeling the need to be near his best friend. *At least she can't send me away,* he thought, feeling depressed again. *Is that why she was sending me away? Because she saw that man and thought it was me?*

"Incoming call from Dante ..." the car spoke to him, pulling him from his thoughts.

"Yeah," Gabriel said, answering the call.

"I need you at the hospital tonight," Dante said immediately.

"Headed there now," Gabriel responded.

"So, Taka and Heidi arrived already? Very good," Dante said, pleased.

"What's happening at the hospital?" Gabriel asked, feeling worried.

"It's precautionary, the Yakim is going to be in public tonight," Dante generously explained.

"Did you learn anything about the photo?" Gabriel asked, trying to take advantage of his generous mood.

"No," Dante said and ended the call.

Limbus
Astra

"It hurts because you're dying," the woman's voice said.

Astra didn't care about the woman's urgings or the panicked quiet voices that spoke over her. She ignored the soft hands and kisses that touched her skin. The woman was either too nice or too angry when it came to the matter of Astra staying or leaving. The ritual she performed hadn't been right and unlike Astra, Angel hadn't seen the bonding ritual performed. Angel was too eager, but she was always eager to look good, so that hadn't been what bothered Astra.

"Are you listening to me?" the woman snapped.

Astra decided she wouldn't the moment Angel walked through that door. The woman was kind enough to show her through the pond that Angel woke up. She felt her sister's tight grip on her hand and Gabriel's gentle caress and kiss. Her sister was well, and Gabriel was nearby to protect her, but it wasn't enough. Something was off, and it had to do with that woman.

What was wrong with the ritual? Astra asked herself because, as time moved on, she slowly forgot herself and the pain grew. She replayed the ritual in her mind she held hands with Angel and the woman tied the ribbon around them. *That was right. The woman said the words. But something was wrong with the way she said them. Too fast? In the wrong order? I can't remember anymore.*

"You're going to die here," the woman said.

"So what if I do?" Astra hissed, turning to face the woman. They were in the meadow where Astra parted ways with Angel. The door Astra was supposed to exit through still sat in the middle of the grass. Waiting and taunting her, she hated the door. She hated how much she wanted to leave, but her gut told her to stay. *There's something wrong here,* her brain reminded her.

"Then you won't see your family anymore. They'll mourn you," the woman said.

"Death is a part of life. They *will* get over it," Astra snapped, rolling her eyes, and the woman tsked at her morbidity, walking away from her. *Was it the way she walked?* Astra thought, trying to find answers in her fading mind. *I shouldn't have forgotten this fast. It's only been a day, hasn't it?* Astra looked down at her hand and wondered when the last time was that someone had touched her.

A sharp stinging sensation warmed her face, and a warm hand enveloped her own. *Gabriel,* she thought with a smile and then almost immediately frowned. *Did he slap me?* She followed the path the woman took to go back to the pond. She was sitting in the grass, glancing down with humor dancing in her eyes. Angel was in the room with Gabriel. They were talking about something and Angel looked frightened. Astra looked up to the woman, and that's when the memories flooded back.

There was nothing wrong with the way she said the words. She placed her hand on top of theirs and added a condition to the bond. She added her megin into the mix, bonding herself to them. Angel pulled megin from both of them officially waking her zawadi. When Angel left Astra felt a pull to leave as well, the longer she stayed, the number she felt. She felt death closing in on her, but it would just be her. The woman caught her staring and smiled at her patting the patch of grass beside her body. Astra sat across from her on the other side of the pond.

"What do you plan to do when you leave?"

"Leave where?" the woman asked.

"Here. This place. Aren't you trapped here?"

"Not exactly, no," the woman responded. "I was trapped here a long time ago, but I learned to send bits of myself out with people when they leave here."

"Is that why you bonded yourself to my sister and me," Astra said, and the woman stared at her, genuinely confused.

"I have no idea—"

"Cut the bullshit. I know what you did," Astra said. "You added a condition to the ritual."

"That your souls find a swift path back to your bodies," the woman clarified. "In the beginning, the soul would find the body, but the body would already be dead," the woman shrugged, "you live and learn, now I clarify."

"I don't believe you," Astra said in a whisper.

"You don't have to. Your sister is proof enough. I mean you no harm, although she may not feel the same towards you with the slap she just gave you."

Astra said nothing to that. Their relationship had always been strained. There was no question that their father preferred Astra to Angel and vice versa with their mother—which would work just fine if Angel didn't need to be reassured that she was loved by both parents. Angel craved their father's attention.

"This boy at your side—what's his name?"

"What's your name?" Astra shot back, and the woman scoffed.

"Midnight," she said with a shrug.

"Why did you lie to my sister?"

"I didn't lie," she said. " I just didn't correct her. I didn't see the point if you two weren't staying."

A cramp in Astra's side made her inhale sharply as she forced herself to breathe through the pain. The woman rose to her feet as Astra crumbled to her side and into the fetal position. The woman grabbed her by the arm and dragged her through the brush and into the meadow, stopping just in front of the door.

"Stop the pain and walk through it."

"Why does it hurt so much?" Astra managed to ask as tears ran down her cheeks. Her warmth was vanishing abruptly.

"Doctor!" Gabriel's voice boomed on the other side of the door, melding with the frantic beeping of machines.

"How selfish are you to allow people to suffer when you can walk away with min—"

"I'm not walking away and allowing you to as well," Astra proclaimed, clawing her fingers into the grass to distract her from her stomach lurching.

"She won't make it through the week," a woman's voice said sadly. "Give her something for the pain. There's nothing more we can do at this point."

"This is the path you want to take," Midnight said with slight interest. "Why do you believe I'm so evil?" she asked with a frown.

"I don't think you're evil," Astra said as her spirit lightened and the pain melted away. "I just know you aren't telling me everything."

"And you're willing to die for that?" Midnight said with a frown.

"You bonded yourself to me," Astra said, rising without pain. "You aren't experiencing any discomfort in being here, and you already told me you let a little of yourself go with everyone that comes through here," Astra said with a frown. "I've been in here for two days—I think—and I haven't seen anyone else. That tells me it's not that easy to get here."

"Well, you have to bring yourself," Midnight said, holding her pointer finger to her thumb, leaving a breath of space between them, "this close to dying. Or put yourself in a coma or be exposed to an unimaginable amount of raw Heka."

"Majik?" Astra asked for clarity.

"Heka," Midnight repeated, "Majik is controlled and diluted heka. Heka exist around us within all natural things," Midnight explained.

"Whatever," Astra snapped, "but then you end up here."

"Here is vast," Midnight stated, "here is limbus, and they have to travel through their own hell to end up here."

"Where is here?" Astra asked.

"Here is the door to lead you back to your body ... or anywhere else." Midnight shrugged. "I don't care to find out."

"If everyone's spirit winds up here when they die, that means your pieces of yourself you let out do too," Astra concluded, "how much are you here and how much are you there?"

"Walk through the door and find out yourself," Midnight taunted.

"No," Astra said and sat on the ground.

"Same conversation tomorrow?" Midnight asked with a raised brow and then turned and walked away.

Distractions
Dante

The council meeting was crowded and nosey because the Yakim permitted the locals to enter the room. Dante arranged with the help of Kaleen secure exits and entrances. Dante wasn't worried about the Yakim's personal safety; he was worried about what might come out of the man's mouth. He had always been a sexist ass, but during this last year, he'd only gotten worst.

"The divorce might have a lot to do with it," Kaleen signed when Dante ranted to her about the Yakim's words for the meeting they had earlier. "No offense to your sex, but when a man's ego gets bruised, every woman is an annoyance."

"I'm not like that," Dante said.

"Every man says that," she signed, rolling her eyes.

Dante shook away the irritation of the brief conversation and checked on the guards on the perimeter of the building. Walking to the back where he'd placed Elizabeth, he noticed she wasn't at her post. He lifted his wrist to speak into the communicator when a branch snapped behind him. Elizabeth walked up to him with her head down, almost as if she wasn't seeing him. Dante cleared his throat, and Elizabeth stopped, saying, "Oh" in a faraway voice.

"Oh," he repeated. "Oh what? Why aren't you at your post."

"I've trapped the door."

"A door trap and your presence aren't the same thing, Beth," he scolded. "Where's your head at?"

"Malina isn't going to make it," Elizabeth said quietly.

"What?" Dante asked and then softened. "Wh-what ... why would you say that?"

"The nurse said her organs are starting to shut down. They don't know what's causing it," Elizabeth explained, covering her mouth.

"I got the go-ahead for her to leave I'm placing her on a ship tonight," Dante said, trying to lift his sister's spirits.

"I just got off the phone with them. It's too dangerous to move her," Elizabeth said tears falling from her eyes.

"Why do you care?" Dante growled. "You kicked her out of your home—"

"That was when I thought she would live! She was supposed to live ... she's such a strong girl. Something like this wasn't supposed to happen," Elizabeth said, wiping at her face with a shaky hand.

Dante blew out an emotional breath. "Okay," he said. "We have to table this and talk about it later." And with that, he began to walk away.

"Dante there might not be a later ..."

"Malina isn't dying tonight," Dante declared.

Just then, a woman's high-pitched scream pierced his ears, freezing him in the spot he stood. Elizabeth snapped out of her depression first and ran toward the noise, freezing the entrance so no one could leave the way she came. Dante ran around the building, noting a wall of fire blocking one entrance and a wall of vines another. The screaming inside increased as people rushed to the main exit of the building where Kaleen stood. Dante walked to her side, and she held a hand up to him to stop.

"Stop," she said in a voice so sweet and alluring that Dante's knees almost buckled. Kaleen walked toward the crowd of terrified people who froze before her with admiration. "Stay here," she added and stopped before a stubborn woman fighting her control. "There's always one," she sang, touching the face of an umber-complexed young woman. Her golden-brown locs were twisted into a bun on top of her head. She wore silver arrow earrings that matched her sharp eyes.

"Not her, Kaleen," Dante warned. "Matoya is off limits."

Kaleen signed "OK" with her dominant hand.

"The Yakim is dead," said a panicked voice through his earpiece. Kaleen looked at Dante at the same time he looked at her.

"Location?" he said into his wrist. "Stay here with them," Dante ordered Kaleen, who frowned with displeasure. After a heartbeat, she turned her eyes to Matoya. As he walked past her, Dante placed a hand on her shoulder and bent down to Kaleen's ear, "No harm may come to her. I'll need her for questioning later, understand?"

"Back room. Elizabeth is guarding the entrance." Informed a voice through the earpiece.

Kaleen nodded, and Dante walked toward the back room. Elizabeth stood stonily although the ice she was producing had started to turn her fingers blue. Dante placed a hand on her shoulder in an attempt to ground her like he had when they were younger, but she rolled him off her shoulder and stepped away.

"Reel it in before you lose a finger," he said in a low tone so no one would hear.

"He died while we were all on duty," Elizabeth hissed. "We're all going to lose—"

"Hush." Dante hissed. "Remain calm and quiet. We don't know anything yet," Dante reminded her.

Elizabeth didn't relax and he couldn't waste any more time.

Dante walked into the back room and paused as he smelled the alcohol and then saw all the blood that waited for him around the corner. The woman who must have been responsible for the scream everyone heard was passed out in the corner, blood covering her clothes and dripping off her face. Dante felt his stomach churn as he took in the sight before him but pushed forward nonetheless. He saw the Yakim's balding head lying on his desk. His face was turned away from him, and Dante could only imagine the sight alongside the smirking face of an Askari woman. The room buzzed with dark humor, worry, and the clicking sound of lens shutting and opening as pictures were being taken.

"Report," Dante said, as a camera flash sounded beside him.

"We don't have one yet," a man said to him with cool indifference and light humor. "The eye witness is passed out and—"

"And you all look a little too happy for someone whose charge just died on them," Dante said coldly. The indifference cleared his face as the room quieted around him. "The Yakim died on our watch. This isn't something I should have to tell you to take seriously," Dante scolded.

"We're taking it seriously. We followed protocol and checked on him in cycles. He was never alone," a woman said from behind him.

"Then there should be more than just one witness," Dante said.

"He told me to leave," another Askari stated. "Wanted alone time," she said, nodding to the girl who was beginning to rouse from her sleep.

"It looks like his stomach exploded ... and then his lungs," the photographer said.

"What could do that?" Dante demanded.

"Megin," said the photographer, dropping her camera lens, her eyes glowing with the power she had inside, and she sighed deeply, stretching.

"It's going to be a long night," Dante said. Then, with a sigh, he placed the communicator to his mouth and spoke.

"Shut down all portals. No way in or out effective immediately."

Philia or Pragma
Gabriel

Gabriel felt his body stiffen as he watched the news by Astra's side. Her body was gradually feeling colder to him, and it worried him. The doctors said she might not make it through the week, but they had another plan. *There's still hope*, he reminded himself. He'd seen the same effects in his mother before they placed her in a majik chrysalis. *The same can't happen to Astra. She still has so much life to live*, he thought as he started to bite his nails again. His phone rang, and he answered it quickly.

"I'm here," Gabriel said briskly.

"By here I imagine you mean the hospital," Dante said dryly.

"Yes," Gabriel responded, looking at the television screen. "What happened?"

"The Yakim was assassinated," Dante said with a sigh. "We're locking down. No one in or out," Dante explained.

"What about Astra?" Gabriel said, holding his breath. "She has a better chance in Serinytas. Remilda said so," he reminded levelly.

"The assassin hasn't been identified."

"Okay and?" Gabriel growled into the phone. "Astra is dying, and she needs help now!"

"She will have to wait until we've captured the assassin," Dante said coldly.

"She can't! What's wrong with you?"

"Finding the assassin takes priority."

"Astra will die if we do nothing!" Gabriel insisted. "Dante, please! My mother didn't stand a chance, but Astra does."

"There's nothing else left to say," Dante stated and ended the call.

"FUCK!" Gabriel growled, throwing his phone. One of the two Askari outside the door poked their head into the room.

"What's the problem?" the male asked with a frown.

"Portal travel is shut down, no one in or out," Gabriel stated his mind racing with the information.

"Damn," the male said and placed a hand on Gabriel's shoulder. "What happened?"

"Donnell, look at the news," the female said, pointing at the television.

Donnell did as he was asked taking a stance beside the woman.

"Shit," they said in unison as the news of the Yakim's death took precedence.

"Breann, look at the bottom," Donnell stated.

"They arrested someone for that shooting that happened this summer," Brenann said, in a hopeful tone. "That's great news for you right Ga—Valor? Valor!"

Gabriel heard them call after him, but he couldn't control the trembling in his hands anymore. His breath was coming fast and hard, the stale and fear laced air was causing his stomach to rebel against him. He stormed outside, feeling lightheaded and dizzy.

"Gabriel," Jezabel's honey voice called.

He waved a hand up at her to stay back. Then, he placed a hand against the white brick, and his megin rushed through him, enhancing his senses and his strength. The brick beneath his hand felt like loose sand as it crumbled and fell between his fingers. He heard Jezabel's tennis shoes squeak as she walked toward him.

"Stay away," he warned.

"Oh please," she scoffed. The smell of burnt tobacco wafted to his nose, shocking his senses as much as her words had. "You think you can scare me?" she asked, amused by the notion.

"I can be really strong Jez," he warned, frowning at how silly the truth sounded. "I could hurt you."

"You can't hurt me more than my sister has," she said candidly. He turned and watched her blow out a big cloud of smoke.

"What triggered you, Son?" she asked gently. "Is it Astra's condition?"

"I told you not to call me that. I'm not—"

"This hospital raised you," she said firmly. "You're a spiritual child of mine. Now, what happened?"

"It's Astra," he said, suddenly feeling very tired. "Dante was supposed to help her ..." sniffing, he turned away. "I'm going to be alone." Gabriel heard the crumbling of paper, and as he turned, the makeshift ball bumped against his head. "What the—"

"After everything that's happened—"

"Jez, it's different with Astra," Gabriel said, wanting her to understand more than anyone. She wasn't actually hurt. He could tell by her even breath and blue aura that she was toying with him. "Astra is my best friend. She's always been there. She was never afraid of me, and she always trusted me. I remember a time before her, and I never want to go back to that," he explained.

"That's called love," Jezabel said with a soft smile.

"It's more than that," Gabriel said, shaking his head. "Love isn't what I feel for her. I don't want to be with her like that," he said quickly. "I want her to be happy, safe, and loved, but I don't need to be the person to love her. I just—" Gabriel ran his hand through his hair. "I want her to be okay, but it seems like I'm the only one that hasn't given up on her," he said with his voice cracking. "I can't help her. I want to, but—"

Jezabel closed the distance between them and embraced him. He froze and then carefully—so as not to harm her—wrapped his arms around her.

His hot tears stung her skin, and his warm breath tickled her neck and ear. Unfazed, she rubbed his back and swayed him until he broke from the tenderness he rarely received.

"I don't know what to do," he sobbed. "Please, help me."

"Of course, I will, Son," she said as he broke down.

Paradigm Shift
Carina

C arina sat in the DJ's Booth of Kore's Palace on top of one of the stereos as the Kipi met below. Today was Saturday, and the girls were supposed to be performing on the stage Tirany now stood on getting paid. However, Margherita had promised that the Kipi would always have a safe place in her club, and she allowed them the privilege to use the venue however they saw fit. On nights like these, the girls were sent home with $200. $100 for showing up and the other $100 as an apology for missing out on the potential for earning more.

Carina watched the last girl leave as Matoya stepped in. A cool breeze whipped through the booth, and for a moment, Carina believed the chill down her spine was a warning from the gods, but as she turned, she saw Margherita.

Margherita slid into the booth with aura hues of orange and purple swirling around her like a storm. She looked down at the crowd, and red engulfed the other emotions. Carina felt an eyebrow raise at the peculiar mood. Margherita marched over to the booth and picked up a microphone.

"Tirany, a word?" Margherita asked it like a question, but there was no misunderstanding that it was a command.

"Rita," Carina said in a light voice. "You good?" she asked.

"No," Margherita responded in a measured voice and began to pace as she waited for Tirany to arrive.

"Mary, what is it?" Tirany asked gently. Lionel looked behind her, but something about his demeanor seemed off to Carina. Margherita never allowed her anywhere near Lionel reading his aura Carina understood why. She shifted away distressed as the malevolent tension grew.

"Where's Jack?" Margherita demanded, and Carina noted when Margherita's eyes shifted to Lionel her irises darkened.

"I don't know," Tirany said, frowning. "Did you interrupt my meeting for something that simple?" Tirany crossed her arms and stepped closer to Margherita, forcing her to stop pacing and hold her ground. "Have you lost your mind? I have a community that's on the verge of storming the capitol."

"Tirany, you and I both know they lack the conviction to follow through with something like that." Margherita sneered and rolled her eyes. "The Kipi are upset that Henrik was arrested, but everyone knew that was bound to happen!" Margherita snapped, her temper overwhelming her. "Even I knew he orchestrated that raid on the Yakim's home, he's been openly bragging about it!"

"Well, I don't know where Jack is," Tirany said with a shrug and turned on her heel to leave.

"Bullshit," Margherita said in a cool voice.

Carina sucked in sharply and slipped off the speaker. Her skin prickled with animosity to the point it pained her to be so close.

"Bullshit?" Tirany repeated, raising an eyebrow and looking back at Margherita.

"You know I always wondered when you would show me who you truly were," Margherita said with a placid expression. "This is it? This is who's leading the Kipi?"

"They killed my boy," Tirany said evenly, "I mourned—"

"We both know you did more than that," Margherita hissed. "When I came by, I knew there was more to Lionel being back than you let on."

"My relationship isn't your business."

"It is when it *fucks* with my life," Margherita snarled.

"It's just one girl," Tirany said. "Let her go—like they let my boy go."

"Tirany, seventy people, including myself, are going to die by the end of the month if you don't tell me where he is," Margherita said levelly.

"What makes you think we give a fuck about your seventy lives," Lionel interjected scoffing.

"Seventy *innocent* people will die because of what *you two* did," Margherita hissed. "Don't make me say the cliche line that everyone is already thinking."

"My, my, Rita," Matoya said at the door frame, smirking, "you sound terribly desperate. I know where he is."

"Shut up," Tirany snapped, turning her back to Margherita.

"Where?" Margherita demanded. "I heard you work in trade," Matoya said, ignoring her mother.

"Now is not the time for games, Matoya," Margherita said, placing her hands on her hips. Her head was down as she bit the inside of her cheek.

"No games. Just a trade," she said too casually.

"What do you want?"

"Gabriel."

"Why?" Margherita said crossly.

"He killed my brother," Matoya scoffed in disbelief.

"They arrested someone else for that already," Margherita said evenly.

"Henrik didn't *kill* Azazel."

"No, he just led eight people to their slaughter," Margherita quipped. "Henrik isn't innocent, and you have no proof Gabriel was there," Margherita said quickly.

"I have a picture," Matoya lamented.

"That's not enough proof," Margherita chuckled. "Have you forgotten the world we live in?"

"I saw him there," Matoya snapped. "Is my word not enough?"

"Not when it's clouded by grief," Margherita said evenly, meeting Matoya's silver eyes. "Mmm, so the rumor is true about you," Margherita continued in a voice so quiet that Carina had to rush megin to her ear to make out the words. Matoya's eyes snapped to Carina. "Your eyes told me everything I needed to know," Margherita explained, stepping closer to her in warning.

"I may be grieving, but I didn't imagine Gabriel there. Astra saw him too."

"She didn't, and she professed as much before she went into her coma."

"Why are you protecting him?" Matoya yelled.

"I'm not condemning another innocent child to death because of *your* family," Margherita hissed.

"We deserve justice," Tirany said, her voice straining against her emotion.

"Not at the cost of innocent lives," Margherita said firmly. "Now, where is Jack?"

"I won't tell you," Matoya said and turned away.

"Lionel, I believe your daughter has something to tell you," Margherita said expectantly.

Matoya stopped walking and Carina gasped at the cruelty that Margherita had just said. Tirany glared at Margherita, but she remained unreadable. Carina watched Margherita's aura dissipate, *this won't end well*, Carina thought chewing the inside of her lip. Lionel's face contorted into a frown as he stared between his daughter and Tirany.

Meanwhile, Margherita walked over to the alcohol cabinet and grabbed a strange vial that was shaped like a pair of feminine lips. She placed it on the table and brought out an empty glass.

"What is she talking about and why did you two get so quiet?" Lionel demanded.

"You know," Margherita said, looking at him with a thoughtful expression that cleared into a pleasant smile when she met his eyes, "I feel like making a deal." Tirany glared at Matoya who turned hateful eyes on Margherita. "An exchange of information," she explained, pouring amber liquid into one cup and then another. "I only deal with *honest* people, and I only deal with *good* information ..." Margherita grabbed her cup and then the other, holding it out to the air. "I want to know where Jack is. I know at least one of you know where he is. After all he's Tirany's favorite cousin." Her eyes wandered to Lionel's violent face and her full lips pulled up into a slight smirk, "Lionel, I'll tell you what the women in your life are afraid to tell you," she baited.

"Rita," Carina breathed.

"The information you're asking for is useless to you!" Matoya snapped. "The Yakim is dead, and they aren't letting anyone leave the country until his murderer is found."

"That sounds like a me problem," Margherita said with a shrug, "just tell me what I want to know and, I'll tell you who orchestrated your son's death." The color drained from all of their faces at that omission. "Matoya, I will make your father forget he heard anything and erase all suspension he has. You three have until my arm gets tired of holding this cup, and you cannot change the offers I gave you."

"Tell me what the fuck you two are hiding," Lionel bellowed.

"If I have to put him down," Margherita said in a dark voice, "all deals disappear."

Matoya glared at Margherita, her silver eyes glimmering in the light. Carina moved toward them, ignoring the cramps that twisted her stomach into knots. Margherita frowned at Carina and dramatically dropped her arm so she would stop walking toward them.

Carina felt another chill course through her at the sight of Margherita's black near-pupilless eyes.

"Don't do this," Carina pleaded in sign.

"If you can't handle it, then leave," Margherita said sternly.

Tirany walked forward and took the glass from Margherita. The amber liquid darkened, and the glass shattered. A shard jammed itself deep into Tirany's hand, and she grabbed her wrist, crying out in pain and falling back. Margherita tsked and sighed, tossing a towel toward her as Carina rushed to her side, closing off her megin so she wouldn't absorb any further emotions.

"What happened?" Tirany cried. "I was going—"

"To lie," Margherita said with a shrug. "I honestly hoped Lionel would be the one I would *have* to make an example of, but he may be the most honest out of the surviving family." Margherita grabbed another glass, poured the same amount of liquid as before, and held it out to them. "Who's next? Tirany you have a good hand left if you'd like to try again." Margherita offered a smile that didn't reach her soulless pitch-black eyes.

Lionel stormed forward, and grabbed the glass tossing the amber liquid to the back of his throat. He dropped to his knees before her, his hands covering his throat in agony as the majik worked through his system. Margherita locked eyes with Tirany whose breathing sped up. Matoya rushed forward to grab her father and pull him back. He shoved her down roughly, making her fall back into the glass.

Lionel rose to his full height and glared at Margherita. "What are they hiding?" he asked, licking his top lip.

"My question first," Margherita said coldly, although the thought of making a deal with him made her stomach churn as she tossed back her shot. "Where is he?"

Lionel opened his mouth to answer as Carina saw Matoya pick up one of the lighter speakers and smash it against her father's head. Margherita's eyebrows rose with surprise. Matoya stepped forward and Margherita shifted her attention to the girl.

"I already have a deal in place," Margherita stated.

"I don't care about my father knowing who I am, I want to know what happened to my brother," she proclaimed. "Please, I want to know who orchestrated what happened."

Margherita settled into a thoughtful silence as she considered this. She looked at Tirany and her pleading eyes wanting to know the knowledge Margherita held. Silently she walked to the cabinet and silently grabbed clean cups. She poured them both new shots before holding the glasses out to Matoya she channeled her megin into the amber liquid. With an inviting grin, Margherita extended the cup to Matoya, whose hand was trembling.

Margherita instinctively knew that she was more afraid of the what-if factor than the truth as it stood before them. *I could confirm their theories or make their realities worse*, Margherita realized but shook it all off with a sigh. *I refuse to allow their fear to dictate my life.* She held it out again, raising it slightly. "Don't be afraid. Just be honest." Matoya grabbed the cup and sighed when it didn't shatter.

"Drink it and tell me what you know about Jack's whereabouts," Margherita demanded.

Matoya nodded and tossed the amber to the back of her throat sighing in surprise when there was no pain. "You—" Matoya couched and began scratching her throat panic settling in.

"The truth, Matoya," Margherita reminded gently.

"Last I heard, he found a way to Hiboria," Matoya rushed out, sighing as the discomfort eased.

"Hib—" Margherita stopped herself and released a frustrated breath, "The how doesn't matter."

"I'm not lying," Matoya said, panicked.

"The potion made sure of that," Margherita said, pointing at the whelps and broken skin on Matoya's throat with little care. She tossed her shot back without a grimace, she looked at Tirany. "Jade Valeno."

"You're lying. Jade is dead," Tirany snapped.

"She's not lying," Matoya said in unison with Carina.

"Then where is she?" Tirany demanded.

"That wasn't part of the deal," she said callously, stepping over Lionel's sleeping body. "The man is resilient," Margherita said with a frown. "Get him out of my club, and don't ever bring him back here," she ordered, looking down at Tirany. "We're done here. I can—"

"We're leaving," Tirany said. "No one needs to help me."

"Don't we all know that," Margherita clipped and stepped out of the booth.

Compromise

"Sorry, we're closed," Carina said, descending the steps surprised to find anyone was still in the club. In the middle of the club stood a young girl swaying side to side to music Carina assumed only she could hear. The girl wore a black hoodie that looked vaguely familiar the hood was pulled up covering ginger curls. "Are you with the Kipi?" Carina asked, when the freckled face girl with amber skin blankly stared at the stages in front of her.

"My ex was," she responded her green eyes finding Carina as she neared her.

"Oh … okay," Carina said, looking to see if anyone else was around, "well he's not here—"

"Of course not," she said bitterly tears springing into her eyes, "he's dead!"

Tracy's face finally fell into place in Carina's foggy memory. "You were Gabriel's friend. We actually met before—a long time ago. You probably have no memory of it because you weren't in the best place then," she said distantly and then thought *she's not in the best place now.*

"In the flesh," Tracy muttered, blowing out an alcohol laced breath that turned Carina's stomach.

"You shouldn't be drinking," Carina scolded.

"I'm eighteen—" Tracy dismissed rolling her eyes.

"I'm *nineteen*," Carina shaking her head with disapproval. "I get it everyone has their ways to cope, drowning at the bottle of a bottle—"

"Save it," Tracy snapped, shaking her head, "that's not why I'm here."

"Why are you here?" Carina asked frowning at the girl in front of her.

"I don't know," Tracy breathed out a tear falling from her eye that she quickly wiped away.

"Let me walk you to the door," Carina offered, and Tracy shook her head.

"I want to talk with Rita," Tracy demanded.

"Why?" Carina asked, taking in the girl's determined green eyes with brown flecks.

"Because I heard Rita helps."

Carina sighed she shifted her weight from one foot to the other. She thought briefly about her own life and how she wouldn't be alive without Margherita. *Yeah, she helped more than she hurt. This girl needs rehab not Rita.* "Erasing your pain won't help you."

Tracy stepped back her fair complexion flushing at the accusation. "How would you know?" she demanded. "You don't know what would help me."

"Rehab, actual food, maybe a shower," Carina said coldly.

"Shut up," Tracy hissed.

"That's the only help we would offer you," Carina said turning away from Tracy.

"Will you help Henrik?"

Carina frowned and turned back to look at Tracy. "Why would we?"

"They're convicting him of Azazel's murder," Tracy stated. When Carina didn't respond Tracy continued, "an innocent person being convicted of *his* murder isn't what he would have wanted. There must be something Rita can do … I've heard the rumors."

"I won't make any promises, but I will talk with her for you," Carina conceded.

"Why can't I talk with her myself?" Tracy asked turning as the front door opened.

The last person Carina expected to see walk through with a clenched jaw and worried expression. She fought her instinct to hug him and rooted her feet to the ground instead. Admittedly, her relationship with Gabriel was strained and complicated. They used to be closer, but now it was like walking on shattered glass. Even though they'd picked up all the big pieces, they both knew that little shards were prone to cutting them when they least expected it.

"Care Bear I need your help," he said gently.

Carina visibly winced and fought the urge to tell him to go fuck himself. "Help with what?" she said with equal gentleness.

"Why are you mad?" Gabriel asked, breaking the charade they were maintaining.

"I'm not mad," Carina said through clenched teeth.

"I don't have to see your aura to know you're mad," Gabriel replied with a frown.

"I'm not mad," Carina insisted with a sharper tone. "Just tell me what you want," she snapped.

"See, you're snapping at me," he said, thrusting his hands forward, exasperated. "I didn't even do anything but walk through the door!"

"Walked through the door and called me *Care Bear!*" Carina yelled. Gabriel rolled his eyes and blew out a long breath. "Oh, now you're breathing hard?"

"I'm sorry!" he groaned loudly. "I'm a piece of shit that forgot I couldn't call you that anymore," he said. "I know, I know. *I'm stupid.* I'm selfish," he complained, triggering Carina's peak frustration.

"Don't forget to add emotional terrorist," Carina snapped. She stepped closer to him and pointed at his face when he took a deep breath.

Silence built, and eventually, Gabriel turned his head toward the heavens.

"I'm an emotional terrorist. I'm literally the worst ex-boyfriend anyone could have," he lamented. He quickly wrapped her in a hug before she could walk away, "I'm sorry you have to even breathe my air I'm so undeserving," he continued.

"Please stop," she groaned and shoved him away.

He backed away, hands held up in surrender.

"I'm gonna go," Tracy said smirking at Gabriel.

"Call me when you get home," he said to Tracy stiffening her spine.

"Yeah," she muttered, closing the door behind her.

Carina's face pulled tight with stress as she watched Tracy leave the club. "She's been drinking Gabe," she said softly.

"I know," he replied, frowning, "she's not driving herself home."

"How do you know?" Carina said frowning.

Gabriel bopped her button nose and chuckled as her eyes widened and her chest heaved. "Jezabel is outside, she'll take care of it."

"Okay … wait why is Jezabel here?" Carina breathed out a frustrated breath and glared at Gabriel's sheepish expression. Carina tapped her manicured nails against the tabletops of the high table she stood next to. "You know, I am sorry for what happened between us," Gabriel said softly.

"Why are you here?" Carina signed her frustration seizing her vocal cords.

"It's Malina," Gabriel said with a heavy sigh.

"She's where all roads lead," Carina signed with a scoff. "What about her?" she added, quickly seeing the hurt in his face and knowing she'd caused him to step on an emotional shard.

"Doctors say she won't make it through the week," Gabriel said in a harsh voice.

Carina's mouth dried. "I ..." she started and stopped. "I didn't ... Gabriel, are you okay?" she signed.

"I need your help," he repeated.

"What do you think I can do?"

"Talk to Rita for me," Gabriel said, stepping toward her.

"Talk to Rita about what?" Carina asked harshly. "What do you think Rita can do for her?"

"She can make a portal to Serinytas," Gabriel explained. "Malina needs to get to Serinytas so she can receive treatment from the Pharaoh's people. Remilda said they deal with these things all the time."

"No," Carina said, shaking her head.

"No?" Gabriel repeated incredulously.

"No, you aren't telling me everything," Carina said standing her ground, "why can't the Shikka deal with it? It's not like Serinytas has bad blood with Ekocia. Why can't they ship her through the proper channels?"

"Because the Yakim is dead," Margherita said with a frown.

Carina looked at Margherita's stoic face with a frown and shook her head. She walked toward the only mother she had ever known and shook her head.

"If the Yakim is dead, opening the portal would be an act of treason," Carina said out loud and glared back at Gabriel, who wouldn't meet her eyes. "You wouldn't ask this of Malina," she hissed.

"Don't make *this* into *that* Care," Gabriel pleaded. "Despite whatever you believe, I do love you," he admitted.

"Just not enough to stop yourself from asking my mother to commit treason," Carina said. "When shit hits the fan, I'll be motherless."

"Join the club," he said with a weak smile. "Carina, If there was another way—"

"There isn't," Margherita said, quickly. "I know there isn't."

"You can't be considering this," Carina said, frowning.

"It's the right thing to do," Jezabel's voice said as she walked into the club.

"You put him up to this?" Carina said dismayed.

"It's my decision," Gabriel said.

"Don't!" Carina snapped. "Don't defend her. What happened in the ritual wasn't even Rita's fault."

"We've been through this," Margherita said and sighed.

"You trusted, the hag!" Carina snapped. "We all did. We all would have done the same thing!" Margherita descended the steps, and Carina moved away. "No!" Carina said, moving so Margherita wouldn't hurt her for disrespecting Old Lady Bella. "Margherita please don't do this," Carina begged. "Ma, please ..."

Margherita stopped, her resolve crumbling.

"She has to make this right," Jezabel said from behind her.

"If you feel like it has to be done, do it yourself," Carina snapped, advancing on Jezabel.

Gabriel stepped in the way, wrapping his arms around her. "I'm sorry," he breathed into her hair.

Carina felt herself breaking. The only people in the world that she loved were ripping her apart, and she couldn't tell anyone. She knew it was the right thing for Margherita to do. She knew that's why Margherita had been distancing herself and spending more time with Jezabel. They'd been plotting this whole thing. The only thing that screwed everything up was the Yakim dying. They would have gotten in trouble before, but now it's treason and kidnapping. Carina held onto Gabriel.

She trembled and he held her tighter. Despite her hatred and pain, she knew he wouldn't let her go until she was ready.

"I'm going with her," Gabriel said into the crown of her head.

"No," Carina said eyes filling with tears and panic. She pulled away from him and met his red eyes. "You have to stay. You can't leave me alone ..." She hadn't expected herself to say that. She hadn't meant to say so much out loud.

"Carina," Margherita said hesitantly, coming up from behind her. She pulled Carina from Gabriel's embrace so she could fully face her. "I will never leave you alone if there was another choice you know that."

"There has to be another way," Carina said squeezing Rita's hands.

"This is the worst mistake I've ever made."

"It wasn't—"

"It is my fault Carina," Ritta confirmed, cupping Carina's face brushing away a stray tear with her thumb. "I have to face this and fix it. You have to be okay with this."

"I don't *have* to be okay with losing you," Carina debated, pulling away from Margherita's comfort. "But I promise I won't stand in your way."

Errands

Carina rose from her bed and carefully stepped over Gabriel's sleeping body on the floor. He didn't want to go home where his rage and Dante were waiting for him. Staying the night at the hospital and watching Malina wasn't an option. Carina's bed wasn't an option either. Civil didn't mean cuddly. Carina grabbed a change of clothes and padded her way to the bathroom. She stopped in the middle of her journey, haunted by the sound of a painfully familiar voice.

"Do you want breakfast?" the voice asked.

No one responded to the question, leaving Carina frowning and feeling crazy, *no way is Lunis here.* Shaking her head, she continued down the hall and into the bathroom. Mindful of Gabriel she showered quickly to not waste the hot water. She was in the middle of her face care routine when a knock sounded on the door.

"Just a minute I'm almost—" Carina frowned when the door opened, and Margherita poked her head in. "Oh, it's just you," Carina said casually. Margherita was wearing her purple silk robe open, revealing her black tank top and white bottoms.

"So, now that he's around, I'm *just you*," Margherita mocked.

"You know it's not like that," Carina said, rolling her eyes while gliding her jade roller over her face. "What's up?"

"I need you to run an errand for me today if you don't mind," Margherita said, leaning against the doorframe.

"I don't mind," Carina sighed, pondering if she was gonna wear makeup. "What's the errand?" she asked while removing the band she used to hold her hair back.

"I need you to pick up some things for the ritual tonight," Margherita said, biting the inside of her cheek. "I made a list ..." Margherita held up the paper and money. "Whatever you don't use, you can keep," she said.

"I already said I would," Carina said, smiling, and plucked the money and list from Margherita's loose fingers. "But thank you for sweetening the deal." She stuffed the money into the back pocket of her denim shorts.

Then, she dipped her hair under the faucet, wetting it so she could work through the stubborn tangles. She bent over, letting the hair that grew to her shoulders overnight hang past her knees as she brushed her hair toward the floor. She grabbed her rainbow bandana that she laid folded in half on the edge of the sink. She carefully tied a knot in the front above her hairline and then leaned up to examine the look in the mirror. She pulled at the curls that fell over her forehead and smiled, satisfied with the way she looked—at which point she noticed Margherita's affectionate eyes on her.

"What?" Carina asked feeling suddenly self-conscious.

"You just look beautiful," Margherita said with a smile and then slowly turned and walked away.

Carina padded back to her room, so lost in thought that she forgot Gabriel was in her room. When she opened the door, she found Gabriel sitting on her bed, looking more tired and troubled than the day before. He looked up at her, and something shifted in his expression as he opened his mouth and a strangled sound eased out. He cleared his throat and rubbed his palms on the sweatpants he slept in.

"Good morning," Carina said.

"Good morning," he responded in kind. "You look ..." Gabriel looked away frowning.

"There's plenty of hot water, so you can shower here if you like," Carina offered, moving into her room and going to her dresser. "I still have some of your clothes from when you slept here last," Carina said, handing him clean underwear, a pair of grey shorts, and a blue shirt.

"Are you going somewhere today?" he asked, taking the clothes from her.

"Uh, yeah," Carina said, sighing. "I'm running errands for Rita," Carina said, standing to face her dresser and pick through the jewelry she left out for the hoops she wanted to wear.

"I can drive you if you like," Gabriel said with a sheepish grin.

"Don't you have an ambassador to guard?" Carina asked with a frown.

"They'll manage if I take the day off," Gabriel stated.

Carina nodded, tapping her fingers on the top of the dresser before meeting his eyes. *Don't get attached. It's a distraction*, Carina mentally reminded herself. "I'll wait for you," she said. She watched his shoulders roll back and lift with his smile as he walked out of the room.

∗∗∗

"So, where is this journey taking us?" he asked, keeping pace with her side as they walked to his car.

"Do you know where Belladonna's fields are?" Carina asked as he opened her door. She slid into his car and looked at him confused when he didn't close the door. "Gabe?"

"I ..." he started and stopped shaking his head. "Of course, I know where my best friend died," he said with malice laced in his tone.

"I wasn't thinking," she said apologetically and then eased out of the car.

"What are you doing?" he demanded, watching her every move. His vigilance made her squirm. "What's orange mean?"

"I'm embarrassed," Carina said with a frown. "It's not fair that you can see me like that," she said, looking past his easy smile to his red eyes. "It's weird that you can see the auras at all ..."

"I know," he said simply. "I want to spend the day with you." He side-stepped and blocked her way from leaving, crowding her so she had no other choice.

"All right, all right," Carina said, holding her hands up, and sat back in the car.

As they rode, they fell back into the simple routine of her picking the music and singing along to her favorite songs. Gabriel teased her when she fumbled the words, but it was mostly laughs and lighthearted jabs. When they entered the parking lot, the mood changed, growing sadder. He stepped out with her and paused before the blood stain on the cement. Crouching down, he touched it with his fingertips and closed his eyes.

"I'll be five minutes," she said gently. "You can stay and pay your respects," she said, rubbing his back and then rested her hand on his shoulder.

"I'd rather do it at the gravesite," Gabriel said, placing his hand on top of hers.

"We can do that after this," she suggested.

"Okay," he said, squeezing her hand. He released it to open the store door for her allowing her to walk in ahead of him.

The store smelled like it always did to Carina. She didn't venture in often, but she knew the layout like the back of her hand. She pulled out the list Margherita wrote down for her and started working down the list. While she gathered the herbs, Gabriel slowly walked around the store, not shopping. Carina smirked. *Once you're trained for danger, you look for it wherever you go.* Gabriel suddenly appeared by her side.

"Gabe. What—" Carina began and stopped when Gabriel tightened his grip on her and backed her toward the door.

"That's impressive," said an unfamiliar female voice to their left. When Carina looked, though, there was no one there.

Where is the voice coming from? Carina pondered, moving behind Gabriel's back, "Reveal yourself," Gabriel demanded in his authoritative voice.

Carina looked at the space beside the exit following Gabriel's gaze and saw nothing. Carina frowned when Gabriel stepped more in front of her. Her heart was pounding violently in her ears as she peaked around him to see the invisible danger. Suddenly, the space in front of them shimmered and revealed a woman in black leggings and a sports bra appeared in front of him. Gabriel breathed in deep, and his back stiffened.

"A very select few can sense me," the woman said seemingly impressed, "what did I do that gave me away?" she asked, turning her back to him and walking up to the front counter.

"Uh—" Gabriel started and stopped. Carina peeked up and found that his face was ashen and frowning with disbelief. She reached for her megin and immediately felt an overwhelming pressure of murderous rage.

Carina wanted to speak, but she was frightened and unsure if she could relax with Gabriel in this state. She rubbed his back, and he blinked, returning to the present. He turned his head to the front counter Carina watched his Adam's apple bob up and down as he slowed and walked toward the counter. Carina followed behind, uncertain about what would happen next. The woman had reddish sepia brown skin and piercing green eyes that were both familiar and unfamiliar.

"Well, I suppose it's in your best interest not to tell me," the woman said with a frown and roll of her eyes. She sat on the stool behind the counter and propped her head up on her fist. "Is that it?" she said, nodding her head toward Carina.

Carina stepped to the side, placed the bags of herbs on the counter, and handed her the money.

The woman looked over the items the way Bella often did when she was guessing what her patrons were trying to make. The woman's piercing gaze landed on Carina a hair too long.

"You have your money. Can we go?" Gabriel asked with no humor in his tone.

"Gabe, is it?" she asked suddenly.

Carina felt her left hand tighten on the back of Gabriel's shirt. His right hand reached back and gave hers a comforting squeeze. He gathered the herbs and handed them to Carina without a bag. He turned his back to the cashier and started to move them toward the exit. Carina turned around and opened the door just as the woman spoke again.

"You favor him, you know," the woman said.

"Who," Gabriel said immediately, but something told Carina he already knew who she was talking about.

"Khalan," she said casually. "Or you may know him as Father or—"

"That man is not my father," Gabriel said, turning back to face her. Carina grabbed his arm in protest, "How do you know him?"

"Not intimately if that's what you're expecting," she said with a sparkle of humor in her eyes. Gabriel stepped forward and Carina pulled back.

"Let's go," Carina signed when Gabriel looked back at her.

"Wait in the car," he said softly.

"How gentlemanly of you," the cashier said, walking around the counter toward them. "I promise not to kill you," she said with a chuckle, opening the door for them. Carina stepped out into the sunlight and looked back at the store where Gabriel still stood and noticed sunlight wasn't leaking inside. "The old woman loves her security measures," she mused and sat on the curb, pulling out a cigarette.

"Carina wait for me in the car."

"You're bossing her around and protecting her like she's a fragile doll. It's pissing me off," the woman said, flicking the end of the cigarette. It caught fire and a plume of smoke curled in the atmosphere.

"I don't ... why should I care how you feel?" Gabriel demanded.

"Gabriel, let's go," Carina said, managing to get out in a whisper.

The woman smirked at that and sucked in a deep breath and blew at the ash that was building on the tip of the cigarette fueling the orange glow. She looked at the two young people before her and then out to the quiet street and the crumbled building.

"Will you send a message for me?" she asked, staring straight ahead.

"What?" Gabriel said, pulling his hand free of Carina's grasp. "What are you talking about? Why are you here?"

"I asked your father that question a few months ago before I gave him his last job."

"Last job?" Gabriel repeated.

"You're a damn parrot," she muttered, flicking the cigarette again when it went out.

"Are you saying that you had my father kill someone?"

"I had your father send a message to someone who was digging their nose into something they had no business looking into," she said coldly.

"Why are you telling me this," Gabriel asked after a moment of silence as he processed what she said. He looked at the blood stain and for the first time felt responsible for his friend's death.

"What does Margherita plan to do about my daughter's condition?" she demanded, meeting Carina's eyes. Carina looked at Gabriel for an explanation, "No, look at me," she commanded. "Answer my question."

"I don't know who you are," Carina signed quickly, her heart thudding in her chest.

"You're lucky Margherita taught me sign," the woman said and ignited the remainder of the cigarette while standing up. "I'm Malina's mother."

"You're Jade," Gabriel said, his eyes widening as his breathing deepened.

"So," she said ignoring Gabriel's clarification. "What is Margherita—" She stopped and concentrated on the hand signs Carina was making. "A portal to Serinytas," she said, looking at the empty street, and then stood and walked back into the store.

"Gabriel," Carina said, grabbing his arm.

"If Khalan killed Azazel …" Gabriel began and then shook his head. "I know Khalan did this …"

"Your father did—"

"He's not my father," Gabriel said, interrupting Carina.

Jade walked out of the store, closing the door and locking it behind her. She wore a black hoodie that placed her face in darkness. She held open a bag to Carina, who dropped the herbs she bought inside. She signed thank you, and Jade nodded her head at that and began walking away from them and the store.

"Where are you going?" Gabriel called after her.

"If you're going to carry out this plan, you need a distraction so you won't get caught right away," she said simply. Gabriel walked after her, leaving Carina behind. Jade stopped and faced him. "Ask what you want while I'm still feeling generous."

"What was the price of his life?" Gabriel asked.

"For clarification," she began, turning her face up like she smelled something bad, "I asked him to send a message not to take the boy's life. And the price was a snapdragon."

"Wha—"

"When was the last time you visited your mother?" Jade pried.

"I *don't*," Gabriel said quietly.

"Perhaps you should," Jade said softly and then turned away.

"What would you have done with Carina? If she didn't tell you what you wanted to know?"

"I suppose someone would have had to send *her* a message," she said with a shrug. Then, she laced her hands behind her head and walked down the street with a slight skip in her step.

The ride back to Kore's Palace was quiet and humorless. Carina didn't have to see Gabriel's aura to tell he was a stormy cloud of anger and confusion.

When he stopped outside of the club, Carina opened her door and paused before stepping out. She looked back at his face and sighed, closing the door.

"I have to go," Gabriel said, staring blankly at the road.

"You don't. We could talk about it."

"I don't *want* to talk about it."

"Gabriel, you aren't responsible for what Khalan did," Carina rationalized. "He's a grown man—"

"Do you know what a snapdragon is?" Gabriel asked, his tone cruel and impatient.

"Snapdragons are a myth," Carina offered gently.

"What's the myth?" Gabriel inquired, meeting her soft gaze.

Carina paused for a moment, unsure if he was joking. "Tell me the myth, Carina."

"The myth is if you hold the flower next to someone dying, the flower will draw death to it instead of the person," Carina explained, and Gabriel nodded.

"If you grind it up and have someone drink it, it will clear out any poison. Burn it and have someone inhale the scent, it heals any ailments of the mind."

"Gabriel, it's just a myth," Carina insisted.

"Does Jade seem like the type that wouldn't hold up her end of the bargain?" Gabriel demanded.

"Well, if it's true, how would you get Khalan to help your mother?" Carina asked. Gabriel rested his head against the headrest and stared up at the ceiling.

"I won't have to," he said in a deeply troubled voice.

"I'm confused," Carina said with a frown, and Gabriel eyed her without turning his head. "You told me Khalan poisoned her."

"Please get out," said Gabriel coldly. When she didn't move, he got out on his side and briskly walked around the car to open her door. Carina eased out but grabbed his arm before he was able to move away. "Let me go."

"Why can't you talk to me?"

"Anything but this," he said, pushing her hands off him.

"You know everything about me," she said, argued, feeling rejected and uncertain. "Why don't you trust me?"

"Carina, you broke up with me because you felt like I was in love with someone else because I blew you off on *one* date."

"It wasn't just *someone*. It was Malina, and it wasn't just *one* date; it was the last one I could take," Carina clarified.

Gabriel released a long breath, and hanging his head low he shook his head.

"I can't do this anymore," he said.

"You won't have to. If you just open up to me and tell me the truth. I can take it, Gabriel I ..." her voice trailed off as the red hue of his eyes darkened. "What is it?"

"Someone I don't know is in the club," he said with a frown.

"It could be no one," Carina said, looking toward the club to avoid his intense gaze. She saw blue, green, yellow, and orange hues emanating from the building in front of them. "I'm pretty sure everything is fine," she said with a sigh and walked away from him.

"What were you going to say?" Gabriel asked. Carina turned back to face him and shrugged.

"I care about you Gabe, and how I feel doesn't just go away."

"How you feel about me can go away," he said coldly.

"How can you say that?" she demanded, more hurt than she'd ever felt before.

"Carina, I care about Dante. I'm not going to kill or die for him, but I would do that for *you* because I love you. I'm not afraid of how you would react to me because that won't change my love for you. You saying I could feel this way about anyone else, hurts. But your jealousy makes me love you even more."

"Bullshit," Carina snapped, feeling her throat tighten and her eyes burn with emotion. He smirked and her rage built. "If you aren't afraid of how I would react, then why won't you tell me what happened to your family?"

"I'm not ready to talk about it."

"I bet Malina knows."

"She knows because she was there," Gabriel said with a frown and shook his head. "That doesn't count."

"It counts for me," Carina pouted. "I'm your girlfriend. I'm supposed to know everything about you."

Gabriel smiled and his eyebrows pinched together. "You're my girlfriend?" Gabriel asked, twerking his head and stepping closer. Carina didn't say anything as he wrapped his arms around her.

Carina hesitated for a moment before holding him tightly against her. "Gabe—"

"Who's that?" Gabriel asked, his back stiffening with awareness. Carina looked over her shoulder and stepped away from him.

"Lunis? What are you doing here?"

Involvement

C arina paced in Margherita's office, bristling with anger as Gabriel sat downstairs having a conversation with Lunis. *What type of conversation are they having? Father to boyfriend? As if Lunis has any right*, she thought as anger, relief, and gratitude took their turn stiffening and relaxing her spine. Carina walked over to Margherita's desk, punched in the code to open the bookcase, and walked to it to slide it open. She closed it behind her and walked down to the lab where Margherita was grinding and boiling the herbs Carina returned with. Margherita looked up to Carina and then down back to the herbs.

Margherita was still wearing her robe and night clothes. Her hair was twisted up out of her face, and she appeared tired and distracted. Momentarily,

Carina wondered if Margherita had gotten any sleep the day before. After meeting Jade and noting how little she cared about Azazel's death, the picture was clearer. She may not have ordered his death, but she hadn't cared either way because she believed whatever message needed to be received was received.

"You're still stormy," Margherita commented.

"I have questions that need to be answered," Carina said with a shrug.

"Ask them," Margherita said with a sigh, lowering the temperature on the eye of her solo burner.

"How long has Lunis been here?" Carina demanded, "Did you know Jade would be there? Why haven't you let me help with any of this in a bigger way until now?"

"I'll answer the last one first. You've been involved since the beginning."

"No, I haven't! I didn't know Jade was Malina's mother! Did she have a fling with Victor? Did Elizabeth always know about this?"

"Victor and Jade are siblings, and just because you weren't privy to all of the information doesn't mean you weren't involved—just out of the loop," Margherita offered with a grin.

"Malina is an incest baby?"

"Gods no," Margherita said with a chuckle. "Jade and Dante were a very cute couple. He's the father. Elizabeth had her tested just in case," Margherita said, rolling her eyes. "Jade had an unfortunate event happen to her. She never recovered," Margherita said, her face drawing down as she refocused on the items in front of her.

"What happened?" Carina asked.

"Another time?" Margherita asked, and Carina sighed and nodded.

"Did you know she would be there today?"

"Yes," Margherita said with a stoic expression.

"You gambled with my life, Rita," Carina said with a frown. She watched Margherita wrestle with something as she pressed her palms flat against the table.

"That's the type of life I lead, Carina; I can't protect you from everything, and I can't tell you everything all the time. Do you still want to help me?" Margherita asked, meeting her eyes with unblinking severity.

"I-" Carina started and stopped. She looked at the herbs on the table in front of Margherita, and she thought of Gabriel upstairs. "This has always been my life."

"That's not true," Margherita said gently. "It may have always happened around you, but you simply didn't realize it," Margherita said.

"How long has Lunis been here?" Carina asked, shifting the subject.

"A few days," he answered at the top of the stairs. Then, with heavy footsteps, he descended.

Carina felt her heart thud in tandem as he neared them. His golden eyes reminded her of the sun, and a familiar pang started to overwhelm her.

"You weren't going to tell me you were here, were you?" she asked as a tear slipped down her face.

He met her eyes and shook his head. "But when I saw you, I couldn't stay away," he admitted. "I missed you. You've grown so much," he chuckled and rubbed the back of his neck.

"If that were true, why didn't you come back sooner?" Carina demanded.

Lunis sighed and looked at Margherita for help, but she shook her head.

"Are you mad at me too?" he asked in his deep voice.

"About what exactly?" she asked, turning off the burner.

"About leaving," he clarified, his tone more measured. Carina frowned at the small exchange. *What did I miss?*

"No, Lu," Margherita said, looking at him, "I understood why you had to leave."

"I didn't," Carina interjected, "so why did you have to leave on my birthday, and what brought you back nine years later? And what gives you the right to interrogate the guy I'm talking to?"

"Just talking to?" Margherita repeated with a raised eyebrow.

"You called yourself his girlfriend earlier," Lunis said with a frown.

"It's complicated," Carina said, crossing her arms over her chest protectively. "And that's not what I want to talk about," she said, frowning.

Margherita looked at Lunis expectantly and then turned back to Carina. She looked over the herbs in front of her and then at the watch on her wrist. She turned and started walking up the stairs. Lunis' face fell, and he turned to follow her, but Margherita glared at him and stopped. She shook her head like she was disappointed, and Lunis' shoulders sagged slightly before rising as he turned back to Carina, who was more hurt now than before.

"Carina, I kill people for a living," he said bluntly.

"That wasn't so hard to say," she said glibly. She swayed as the picture of the man in front of her altered.

She loved Lunis. He'd raised her just like Margherita had. Taught her right and wrong. Taught her how to control her megin and how to sign. Taught her to speak and protected her until the day he left so suddenly she questioned if he had ever been there. *Carina, I kill people for a living.* She thought about that for a long moment.

"Do you remember that man that I threw onto a pole?" Lunis asked. Carina nodded she'd been taught to tell people that so fewer people would come by and mess with them. "His family was coming to take revenge. I wiped them out," he explained, and despite the queasy feeling in her stomach, she nodded to learn more. "After that, I was approached by Jade to finish out my contract. We made a deal that I could be released if I could show her that I could live out the rest of my time without killing. I failed when I killed that man and his family, so I had to leave."

"You could have broken his arm—"

"Or legs, yeah. I know," he said, blowing out a frustrated breath that shifted into a chuckle. "Rita and I had the same argument," he said and rubbed at the back of his neck.

"Were you not allowed to visit?" Carina asked.

"I was," Lunis said gently, "but it was safer if I didn't."

"Safer or *easier*?" Carina asked, suddenly feeling angry.

"Both," he said, nodding. "I didn't want you or Rita hurt if I got sloppy, and I was ashamed of myself for doing what I did."

"You protected me," she said softly.

"I didn't break his arms or legs because I knew it would feel good to kill him because I missed killing men like him." Lunis looked away, "I chose a life without you because I'm a selfish man, Carina."

"But you're back now," Carina said, rubbing the goosebumps from her arms, "right? Isn't that why you're here?"

Margherita walked back down the stairs with a wooden totem of a baboon, moonstones, and cookies with icing drizzled decoratively in the shape of crescent moons.

Lunis watched Margherita's movements—the silent way she arranged everything carefully—and then looked back at Carina. He shook his head sadly and rubbed the back of his neck.

"I have to go back to Hiboria."

"Hiboria is a myth," Carina said defiantly.

"Carina ..."

"You want to stay," Carina reasoned, "so stay. Margherita and I want you to stay."

"Carina, speak for yourself," Margherita grumbled as she carefully poured the tea-like mixture into vials.

"Rita," Carina complained, "tell him he doesn't have to go."

"Lunis is an adult," Margherita said sternly, meeting Carina's eyes. "He's aware of where he's wanted and needed," her gaze shifted to Lunis. His golden eyes directly communicated with her soul. "As an adult, he knows when to put his wants first."

"Ma-"

"Carina, enough," Margherita said, exhausted. "I need you to take a few things to Jezabel. We only have one shot at this portal to get Malina to Serinytas."

"Gabriel left to talk to a Remilda," Lunis said, looking at Margherita. "He said she needed to get home for everything to work smoothly. She has access to her own portals."

"Guessing by how smug you look, she's one of your disciples?" Margherita said with an annoyed expression.

"No, but her vizer is. Safety is having friends in high places," Lunis stated.

"How warm do those friends keep you at night?" Margherita asked with a frown.

"Ice cold," Lunis said with a straight face.

"Hmph," Margherita grunted and held a bag out to Carina. "Go straight there and then call me when you make the drop; as soon as she has everything, we're going to start, okay?"

Carina nodded. "Why do you have so much?" Carina asked observing the difference.

"Because, Carina," Margherita started and stopped. "... I'm leaving to go to Hiboria tonight."

"What?" Carina demanded. "Why?"

"I'll need you to run the club while I'm gone. I only expect to be gone for a week to a month."

"Stop talking so casually."

"I have to do this."

"Why?"

"Jack—"

"I don't care about—"

"If they fail in Serinytas, I need to have a plan B. Enough people have died because of this mess. Do you understand?" she asked in a no-nonsense tone.

"I don't like this."

"You don't have to, Carina; you just have to stand aside and let me save these people." Margherita pleaded.

"Can't you kill her?" Carina asked Lunis bluntly. "Jade I mean."

"It's not that simple; I can't kill her," Lunis said with a sigh. "She has an entity inside her, and if she dies that entity will be released into the world."

Margherita rounded the corner with the bag of packed objects for Jezabel and placed it in her hand. Carina sighed and fisted the straps, knowing she no longer had a choice or argument for Margherita. She had to help her or she would get caught trying to help the people she inadvertently placed in harm's way.

Carina placed the strap on her shoulder and Margherita placed her hands on either side of Carina's face.

"Ma?"

"Whatever happens *do not* perform the ritual."

"You can put your life in danger for Malina—" Carina began.

"Carina!" Margherita snapped, interrupting what she was saying. "This isn't the time for games.

He wants you more than any priestess before," she warned. "Just ... just leave it to Jezabel. It'll take time, but just let her do it, okay?" Margherita pleaded.

"Yeah, okay," Carina conceded and hugged Margherita tightly.

Demons
Gabriel

Gabriel stepped out of his car feeling more troubled than he had before. *Khalan killed my best friend. Did he know that when he was killing him? Did Dante know what happened before I showed him the picture?* Gabriel looked up the steps and to Remilda's temporary house and sighed. Breathing in deep, he tried to clear his mind, but his head hammered with the smell of iron. Gabriel rushed up the steps and stopped at the sight of Taka's slumped body. Gabriel knelt down and went to touch his neck but stopped at the claw marks that dug deep into his jugular. A crash on the inside forced his jumbled thoughts onto autopilot.

Message to Dante: Taka is down. I'm at Remi's headed in now.

Gabriel sent the message and pocketed the phone; he eased through the door, which stood ajar. Gabriel's eyes landed on a foot that was turning blue from lack of circulation. He walked through the broken glass and wood to where the foot was connected to a crumpled body. Heidi's pale face looked up at him with vacant eyes as blood poured down her throat. Gabriel reached out to close her eyes when a crashing sound followed by a grunt came from the back room. Gabriel rose from his kneeling position, channeling his megin through his limbs, keeping his body light and agile.

"You weren't running earlier when you called me here ..." Gabriel's heart thudded in his chest when he heard the man's voice. It had been years, but the low rumble was unmistakable to his ears. *Khalan is here, and he killed two Askari soldiers, and he is about to kill Remilda.*

"I summoned you here, yes," Remilda responded as Gabriel walked into the room. "Not to kill these people. Kalair! You're supposed to protect—"

"I'm not my brother," Khalan said, crouching down low and spreading his fingers, which were dripping with thick sticky blood.

"What?" Remilda demanded.

Gabriel watched Remilda's eyes glow yellow as her skin warmed and glistened. Khalan lunged at her; Gabriel rushed into the room, but before he could get to her, Khalan had his hand around her face. Gabriel channeled his megin into his hand and punched Khalan in the kidney. Unfazed, Khalan looked back at him in annoyance, and Gabriel felt like he was ten and powerless again. Khalan knocked Gabriel to the floor and pinned Khalan to the wall with vines that grew up from the floor.

Remilda's had a cut on her lip and light bruising on her cheek. Blood trickled from her nose, and she wiped it away briskly with the back of her hand. She glanced down at Gabriel solely to acknowledge his well-being before diverting her attention back to Khalan. Khalan roared against the pain of needles that dug into his skin and clawed at the plant freeing himself from the wall.

"A botanist," Khalan mused his lips widening into a smile that relieved his sharp canines. "I guess it runs in the family," Khalan grumbled. He looked at Gabriel and narrowed his eyes as he thought through something. "Your mother will come back to us, but we need her," he said, nodding to Remilda. Remilda stiffened and stepped back from both men.

"What are you talking about?" Gabriel demanded.

"I have snapdragons," Khalan explained.

"What?" Remilda said, and stepping forward, she held out a hand. "Show me."

"You have to come with me," Khalan said. "That's the only way you'll see them."

"Snapdragons are a myth," Gabriel said thoughtfully.

"Not a myth," Remilda interjected. "Just native to my homeland and not meant for outsiders," she said in a hateful tone.

"The ones I have are dead, but you could bring them back," he said with a level of concentration that made Gabriel uncomfortable.

"I will not," Remilda protested.

"Not even to save Gabriel's life?" Khalan asked.

"To save Gabriel?" she asked, bewildered.

Khalan's nails turned to claws as they grew rapidly he swung down toward Gabriel's throat. Gabriel moved out of the way, and Khalan's hand went through the floorboard.

Khalan lifted his head, locking his eyes on Gabriel, and he lunged forward.

Gabriel channeled his megin to his bicep and shoved Khalan away from him.

Khalan rolled with the momentum, landing on his feet, and lunged again. He was as agile as a leopard and as viscous as a bear. It took all of Gabriel's concentration to dodge and remain on his feet.

The room was small and cramped, and Gabriel had no weapons and no time to attack. Khalan was relentless and not looking to stop his attacks anytime soon. Gabriel bumped into Remilda, and Khalan took advantage of the small distraction. He dug his claws into Gabriel's forearms, tearing into his muscles. He threw his head back revealing his jugular, and Remilda's vines wrapped around his throat. The vines grew thick and fast, the thorns as big as pocket knife blades, and when she pointed to the wall, the vines threw him through it. The vines retreated back to the earth they sprung from where Khalan made a hole in the floorboard.

Remilda knelt beside Gabriel and reached out to touch his wounds but stopped herself and rushed to her dresser. When she returned, Khalan was rising to his feet, and Remilda quickly handed Gabriel a jar filled with thick cream. Khalan stepped through the hole, shaking his head to get some of the dust out of his hair. The gray shirt he wore was ripped, and in front was a triangle-like shape from the blood that poured down his neck. Khalan looked at the jar Gabriel held and chuckled.

"You see," Khalan scoffed. "All of you botanists are the same."

"What do you mean?" Remilda asked with a frown. Khalan pulled out a knife and settled into a boxing position.

"I'll kill everyone in this neighborhood if you don't come with me," he said, all humor leaving his face. "If you do, I'll tell you where *she* is," he said with a smirk.

"Tell me now, and I'll allow you to leave here," Remilda rebutted.

"I like my plan better," Khalan said and flicked his wrist, releasing the knife.

Remilda's vines sprung up from the earth to stop the knife that was headed toward Gabriel's right eye. The instant the vine made contact with the knife, it shriveled and died. Remilda cried out in pain as the pain spiked up her arm to her elbow. Gabriel managed to catch the blade, but it sliced into his fingers, making his right hand completely numb.

Khalan walked toward Remilda, who had collapsed to the ground, holding her right arm in pain. Gabriel moved in front of her, wielding the knife as he crouched, low ready to defend her.

Suddenly, Dante's voice boomed, "Stop."

"Took you long enough," said Gabriel.

"Dante!" Khalan barked with laughter. "You're working for *him*?" he inquired. "That bastard tore our family apart."

"How I chose to live my life became none of your business the day you left," Gabriel retorted, coldly pointing the knife at him.

"Oh, you mean the day you failed to kill your mother?" Khalan said, and the room grew quiet.

"Gabriel?" said Remilda.

"Oh?" Khalan said as a chuckle escaped his throat, "was I not supposed to tell?"

Gabriel's fist tightened around the hilt in his hand. He tossed the knife up and as Khalan had taught him in the past, he skillfully caught the blade by the tips of his fingers and flicked it toward Khalan's chest. Dante ordered him to stop, but the blade was already gone, and he had no desire to stop it. Despite being stabbed, Khalan lowered his body to line the knife up to his throat. The vines shriveled, and with agile grace, Khalan moved to the side just in time, only getting grazed by the blade.

Remilda was on the ground, cradling her arm to her chest, screaming into the carpeted floor. Dante pulled out his gun and shot once at Khalan. Khalan took the bullet to the shoulder and yanked the blade from the drywall.

"Blade vs bullet which of—" Khalan stopped talking and clutched his chest.

"Valor bullets," Dante said, showing the distinct black metal. "The next one goes through your heart," Dante said. "Deux and Poe get in here," he ordered without taking his eyes off Khalan. Two Askari men stepped inside with handcuffs.

"Where are you taking him?" Remilda asked, rolling up from her side to her knees.

"He's going to the Shikka base," Dante explained coldly. "You aren't authorized to know any more."

"He knows about my mother," Remilda said, rising to her full height on shaky legs.

"Remilda, what are you thinking?" Gabriel asked, stepping closer to her. "Khalan doesn't know anything about your mom. That was just a ploy."

"Like him saying you killed your mother?" Remilda rebutted. "Was *that* a ploy?"

"Get him out of here," Dante ordered.

"I can't let you do that," Remilda said, breathing in a deep unsteady breath as the house shook and split.

"Remi, don't do this," Gabriel attempted to reason.

Yet, a large vine sprung from the earth, wrapped around Khalan, and shoved the other Askari into the wall, knocking them out. Dante aimed his gun at Remilda, and a vine branched off, twisting his wrist until he dropped the gun. As the vine pinned Dante to the wall, Gabriel grabbed Remilda by her shoulders and shook her.

"You're hurting innocent people."

"This wouldn't have happened if you just allowed me to talk with Malina!" Remilda snapped. "I won't allow you to keep another clue from me."

"Remi, that's not what we're doing. Malina," Gabriel attempted to reason.

"Could have been forced," Remilda snapped. Khalan chuckled at that.

"Well, aren't you feisty," Khalan said in a low rumble. Remilda made a disgusted face pulling him back toward her.

"Remilda let him go, or I will have to force you to," Dante promised struggling against the thick plant wrapped around his torso. Gabriel left her side, rushing toward the knife he picked it up and held it up to the vines around Dante's torso.

"I'm not giving up a chance to find my mother," Remilda said, and her head rose, but doubt flickered in her eyes.

"Remilda," Gabriel said as the heady smell of majik filled the air.

Without another choice, he cut into the vines. Remilda held her head as pain shot through her nerves, but she only had to hold on a few heartbeats longer. The vines shrunk back and hid in the earth, and Remilda knelt at Khalan's feet, clutching her stomach as Dante's feet landed on the floor.

Dante released his megin, and his darkness—aimed like a bullet—rushed toward Remilda. Bright-red flames erupted around Remilda and Khalan, and the darkness of Dante's megin shriveled in the light of the fire. The portal swallowed them and closed as abruptly as it opened.

Silence filled the room as the smoke cleared, and the smell of majik disappeared. Gabriel walked over to where Remilda once stood and noticed the burnt vines in the shape of symbols on the floor. Gabriel looked back at Dante whose eyes were stormy blue, as his hands clenched into fists. The two Askari soldiers slowly rose to their feet.

"Leave," Dante ordered the men, and without hesitation they obeyed. "Why weren't you here?" Dante asked in a low dangerous voice.

"Why would that matter?" Gabriel asked, "Heidi and Taka were—"

"They were green!" Dante growled. "You were more experienced. You were supposed to be here too."

"Are you saying their deaths are on *me*?"

"If you were here they may still be alive."

"That's not fair! You saw me! Look at me!" Gabriel yelled, holding up his bloody shaking hands. "I would have died too!"

"Why was he here?" Dante demanded, changing the subject.

"He mentioned Remilda summoning him," Gabriel said quietly, lost in thought about Taka and Heidi. *They're dead, and that's on me.* "Khalan killed Azazel," Gabriel said, his thoughts far away. "We have to tell the Carabinieri."

"They already arrested someone for that," Dante said coldly, walking around Remilda's room. "You didn't tell me she wanted to speak with Malina."

"It wasn't important," Gabriel said. "Henrik didn't do it! Why not tell the truth?"

"Khalan just got away with the stand-in ambassador of Serinytas," Dante stated.

"We should tell people—"

"Tell people what?!" Dante barked, interrupting Gabriel, "What evidence do we have that he did it except for a picture that he was in the country? What proof do we have that he's killed anyone?" Gabriel remained silent, so Dante continued. "Do you really want me to go to the Carabinieri and tell them that who they arrested is the wrong man? That under the Shikka's watch, not only was the Yakim killed, but the prime suspect of a teenage murder vanished. Oh, and let's not forget he's escaped through a portal in front of a Yeoman under a portal ban."

"Bad press?" Gabriel said in disbelief. "That's what's stopping you from telling the truth?"

"My job? This country! This country was found on the frayed rope of trust between Gios and Bahkir. If we can't show them that we'll protect them from us—*at the very least*—the state will crumble."

"So you're just going to bury it? Like it never happened?" Gabriel asked in disbelief.

"You didn't have any complaints when I did it for you all those years ago," Dante challenged. Gabriel swallowed down the bile that rose in his throat.

"What if we do give them someone?" Gabriel offered, and Dante blew out a sigh.

"Who did you have in mind? Yourself?" Dante asked with a scoff. "The Shikka can't interfere with a Carabinieri case unless invited in or if we have another probable suspect that's a Bahkir. We can't interfere."

"We have Jade," Gabriel offered, and it felt like the air was sucked out of the room at the mention of her name.

"Say again?" Dante requested.

"I went to where Azazel died today. Jade was there," Gabriel explained. "We could offer them Jade."

"She's mentally ill. She won't serve time."

"Henrik won't be put on trial for something he didn't do."

"A mental hospital isn't good enough for the Kipi. They want blood."

"I'm sure they're more agreeable than you give them credit for."

"Why does Henrik matter to you?" Dante demanded.

"He was Taka's brother. He was one of us," Gabriel said, "and it's the right—"

"Will you shut—" Dante growled and then walked away. Punching a hole through the drywall, he shouted, "Well, where the hell is she?"

Memory Lane
Jade

As Jade walked to her brother's house she found herself reminiscing of the life she had before Midnight's hateful energy twisted her mind. *This is all Ralceo's fault,* Jade thought with a venom that she no longer fully believed. Ralceo is the reason that Jade missed out on seventeen years with her family, but now with the clarity she didn't have access to before she could see that fear is what kept her from Ekocia. Kept her from the only person that would understand and blindly help her.

Tell me, what greed brought you here? Midnight asked her in Limbus. *A favor to a friend,* Jade responded. excruciating pain was all she knew that first day. On the second day, as her organs shifted themselves to make room for the fetus that was forcing itself to life. *Is your friend's greed worth all of this pain? Who is your friend?*

"Bella," Jade said, and the pain stopped like she was washed in the strongest opioid known to man.

Midnight a visual of her in the pond. "Is this her?"

"Yes," Jade answered numbly, "she helped raise me. Showed me a better path."

"Her true name Ralceo," Midnight said with tired eyes. "She trained my abilities as well ... and with the aid of others, she placed me into the chalice you released me from." Midnight looked at Jade grimly. "When Ralceo has her visions, she can see and live through each path a person may take." Midnight's watchful eyes examined Ralceo's image before looking back to Jade. "I wonder which path you took that worked out in her favor. I suppose you live through this; otherwise, it will have been a total waste of my time."

Jade stopped walking and looked up at the house in front of her. It was night now. The moon hung high in the sky, and through the curtain windows, she saw light where she predicted the living room would be. *The perfect house for the perfect family*, she thought bitterly, regret seeped in as thought about the tragedy that they don't talk about. Jade channeled her megin at the lights in the house. First, she slowly brightened them until they were nearly blinding, then dimmed them once again. Jade walked up the steps, tapping her finger against her thigh as she waited for the front door to open.

Victor stepped out agitatedly as he rubbed his eyes. Her heart stuttered at the sight of her elder brother. From the distance they stood apart, he reminded her of their abusive father. Regulating her breath, Jade walked in, moving past him and into the living room. She plopped down on the couch beside a young girl who appeared to be the same age as her daughter and looked like a nicer version of Elizabeth. She rubbed at her hazel eyes, blinking when she looked at Jade.

"Astra?" she gasped and pulled Jade into an embrace, shoving her cheek against Jade's, and then immediately moved back. She scrambled back, eyes wide, and clear mouth hung open, but no noise came out.

Midnight's entity is in the girl … what does that mean for Malina?

"Jade, what the hell did you do?" Victor snapped.

"I just sat down, Big Brother. What's with all the fuss?" Jade asked, laying her head back against the cushion, appearing bored, but her mind wandered thinking working through possibilities.

"Angel," Victor said soothingly.

"Angel!" Jade mimicked with a chuckle.

"Jade, just hush."

"I could put her to sleep if you like."

"Don't touch me," Angel said, tears streaming down her face as she cowered behind Victor.

"I think I would like for her to go to sleep," Jade mused, staring up at his ceiling. "No popcorn ceiling?"

"Jade," Victor scoffed. "Angel, stand up. Your aunt isn't going to hurt you. Stop being so dramatic."

"You suck," Jade said with a frown. "I remember you being a lot more caring," Jade said, resting her elbows on her knees.

"I'm not his favorite," Angel said with a pout, regaining her composure. "My sister is. He's much nicer to her."

"Sister?" Jade said, testing the word on her tongue as she thought the circumstance she placed her daughter into. "Surely you aren't talking about *my* daughter," Jade challenged.

"Jade," Victor snapped, rising as his temper flared. "Shut. Up," he said calmly as he knelt before her, looking into her eyes. "Don't do this in front of *her*."

"Daddy, what does she mean?"

"Go to your room Evaline."

"But Dad," she whined.

"Now!" Victor shouted.

Angel rose to her feet and stomped upstairs, slamming the door behind her.

Victor sighed, and Jade lifted an eyebrow, and Victor lifted a finger as her door opened again.

"I'm telling mom!" she yelled and slammed the door for the second time. Victor rose and dropped onto the couch beside her.

"Why did you raise them as sisters?" Jade asked, feeling vulnerable.

"Why didn't you give her to Dante?" Victor asked.

Jade sighed and nodded upstairs. "Is she right? That my girl is your favorite," she asked with a smile.

"For the record, she's mine," Victor said with a sad smile that darkened his green eyes. "I love them the same in different ways. Malina is just easier. Evaline takes a lot more work," he said with a sigh as he rubbed his temples.

"Mmm," Jade said and sat back to rest her head on the cushion behind her.

"What are you doing here?" Victor asked.

"Working on a distraction," Jade said with a sigh.

"Distraction for what?" Victor asked with a frown. "What are you planning?"

"Offering your assistance, Big Brother?" Jade asked, rolling her head side to side. She felt lighter in her brother's presence—like they were children again and she was teasing him about his latest crush.

"Jade," he said in a dark tone.

Jade muttered her brother's words to herself: "We're the loose gravel that makes their bricks."

Victor sighed deeply and sat up, resting his elbows on his knees. "I can't believe you remember that," he replied thoughtfully. "Tell me what you're planning?" Victor asked, looking to Evaline's room and then back at her. "Are you trying to hurt Elizabeth?"

Jade blinked processing his words, considering the chain of events that could play out. Then, she rose to her feet and walked out of his house.

"Jade where are you going now?"

"I just wanted to see you," Jade admitted plainly. Turning to face him on the sidewalk she stopped staring at him as he stood in his doorway. "I missed you."

"You didn't have to," Victor snapped closing the distance between them. "What's going on in your head, Little Sister?" he asked tenderly and cupped her face.

Jade flushed with embarrassment. "I did," Jade started and stopped when his intense gaze started to remind her of her father. She closed her eyes and pulled away, her heart hammering as adrenaline flooded her nerves. "I wanted to see you while you still didn't hate me," she said, still trying to catch her breath.

"I couldn't ever hate you," Victor said maintaining his distance.

"You almost did when I killed mom and dad," she said, looking at him.

"I was afraid of you, but I didn't hate you," he explained. "Who do you plan to kill?"

"No one," Jade said quickly. "I don't plan to kill anyone. I just planning a distraction," Jade stated.

"Why? What for?" Victor asked, alarm lacing his otherwise calm tone. "Does this have to do with Malina?" he inquired.

"Have you even visited Malina?" he asked, and Jade vehemently shook her head.

"I told Dante I would leave town, Vic," Jade said, pulling in her megin. "He would have been alerted as soon as I stepped into the parking lot."

"That's why he increased security at the hospital," Victor mused. "I could take you, and because I'm beside you, they'll let you see her."

Jade pursed her lips, and shook her head. "Nah, that seems like an easy way for you to get hurt."

"I'm the older brother," Victor said with a frown, causing Jade to sigh. "Come on," Victor said, stepping closer and holding a hand out to her. "Try it my way first."

Jade hesitated, eyeing his hand that might mean her harm. "What about Elizabeth?" Jade asked, meeting his sincere eyes.

"You're my sister. She'll just have to understand," Victor reasoned.

"Women aren't that easy," Jade said, crossing her arms.

"Admit yourself," he bargained.

"I'm not crazy!" Jade snapped with a frown.

"But you're one of the best people I know," he teased, "and aren't the best people a little crazy?" Jade frowned, tapping her index finger against her bicep. "This will be the best solution," he insisted.

"No, drugs."

"I can't promise that," Victor said, letting his hand fall to his side.

"Then this is where we part," Jade said with a reluctant sigh, pausing when sirens wailed in the distance.

"Evaline said she was calling her mother," Victor explained. "I'll you tell them it's a false alarm."

"Vicky," Jade said with a smirk, "I told you I need to create a distraction this will be as good as any other."

Victor sighed at that and walked closer to his sister. "Why don't you want to see Malina?"

Jade faltered suddenly feeling overexposed. "It's not that I don't want to…" she said her voice trailing away as her thoughts came short of giving her a good excuse.

"What is it then?" Victor prodded.

"Malina," Jade started and stopped, turning to walk away as the sirens drove closer.

"Jade?" Victor called.

"I'm not good enough," Jade snapped whirling on Victor. "My hands drowning in blood. You saw the way Angel reacted! What if Malina does the same?"

"She won't," Victor said with finality.

"She will," Jade said shaking her head. "She will because she's cursed because of me."

"What do you mean?"

"The night Margherita performed the ritual; she removed an entity from me and placed it in Malina."

"How certain are you of this?" Victor asked, feeling terrified.

"I feel sane, Vic," Jade said levelly. "I know she's gone." The sirens were closer now.

"I don't think I'm going to make it through the night," she admitted with a sigh. "I just wanted to spend some time with you, before I couldn't anymore." She shrugged. "I'm getting sentimental in my old age."

"I won't tell anyone," he said with a chuckle.

"I wouldn't kill you if you did," she said with a smile and chuckle as she held her head up to the cool dark sky.

Aletheia
Astra

Malina felt like she was part of the earth at this point. She'd watched so many sunrises and sunsets, she was sick to death of them. She only wanted to see the night sky. She only wanted the cool embrace of night and to welcome the endless stars in her mind. *Were these lights even stars? I've never seen these constellations.* Malina found herself marveling for what felt like a year. Midnight claimed that she wouldn't last much longer, but Malina didn't care anymore. She wanted to be left with the painless nights that soothed her. She didn't feel the phantom warmth from hands holding her own. *That means they stopped caring right?*

The soft jangle of metal against metal and the slight give of moist dirt beneath Midnight's weight alerted Malina to her presence. Malina forced her body to rise, and she turned her head as Midnight stopped in front of her. Midnight offered Malina her hand, and as she took it, they walked hand and hand through the forest to the looking glass pond. Malina realized she had never asked Midnight what the pond was or if it was located in the other world. She didn't care to know anything other than the looking glass pond she thought would be lame.

Midnight released her hand for the first time Malina realized her body was starting to feel more solid here. Malina knelt by the body of water, and she waved a hand over it like she had seen Midnight do countless times before. The Heka-infused water shimmered and formed an image of a woman she had never seen before yet was too familiar to ignore.

"Who is that?" Malina asked but then shook her head. *Why on earth would she know?*

"Jade Lina Valeno," Midnight said fondly. "She spent a lot of time here, too."

"Why?" Malina asked, studying the concern and concentration on Jade's face as she looked at Malina's body. *That's my aunt, my dad said I was named after her,* Malina thought as she noticed Jade's mouth move. She looked up at Midnight with a frown. "What's she saying? I can't hear her."

"She said she's fading fast. Are you sure it's only been three days," Midnight said, studying the water closely.

"It's felt like years," Malina commented. "Why did Jade spend time here?" Malina asked, again realizing she'd never gotten her answer.

"She was tricked by a close friend. She went after a relic that was infused with my megin that was too much for her to handle. It altered her, and during her metamorphosis, her soul escaped her," Midnight explained.

"What aren't you telling me?" Malina inquired. Midnight smiled and chuckled as she shook her head and looked away. After a time, she looked back to Malina and tilted her head.

"Why do you want to stay here?"

"Wh–" Malina started and stopped. She looked at the looking glass pond, then scrutinized her father's sad eyes.

"Why are you running from these people?" Midnight pried.

"It should have been me that died," Malina said, pulling at the grass on either side of her as she balled her hands. "The bullet that killed my friend only missed me because I tripped on the cement," Malina explained. "Can you believe that? Saved by clumsiness," Malina mused.

"So, you're killing yourself because you survived by a fluke?" Midnight stated, unamused.

"How can I continue to live life like everything is normal? Why do I deserve to live and he doesn't? He wanted to be—"

"It doesn't matter," Midnight said, interrupting her. "Greed killed him, and guilt is killing you."

"Azazel was selfless," Malina argued.

"Maybe," Midnight said with a shrug, "but the person who killed him wasn't."

"Do you know who killed him?" Malina asked, moving closer to the water. Midnight looked down at the woman whose hand began to glow as it waved over her.

"A man she hired named Khalan."

"Khalan," Malina repeated, playing with the name on her tongue to try and stir the faraway memory. "Do I know this person?" Malina asked.

Midnight frowned and shrugged. "I could use Aletheia to show you but only if you promise me something," Midnight bargained.

"What is that?" Malina asked, feeling guarded but vulnerable.

Midnight pointed to the pond, "Once I show you this, you *must* choose to live."

Hygeia Hospital
Carina

Carina arrived at the hospital feeling edgy and on guard. The amount of Askari around bothered her. *They've doubled their numbers since yesterday. Jezabel must know this, does she still think they can pull this off*, Carina thought, walking through the front door to the front desk. She smiled at the man at the front desk, and he rose and left to retrieve Jezabel. Jezabel wasn't only Margherita's oldest and longest friend but her oldest sister.

Over the years, she spent a lot of time at Hygeia because of Jezabel's profession as an RN. When Carina was growing up, Margherita would drop her off with Jezabel so that she would be entertained. Carina hated it at first, but over time, she came to love it. She watched Jezabel bring someone back to life and realized that this was what she wanted to do with her life. Be helpful and strong so she could save anything and anyone.

Gabriel believed in her and encouraged her at every turn. She remembered meeting Gabriel for the first time behind these walls. *Timing is everything.* Carina remembered Margherita often telling her that. It didn't ring true to her until the day she met Gabriel.

"Why are you risking your life for this girl?" Carina asked Jezabel when she emerged at the desk.

"I risk my life every day for strangers, Carina," Jezabel responded with a raised eyebrow. "This is no different." She said walking down the hall to the elevator.

"This is *very* different, Aunt Jez," Carina said with a frown, crossing her arms over her chest. "Did you not see the army of Askari outside? They're going to arrest you and lock you away for opening a portal."

"Carina, what are you really concerned about?" Jezabel asked, stepping into the elevator as the doors opened.

"Just voicing my concerns," Carina grumbled, "I don't want to lose my family over a lost cause."

Jezabel's breathing hitched and her spine stiffened. Turning on Carina her eyes glimmered sliver-white like the moon. Carina lifted her chin unapologetic about her comment, but activated her megin to protect herself. Jezabel was hard to read; how she felt rarely matched how she portrayed herself. She'd mastered the skill, unlike Margherita. Although their backgrounds were similar, Jezabel's abuse lasted longer and came from someone who was supposed to protect her.

Despite the fiery orange and red hues that engulfed her. Jezabel smiled calmly and peacefully said, "This girl has a chance to live. I refuse to be the coward that watches her die," she pulled the bag from Carina's grasp and exited the elevator "You can go."

"I'm not letting you do this alone," Carina argued, ignoring the words of caution and followed Jezabel to the room.

"Then stand watch," she said, looking forward through the glass window. "Your attitude will only distract me from what needs to be done," she said and opened the door. Carina stood outside, feeling low and alone. "You two aren't supposed to be in here," Jezabel said, and Carina walked in.

Before them stood Jade and Victor. Victor appeared exhausted, content, and concerned. He stepped between Malina and Jade with open hands raised.

Jezabel dropped her bag full of what was needed for the portal on the floor. She placed her hands on her waist and looked past Victor to Jade.

"What are you two doing?" Jezabel asked.

"Visiting," Jade answered, peering down at Malina.

"We were looking at the rune that was placed on Malina," Victor directed to Jezabel. Jade glared at him and shook her head, "she can be trusted," he assured.

"You trust anyone with a sweet voice and assuring smile," Jade criticized. Jade pointed to the bag in Jezabel's hand, "What's in the bag?"

"I'm calling security—" Jezabel threatened, turning on her heel and bumping into Carina, and dropping the bag.

"Jez, that's not nes—what's all of that?" Victor inquired as Jade opened the bag and pulled out a wooden totem.

"They're moving her to Serinytas," Jade explained, placing the totem back into the bag. She back to Malina and illuminated her pointer finger.

"What are you ..." Jezabel started and stopped when Victor placed his hands on her shoulders.

"She's removing a rune. She needs to concentrate," Victor said gently and released her to stand at Jade's side.

Jezabel sighed and began setting up for the ritual. Carina knelt beside Jezabel, and helped her empty out the bag. Carina held onto the wooden totem of the baboon that mirrored the one Margherita had as Jezabel set up every other item for the ritual. Jezabel held out her hand for the totem; Carina hesitated but handed it to her. Jezabel placed her hand over Carina's and squeezed.

"Wait outside," she urged but spoke more gently than before.

Carina stepped out into the hallway feeling alone and fidgety. It had only been three hours since she last saw Jade, but Carina felt there was a difference in her. *A good difference,* Carina thought as her phone buzzed. She pulled it out of her pocket and placed it to her ear.

"Hello?" Carina answered.

"Are you on your way back?" Margherita asked.

"No," Carina sighed, "I'm gonna make sure everything goes okay before I go."

Margherita sighed and didn't say anything for a long time, "Carina," she said finally.

"Yes?"

"Under no circumstances do you perform this ritual," Margherita warned.

"I promise," Carina swore. Rapid beating from Malina's heart rate monitor caught Carina's attention. "I have to go, I love you Ma," she said and hung up the phone sticking her head in as Jade turned off the ventilator.

Victor rushed to her side, and she held him back. "Why would you—" Victor growled, reaching over her, and then noticed Malina's finger twitch and her chest rise and fall on its own. Victor grabbed Malina's hand and squeezed as he rubbed the crown of her head. "Baby girl, it's Daddy. Can you hear me?"

"Vic, I didn't pull her out of her coma," Jade said with sincere regret. "I didn't mean to give you false hope."

"I just thought," Victor said and then cleared his throat. "I saw her finger move ..."

Jade touched his arm. "I did all I can for her. She will come out of this, but it won't happen while she's staying here. Her soul is stuck in Limbus. The people in Serinytas will understand."

"How certain are you about her being in Limbus?" Jezabel asked, meeting her eyes.

"As certain as I am about Vic being my brother," Jade said and then turned her head abruptly. A bright light bloomed outside the window. The lights flickered and then went out completely. "This won't end well, Brother," she said with a sigh.

"Let me talk to them," he reasoned. Carina felt a rush of cold air and bone numbing malice. Her heart hammered in her chest as tears peppered her eyes. *So much death so much sadness.*

"What is it?" Jezabel demanded when Carina stood silent and shaking.

"Dante is outside," Jade stated.

Chosen

Carina paced beside Malina's sleeping body. Jade and Victor left the room to face Dante. Carina's nerves spiked with discomfort as she tried to push out the death creeping around her. *Will they really buy us enough time?* Carina wondered, watching Jezabel reset the altar for the third time. *Why isn't he coming? Is he still with Margherita? It shouldn't take this long,* Carina thought, tapping her finger impatiently against her bicep. The electricity in the room flickered back on and the cold numbness in her bones eased away.

Jezabel frowned, looking back to Carina and then to the door. *Did she just break out of the trance?* Carina thought in disbelief. *Where is she going?*

"Margherita didn't happen to teach you how to pray to Khonsu, did she?" Jezabel asked, rising to her feet.

"You know she did," Carina said, feeling more than a little overwhelmed.

"I have to check on my patients," Jezabel said walking to the door.

Carina blocked her exit, "You can't leave," Carina signed as frost covered the window.

"Do the ritual or don't I'm checking on my patients," Jezabel said, pushing Carina to the side.

"What about Rita?" Carina said, pushing Jezabel back.

"Rita isn't dying right now and neither is Malina, but those patients dependent on life support are. I have to help the other nurses reset the machines so we can save as many lives as we can. Now move," Jezabel demanded and shoved Carina so she could race out the room.

Carina stood stunned in place, "I promised Rita I wouldn't," she said to the empty room.

She thought of Gabriel and Margherita who most likely is doing the ritual right now. *How fast would they close in on her? With all the attention drawn there would she be able to get away?* Carina faced the altar. *If she would have just focused, she could have finished it*, Carina thought, feeling overwhelmed. *She knows what could happen to me, and she left anyway.* She looked at Malina's body and then to the altar. Carina rubbed her sweaty palms against her thighs and grabbed the chalice Jezabel had prepared for the ritual. Opening the bag of ocean water, she scrunched her nose up at the smell and began to pour.

"Khonsu, I summon you out of reverence and need. Please come," Carina said, pulling back the water flow and bowing her head. She closed her eyes and imagined the push and pull of the tide, mirroring the flow with her breath. She poured and bowed and repeated the plea until the ocean water filled the chalice.

Carina dabbed her finger into the ocean water and drew a crescent moon on her forehead. She felt a cool power flow through her body as she repeated the plea. She was uncertain if that was the power of Khonsu or Elizabeth's veil surrounding her. The shouting outside was harder to ignore, but she reminded her this is what needed to be done to save a life. Everyone around her was fighting hard for Malina, so it would be remiss of her to let them down. But what did she care about the girl? *I wouldn't shed a tear if she died*, Carina thought absentmindedly.

The sound of an ocean wave vocalized in her ear: "Then why have you brought me here?"

Carina froze, terrified of the mistake she had just made. *A priestess must have a clear mind when in front of a god, Carina.* As Margherita's urgent reminder echoed through her mind, Carina slowly rose to a kneeling position, her eyes glued to the midnight blue and speckled with bright white stars.

"Meet my eyes," the young man demanded.

Trembling, Carina obeyed.

The young man had midnight blue skin and eyes so white they glowed like the stars above. The hair on his head was gray and shaved except for one patch, which was braided down to his shoulder. His long gray beard was groomed and curved at the end, signifying his god status. He hadn't aged at all since the last time she saw him.

"You're still strangely beautiful," she said aloud.

The god smiled and offered her his hand. "Where can I take you?" he asked.

"It's the girl," Carina said, keeping her hands on her thighs.

"The one you don't care for?" he asked, tilting his head to the side. He dropped to one knee and touched her hand. His nighttime hue faded into a muddy dark-brown complexion, and his stary eyes faded to a soft gray. "Why do you want me to save her?"

"Someone I care for wants her to live," she said honestly.

"I see," Khonsu replied, grabbing her hand and flipping it over, proceeding to rub his fingertips lightly over her palm. "To Serinytas," he said, staring with bright near white eyes.

"Yes," Carina said softly, the hair on her arms rising—almost pulling her from the trance. "Will you do this for me?" she asked, pulling her attention back to the man in front of her, tightening her hand in his. He blinked, looking down at their hands.

"If you come, too," he said.

The saliva in her mouth dried, and her heart pounded, but she nodded.

"Voice your response," he demanded.

"I'll go to Serinytas if you bring along Malina," she said intentionally. He smiled at her and released her hand, walking past her to Malina.

The baboon totem cracked open, and a white orb with grey spots hovered in front of her body. The orb began to rotate and mimic the lunar phases. The flickering light grew, and then the room was enveloped in darkness. A chill fell over Carina, and when she looked up beside her, Khonsu mirrored the night sky. Malina hung haphazardly over his shoulder, and he held out a hand to her.

"Rise," he ordered. Carina obeyed immediately, taking his hand.

"Carina," she heard the awe in Jezabel's voice and wondered briefly if this was her plan all along.

Carina stared into the god's eyes as the moon-like orb engulfed them, turning through the phases of the moon, and she felt a wave of heat warm her. Khonsu dropped Malina on the sandy floor, and before Carina could determine where they were, the orb engulfed them again. When the orb opened, she was met with the same heat. She appeared to be in a temple dedicated to the old gods. Margherita often spoke of the place, but Carina had never believed it would look like this. The temple had high ceilings, and the walls had artwork that told the stories of the gods that once walked the earth in this region. Margherita had told her they used to appeal to other gods that protected those who gave up pieces of themselves as a sacrifice. Margherita's mother was a priestess and knew the gods intimately Margherita would have too, but Jezabel spirited them away.

Carina looked at the murals that depicted the moon and starry night sky. A blue young man with a staff and braided locs. He had a moon disk on his head, and beside him was a woman with dark-brown skin and red-brown eyes. Her dark-black hair was curly, and thick on top of her head was a golden crown of a vulture, on top of which rested a peculiar hat. To her, it looked like a red throne and a white wine bottle that sat on the throne. A thin spiral fabric branched out from behind the throne. To the left of the night-sky man was a man with the complexion of a cloudless blue sky. On his head was a sun disk and what looked to be two large goose feathers.

Underneath the art was an altar that sat a bowl of water, bread, a board game, and a peculiar soft rock that reminded her of the moon. Carina reached out to touch an item on the altar when Khonsu grabbed her hand and pulled her away from the altar.

"That's you," Carina said.

Khonsu nodded.

"Does this mean I'm a priestess now?"

He nodded again. "She's here," Khonsu announced and then faded away into an orb of light that floated into a skillfully carved statue.

Carina watched him fade into the statue she was about to touch as footsteps neared where she stood. A woman in a robe stood before her when she turned. As she dropped the hood from her head, a dark-complected woman with shiny purplish-blue eyes was revealed. She had a crescent moon drawn on her forehead and a head full of locs.

"Welcome to Kanrak."

Resentment
Elizabeth

For the second time in twenty years, Elizabeth felt butterflies in his stomach. She was going to kill Jade, but despite everything she had done, Elizabeth wouldn't find comfort in her passing. Dante, who stood at her side, felt differently. He itched to cage his only love, and as the elevator slowly climbed, she wondered how it had come to this.

"We all used to be family," Dante said suddenly.

"What?" Elizabeth asked, stunned. The elevator warmed, and as she thought over what he said. "You don't consider us family?"

"You'll always be my sister," he said as the elevator came to a stop, "but you know that's not what I mean." The lights flickered, and he stepped to the back of the elevator, bracing himself in case the whole thing fell.

Someone's frantic voice came over the radio. "Electrokinetic spotted."

"Detain them and get these elevators working!" Kaleen demanded.

"She spoke. Will we be affected?" Elizabeth asked alarmed.

"No. Her megin doesn't carry like that," Dante said. "She must not like closed spaces ..."

"Everyone has a weakness," Elizabeth stated, looking around the metal death trap they stood in. "If you give me a boost, I can open the hatch to see if we're close to the next floor."

"No. We need to talk about what will happen when we see Jade," Dante said, and he felt the temperature drop around them again. "Liz?" Dante said carefully.

"Jade doesn't need your protection, Dante." Elizabeth said.

"That type of thinking is the reason we're in this mess in the first place—because no one wanted to protect her."

"Because she doesn't need it!" Elizabeth snapped.

"She does!" Dante reasoned. "Jade has been through more shit than the rest of us combined."

"You forget Victor is her brother and he was right there with her through the same abuse."

"He wasn't forced through a five-day pregnancy," Dante said, rolling his eyes.

"It's been—"

"Fifteen years isn't going to erase that pain, Liz. What if you had to give up Evaline?"

"Evaline had a sister that died," Elizabeth reminded bitterly, "I didn't have go off on a killing spree when my child was taken without my consent." She seethed. "I didn't recruit a group of misfits to kill on my command while forcing my brother to raise my child! You claim she must be so tortured or insane because of what she went through, but it all seems calculated to me. So, while you and my idiot husband defect, trying to protect her, I'm going to do what neither of you can and put her down for good."

"Elizabeth, I'm not going to let you do that," Dante said in a dark tone.

"Did you know Malina is hooked up to a ventilator because she can't breathe on her own?" Elizabeth said matter of factly. "It's been three minutes, and the elevator still isn't working. How do you think that ventilator is doing? Who do you think that electrokinetic is working for?"

The elevator jerked, and Elizabeth squatted to brace herself, sighing when it started to move up. She didn't look back at her brother and he didn't say anything else to her. Elizabeth passed the time by watching the floor numbers illuminate until they settled on the level they needed to be on.

"What do you mean we *used* to be family?" Elizabeth inquired.

"Things changed when Jade left," Dante stated.

"That was her choice," Elizabeth said as the doors opened.

"Jade you can't keep running off ..." Victor's voice drifted to Elizabeth's ears from her right.

Elizabeth stepped out of the elevator, her megin concentrated in her hand, which she pointed at Victor's back. A bright light blinded her, making her instinctively pull her megin back. She covered up to her eyes to protect them from further damage. A small hand punched her, making her stumble toward the wall. She heard her brother yell, but her mind was still reeling from the light and pain. A hand gripped her arm, and she gripped that hand with her own channeling megin into her flesh.

Jade's melodic voice sounded: "Tricky tricky."

Elizabeth pushed her megin harder against Jade's skin, but instead of the usual screams of discomfort she drew from her victims, Jade just laughed. Elizabeth snatched her hand back at the sting of heat that emitted from her skin. Jade swung her fist and Elizabeth dodged, using her megin to feel the heat in the room. She crouched down, ducked her head, and lunged at Jade's stomach, slamming her against the wall.

Jade's hot hands grabbed Elizabeth's shoulders, burning through her clothing and melting the leather to her skin. Elizabeth cried out, and strong arms wrapped around her waist, picking her up off Jade. Elizabeth fought against the warm body, ignoring the grunts of pain. As soon as the man dropped her to the ground, she attempted to move him out of the way. His grip tightened on her biceps, and he pressed her against the wall.

"Lizzie stop," Victor pleaded, low and rough against her ear.

Elizabeth flinched away from his warmth. "Vic, get away from me," Elizabeth warned, pressing herself against the wall, not wanting to hurt him.

"If she hurts my brother, I'm killing her, Dante," Jade yelled.

"Lizzie isn't going to hurt me, Jade," Victor said in an exasperated tone. "Can you open your eyes?" he asked, releasing her bicep to touch her face.

"Vic, don't," Elizabeth warned again.

"Vicky, you saw what I saw. She was going to blast you in the back," Jade said.

"Is she permanently blind?" Victor asked, touching Elizabeth's cheek despite her protest and the cold nip that met his finger.

"She will be if she tries that shit again," Jade warned. "Dante, you're next if you keep—"

"Did you try to kill Malina?" Dante interrupted.

"She didn't," Victor said at the same time Jade said, "I didn't."

"The electricity went out," Elizabeth stated, blinking her eyes open her vision slowly returning.

"That wasn't Jade," Victor said quickly.

"I don't control electricity," Jade reminded them impatiently. Elizabeth's eyes landed on Jade stepping away from Dante as he stepped closer. Jade rose a glowing hand to his face. "Stop."

"No," Dante said, taking her hand to cool it with his darkness. "Did you hire Khalan to kill Azazel?"

Jade quieted stepping further back into the hallway as Dante...

"Yes or no, Lina." Elizabeth heard her brother's deep voice say.

"It's not that simple," Jade said, pulling at her hand. "Dante stop," Jade demanded and lifted her other hand—filled with megin—to his face.

"No," he said, taking that hand as well and dimming her light with his darkness. "Not this time. You had your chance to leave. If you wanted to face this, face me."

"No, I wanted to see her," Jade said, shaking her head. "I can't do *this*. Let me go," Jade said, frantically pulling at her hands and backing away from him.

"Jade!" Victor yelled.

"Let them go," Elizabeth said with a grunt as she tried to rise to her feet. Her head swam and vertigo refused to allow her to find her footing. "Help me?"

"I am," Victor said his voice laced with concern as he held her tighter.

"Walk me to Malina's room," she said closing and covering her eyes.

"You're crowding me," Jade complained. "You didn't use to be this dark."

"You were my light, Lina," Dante said. Elizabeth rolled her eyes feeling more steady as the pain subsided. She placed a hand on the doorknob chancing a glance toward her brother.

"Let go of me," Jade hissed.

"I can't," Dante said with a frown. "I have to take you back to base. No one else can handle you," he reasoned.

"You can't handle me, Dante," Jade said softly.

Elizabeth stepped toward them when she noticed her brother tense and cover his eyes. Victor's hand on her body stopped her from leaving his side. Elizabeth heard light and fast footsteps rushing away she walked toward Dante and Victor pulled her back.

"Let me go," Elizabeth said, turning back to her husband.

"Dante, don't make me do this," Jade warned.

A flash of light warmed the back of Elizabeth's skin guilt filled her as she watched him grimace with pain. She wrapped them both in her megin and rushed them into the room. In the room she knelt before Victor who still grunted with pain.

"Lina, you can't keep hurting people!" Dante yelled.

"Are you okay?" Elizabeth asked Victor cupping his squirming face as she tried to look at his eyes.

"She's gone," a haunted female nurse said snatching Elizabeth's attention.

Elizabeth looked around the empty room and rushed to the bed that was still warm. Elizabeth grabbed the nurse's arm chilling it to cause the right amount of pain that pushed away shock and focused the brain. The nurse snapped out of her daze and focused on Elizabeth.

"Let me go," the nurse demanded pulling away from Elizabeth, but her vise grip was stronger.

"Where did she go?"

"I don't know," the nurse said through chattering teeth.

Elizabeth found Victor with his back facing her as he knelt in front of an altar. *He knows something,* Elizabeth thought with displeasure.

"Victor, stay with her," Elizabeth demanded, "we're taking her in."

"Okay," Victor said cuffing her with robotic motions.

"Dante, she's gone," Elizabeth said, anger lacing her tone at the sight in front of her.

Dante had Jade in his hold. One hand cradled the back of her head as he kissed her like his life depended on it. He pulled away and wrapped his arms around her holding her tighter.

"Dante did you hear me?" Elizabeth snapped Victor coming to stand beside her.

Dante stiffened against Jade. He sighed and pushed her away slightly to look down at her. She stared up at him with defiant eyes, despite the hand he had on her throat, and she lifted her head, taunting him. He shook his head at her, grinding his jaw.

"Where is she?" Dante demanded.

"Safe," Jade promised, "I had to buy her time."

"From us?" Dante asked.

Jade shook her head. "From Ralceo."

The Messenger
Tracy

Tracy stood in before the Fields of Belladonna store front and nervously tapped her fingers against her thighs. The past three months had been a roller coaster of emotions. Her best friend and the love of her life died; her other best friend ghosted her and then fell into a coma the day they reconnected. Gabriel checked in when he could, but he wasn't enough to satisfy her sadness. Not when he could have killed Azazel.

Gabriel could never do that! Tracy argued with Matoya almost every day for months—to the point that Matoya and her family stopped bringing it up around her. Tracy didn't know what all was said at Kore's Palace, but they were being more distant. She wanted to talk to Matoya about Astra being in the hospital. She wanted to visit, but she didn't want to go by herself, and Gabriel wasn't answering his phone.

Tracy pulled out her phone and looked at Matoya's location to make sure that she was in the right location. *Is she in the forest? There's her car,* she noted spotting the beat up red car off to the side. Tracy hesitantly walked to the edge of the forest and heard distant loud voices. *I think that's Lonnie,* she thought fondly swallowing the guilt that came with the butterflies in her stomach. Taking a breath she slowly and carefully followed the his voice through the unruly forest floor.

"Why are we here and not at your shop?" Lionel complained.

"Lonnie I told you, Bella can't be seen in town," Tirany said gently.

"Why?" he demanded.

"Because I'm finishing what you couldn't," Bella explained, making Tracy falter in her step and break a branch.

"Who is that!" Matoya yelled.

"It's me," Tracy said coming out of the darkness into the clearing in the meadow.

"Wh—Tracy what are you doing here?" Matoya demanded.

"I wanted to talk to you, and you weren't answering," Tracy said shyly. She chanced a glance at Lionel, but his stiff back was turned away from her.

"So, you just showed up? How did you know where I was?" Matoya asked with a frown.

"Never mind that," said Tracy dismissively. "What do you mean you finishing what they couldn't?" she directed Azazel's grandmother.

"Tracy, you can't be here," Tirany said, stepping between Tracy and Bella.

"I'll only answer questions to Tracy," Bella's raspy voice said.

Tirany stilled, and Matoya's eyes glowed briefly with irritation. Lionel, walked to the old woman glaring down at her face. Tracy walked past Tirany and shoved Lionel in the chest like she had often since being at their home.

"Back off, old man," Tracy demanded, chasing the buzz of fighting someone so unstable and violent.

"Tracy," Tirany said in warning.

"She could have said Azazel's life," Lionel growled.

"Where is he?" Tracy demanded, ignoring the tightening in her throat.

"What?"

"I don't see him," Tracy continued, "so it seems to me that this abuse isn't bringing Azazel back," Lionel clamped a hand around her throat his eyes darkening with his violent intent.

"I'm getting tired of you clinging to my family and acting all high and mighty," he growled. "You aren't a part of this family and you aren't wanted around here. If we thought you *deserved* to know the truth about Zay, we would have made sure you were here ourselves."

"Lonnie, let her go!" Tirany demanded.

"Dad, what the hell?" Matoya said.

Lionel squeezed her throat and then gently released his rough thumb scrapping her smooth skin. Tracy took a physical step back, feeling more harmed by his words than his actions. It wasn't the first time she'd been abandoned, and she knew it wouldn't be the last. She did, however, believe this would be the first time it shocked the air from her lungs, as it shook her reality. *"Dad, what the hell?" wasn't a denial,* Tracy thought as she blinked away the pain and lifted her head. Tracy turned to face the old woman, remembering the raspy words she spoke earlier.

Tracy released a sharp breath taking in the sight of the old woman. She had bruises on her wrist, and her brown skin and gray eyes reminded her of Azazel. She blinked, feeling extremely stupid. *This is Azazel's grandmother.* Tracy looked at Tirany and frowned, horrified at the thought.

"How could you let him do this to your mother?" Tracy exclaimed.

"We need answers," Tirany interjected gently. "That makes it better?" Tracy asked and then blinked in shock.

"What do you want to know Tracy?" Bella said with a disinterested sigh.

"Ask her—"

"Is your name Tracy?" Bella snapped.

"She doesn't know what to ask! She doesn't know what we need to know!" Tirany exclaimed.

"Not my problem," Bella said with a shrug. "She loved him too ..." her words quieted the room.

"This is bullshit," Lionel said, shaking his head.

Lionel pulled out his phone and tapped on the screen in an angry fast rhythm. Bella sighed and raised an eyebrow, as a ding sounded on Tracy's device. A smile tugging at Bella's face in amusement. Tracy pulled out her phone and looked over the questions.

"How could she know about Azazel's death before it happened?" Tracy inquired.

"Because I'm a seer," Bella said rolling her eyes, "and yeah, I did know," she said sadly.

"Why didn't you say anything?"

"I saw his death the day he was born," she clarified. Tirany gasped, and Matoya went to her side. "There was nothing that could be done but enjoy the moments I did have with him," she said sadly.

"Do you know who killed him?" Tracy asked.

"That's not a question we wrote," Lionel said.

"That's the question I'm asking," Tracy snapped.

Lionel's eyes flared. "You're wasting our time!"

"I have nothing more important to do today," Tracy stated, throwing her hands up. "What's the rush?" she demanded.

"Yeah, Lonnie," Bella taunted. "What's the rush?"

Lonnie stepped toward Bella, and Tracy grabbed his forearm in warning. He looked back at Tracy with rage-crazed eyes. Lionel pointed to his chest, which heaved with every breath he took, and then brought his index finger and thumb a breath apart.

"I'm this close to knowing why Gabriel killed my boy," Lionel said.

"Gabriel didn't—"

Lionel grabbed Tracy's jaw, squeezing it painfully, stopping Tracy from talking. Tracy swung at and hit Lionel's arm in an attempt to make him loosen his painful grip—but to no avail.

"She isn't wrong," Bella said, rolling her eyes.

"What?" all three people said, and Lionel dropped Tracy's face. Bella raised her eyebrow and looked at Tracy expectantly.

"I'm not asking anything else until Lionel leaves," Tracy said, touching her sore jaw with her fingertips.

"I deserve to be here a hell of a lot more than you!" he protested.

"My face says otherwise," Tracy said coldly.

"We need him here," Matoya said.

"You said without a doubt it was Gabriel!" Lionel roared, turning his anger on Matoya. Tirany stepped closer to her daughter. "I'm talking with her," Lionel growled.

"You will not lay hand on my child," Tirany declared protectively.

"I know what I saw!" Matoya snapped. "It was Gabriel!"

"It wasn't! She just told you it wasn't!" Tracy said, shaking her head in disbelief. "No wonder Henrik is facing time for this," Tracy muttered.

"What the hell is that supposed to mean?" Matoya demanded, walking toward Tracy.

"69 percent of wrongful convictions are due to misidentification by an eyewitness," Tracy explained.

"I wasn't wrong. There's a picture—"

"We live in a world where people can see into the future," Tracy said, pointing to Bella. "How crazy would it be that someone forged that picture?"

"But Henrik wasn't there!"

"Neither was Gabriel! He wasn't in the country!" Tracy argued. "Who killed Azazel?" Tracy asked, directing the question at Bella.

"Khalan," said Bella matter-of-factly.

"You see," Tracy said with sweaty palms and a queasy stomach. "Khalan isn't Gabriel."

"No, just his father," Lionel said with a somber expression.

"Khalan killed my boy?" Tirany asked in a pained tone. "I thought he was your friend," she added, looking at Lionel. "Did you do something to Khalan?"

"How could you ask me that?"

"He was your friend!" Tirany snapped, "He wouldn't have—"

"Jade," Matoya said, "don't forget she had a part to play in this ..."

"Who is Jade?" Tracy asked.

"Malina's mother," Bella said, staring up at the ceiling.

"Malina's mother?" Tracy repeated, "but Malina's mother is—"

"That's not important. We aren't here about your friend," Matoya said.

Tracy looked down at the phone in her hand and sighed. She burned with all the questions she wanted to ask. *Why are they rushing me? Who is Jade? Because Elizabeth is Malina's mother. Why would Azazel be important enough to kill? Why won't Bella talk to them directly? Why am I so important?*

"Why am I important?" Tracy asked.

Bella dropped her eyes from the sky to Tracy's face. "You *aren't*," she said simply.

"But then why—"

"Can you *please* stick to the fucking questions that I sent you?" Lionel asked.

"What are you buying time for?" Tracy demanded, ignoring Lionel.

"The portal," Bella said.

"Portal to where?" Tracy asked as Bella's eyes glowed, near white, and a smirk tugged at her lips.

"Serinytas. She made it."

"She who?" Tracy asked and stepped closer to Bella, feeling the sudden need to hold onto her.

"Malina," Bella explained, looking at her as Tracy held her hand.

The hair on Tracy's arms rose, and goosebumps pimpled her flesh. Tracy felt a surge of electricity course through her. *What is this feeling*? Tracy wondered, suddenly feeling afraid, and pulled away. Bella held her hand tighter and pressed her thumb to Tracy's head. Tracy's eyes rolled to the back of her head as her mind blanked and she saw Malina's flushed face ... with a bloody hole through the top of her head. Tracy jerked back and fell on her butt as more images flashed through her mind. "What is all of this it doesn't make sense?"

"Where did she go," Lionel's deep voice barked.

A soft hand touched Tracy's shoulder, when Tracy looked to her right she saw Matoya's worried gaze. "Are you alright?"

"I-I think so?" Tracy stuttered out her mind felt like it was being split into.

"Did she show you something?" Matoya asked.

"My head ..." Tracy replied placing both hands to either side of her head when the pain started to become too much.

"Too damn bad," Lionel's impatient voice said.

"Lonnie—" Tirany began.

Tracy felt his rough hand in her hair yanking her face up to meet his, "Tell me what you saw!" he barked.

Despite the blinding pain that greedily stole her vision and voice Tracy managed a steady, "No."

The Incident
Astra

Midnight stood before Malina and lifted her to the moon above and then down to the pond where the moon sat beautifully in the middle. She hovered her hands over the looking glass, and then her hands shimmered with purple fog. Malina stared at her reflection in the pond until it disappeared and another image appeared.

An older man lay on a dock of the ship. He had thick curly black hair, a reddish brown complexion, and red eyes. *Gabriel?* Malina thought with a frown and then shook her head. *No, this man is someone else*, she concluded, suddenly feeling shaky. Across the dock were white candles with various symbols carved into the wax. Without warning, the orange flames took on a purple hue as a white light snapped into the atmosphere. Emerging from the light was the woman she'd seen before, but there was something different about her. The green eyes she saw before had gray flecks in them now. *Interesting.*

Jade walked toward the man and sat beside him, gazing up at the sky above.

The man beside her smiled and released a soft chuckle.

Jade raised an eyebrow and looked down at him with intrigue. "What's funny, Khalan?"

"Just thinking about what the end would feel like," he mused.

"Khalan is Gabriel's father," Malina said with sudden understanding, looking up to Midnight's emotionless face. "I didn't realize he looked so much like that man ... He always looked like his mother to me," Malina said thoughtfully.

"I've found you only see in people what you want to believe fits your narrative of them best," Midnight said objectively.

Malina smiled weakly and redirected her attention to the pond of Aletheia. Jade was standing and stretching. Then, she stilled herself and pulled out a piece of paper and three black boxes with a ribbon wrapped around them. *What's that?* Malina thought, shifting her weight.

"What have you got in the boxes?" Khalan asked, rising to his feet, his body bobbing and swaying in tandem with the sea.

"Incentive," Jade said with a soft smile.

"Incentive for what?" Khalan asked in a hard voice. "I always finish my contracts."

"This one is special," said Jade. She held the paper out and then pulled it back when he reached for it. "You might not have the stomach to finish it."

"Give me the damn paper," he snapped and snatched the contract from her hand.

As Khalan read over the contract, Malina thought distantly, watching Jade's body language while she walked to the railing of the ship. *Did she hire him to kill Gabriel's mom?*

"Kalair Valor?" he said incredulously, staring at the back of Jade's head. "Jade," he said in a dark tone when she didn't turn back to him.

"Yes?" she said with a bright smile that never extended to her dead eyes. She turned to face him, leaning against the side of the ship.

"You can't expect me to kill my twin, you psycho," he snarled and Jade pouted.

"You know I don't like that word," she said in a sad childlike voice.

"Jade!" he barked.

She rolled her eyes and walked over to him, plucking the contract from his hands and rolling it up.

"What are you doing?"

"I'll give the job to someone else," she said, shrugging.

"You can't kill my brother," he argued. Jade rolled her head back and looked up at him. "I'm pretty sure I could," she said with raised eyebrows.

"Damn it, Jade!" Khalan yelled and grabbed her arm.

Malina watched a silver hue roll off Jade into Khalan, whose knees wobbled as his skin flushed. He released his hold on her and looked up at her face. Jade placed a hand over his face and tsked, guiding his head down until he dropped to his knees. She moved her hand away from his face, and he glared at her with defiant hatred. She held up two fingers, eyeing him carefully before she spoke again.

"You have two choices Khalan," she said slowly so there was no misunderstanding. "You take the contract or allow me to give it to someone else," she stared at him with an unwavering enjoyment as she watched his anger and frustration build. "Tick tock," she taunted.

"What's in the boxes?" he growled. Jade channeled her megin to her finger and drew a rune on the box before opening it. "Snapdragons," Malina and Khalan said and gasped in unison. "You found them," he said in awe.

"I thought they were a myth," Malina muttered.

"Yes," Jade said with a little smile. "I do apologize for the wait," she said with what seemed to be legitimate remorse.

"I can't believe ..." Khalan reached for the box, and Jade pulled back immediately, her face hardening with displeasure.

"Incentive," she reminded him.

"Can I bargain?" Khalan said, resting his hands on his thighs.

"Unfortunately not for your brother or Juniper."

"Juniper?" Malina muttered with a sense of grief.

"They're too close, but Azazel ..." Her face softened into something reminiscent of regret—or hope. Malina couldn't tell. She shook her head and sighed. "Give Azazel a message ..."

"What message can I give him that I can't give to my own twin?" Khalan demanded.

"Stop looking for Hiboria," Jade said simply.

"You don't think Kalair will listen?" Khalan asked with a frown.

"They found Hiboria," Jade said and shook her head. "They won't stop traveling there now."

"But—" Khalan began and stopped when Jade showed him the box. The rune she drew brightened and then disappeared.

"Take the contract on these terms, and I'll give you one box now," Jade said.

"And the others?" he repeated.

"At the very end of your contract, so if you mess up ..." She shrugged, leaving him to interpret the rest.

"I don't mess up," he said firmly.

Midnight waved her hand over Aletheia, and the image changed.

Khalan was standing on top of an abandoned building a block away, pacing on the roof. His hands twitched with what Malina imagined to be impatient nerves. He cracked his knuckles, and the view suddenly altered, so Malina could see what Khalan saw.

A bobbing head of locs. *Azazel's head*, Malina thought with her heart in her throat. He settled the gun on a stand and set the timer and controls before pulling out a remote that had a camera that showed his target.

"He could have just talked to Zay," Malina said in a thick voice of emotion.

Khalan walked to the edge of the building, channeling his megin as he dropped off the building. Landing on his feet in a crouching position, he looked at his device, watching Azazel walk out of the building. Khalan adjusted the sights, accounted for the wind, and then set the timer for five seconds and began walking away.

"You chose to kill him," Jade said, making him stop.

"I didn't hear you walk up," Khalan commented. Jade shrugged.

"I don't pay you to sense me," she commented.

"Why are you here?" Khalan demanded.

"I'm here to make sure you completed at least one of the tasks presented to you," she said with bored displeasure.

"What?" Khalan demanded. "Everyone on the list is dead," he said evenly and advanced toward her.

Malina looked away from the pond. "I don't want to see—"

"You should watch until the end," Midnight suggested.

Malina frowned and looked back to Aletheia.

The gunshot rang out, and then there was silence, which was broken with screaming and wailing. Jade frowned in front of him—something akin to agony twisted on her face. She began walking toward the noise in a dreamlike state.

"SOMEONE, HELP ME! PLEASE!" Matoya bellowed.

"I'm supposed to be the one screaming," Malina said with a frown. She watched Jade squint her eyes and then flushed with anger and hurt.

"What?" Khalan said, almost amused "You don't want to be faced with ..." Khalan's breath caught, and pain spread through the back of his head. Jade was squeezing his throat and pinning him to the wall. "J ..." he tried to breathe out. He was equally terrified and furious. Jade's eyes were a silver-green, gleaming with pure megin. Her hold trembled. She closed her eyes and then released him. He fell to his knees and caught his breath, bringing both hands to his throat, as he yelled after her—"Jade!"—but she was gone.

"She was crying," Malina commented coldly, "but she's the one that gave him the choice. She doesn't have a right to be upset ... wait what?" Malina said, near breathless.

Khalan walked closer to the shop, ignoring the young woman crying over Azazel, and knelt beside Malina's still body. Malina had a small hole in her head, and a small trail of blood leaked from the wound. Khalan reached out and caressed her cheek and rubbed his hand over her eyes to close them.

"Little Malina," he said in a tender voice.

"I don't … this doesn't make sense," Malina said her fist digging into the grass blades on either side of her legs. Her stomach flopped with queasiness and anger. She studied the image before her and noticed a golden glow from his pocket. *You're joking*, Malina thought bitterly.

"Gabriel, how could you?" Matoya yelled and raced toward him.

Khalan turned and watched her close the distance between them and then backhanded her when she was close enough. Matoya fell back and wiped at her bleeding lip and rose to her feet. Her eyes were filled with unshed tears, blurring her vision as she rose again and he grabbed her by the throat, pressing down on a pressure point and knocking her out.

"What have you done!" an older woman demanded, coming out of the shop.

Khalan sighed and pinched the bridge of his nose. He began to walk away when he felt a small tap against his foot. He knelt down beside Malina again, and she let out a small gasp and slow blink.

It was the snapdragons, Malina thought, seeing herself staring up at the sky with tears running down either side of her face.

The vision of herself chuckled, relishing in the anger on his face as he pulled out the black box and his once pink and white snapdragon bulbs wilted into tiny skulls.

With cold disassociation, Malina watched herself heal, strangely entranced by the way the bullet pushed out of her head and her flesh knitted together. The snapdragon flower was said to ward off death but watching necro majik in action sent chills down her spine. Her past self looked at Khalan with unfocused recognition as she moved to sit up. Khalan channeled his megin to his finger and drew the same symbol on her chest that Jade had drawn on the box.

Satisfied with the truth, Malina rose to her feet and turned away from Aletheia. As she walked through the brush, she could hear Midnight's quick feet follow behind her.

"Malina," she called, and Malina turned on her with raw emotion.

"He killed me," Malina snapped.

"It appears he also healed you," Midnight offered with a stoic expression stopping just in front of her.

"It was on accident," Malina commented, "he killed Azazel!" she said rage building.

"On the orders of Jade," Midnight said.

"She gave him an out!" Malina cried, shaking her head. "She gave him an out and decided to kill two innocent children!"

"You were an accident," Midnight said, but Malina shook her head.

"No, I'm vengeance," she declared.

"Malina," Midnight said, seeking to caution her.

"What is it?" Malina asked, standing right outside the door.

"Don't use your second chance at life to be weaponized for the sake of vengeance," Midnight warned.

"No," Malina said with a tight jaw. "I already did. I used it to cower and be afraid, but with this third chance, I *will* live with purpose," Malina said and walked through the door.

Revenge

Malina groaned and coughed, tugging at the plastic tubes on her face. She blinked her eyes open and yanked at the plastic stickers on her chest and temples. A hand grabbed at her, trying to shove her down, but she fought them off. Sounds were slowly echoing within the labyrinth of her consciousness. She opened her eyes but was met with nothing but darkness.

"Malina! Malina, please stop!" an unfamiliar male voice said.

"Let me go!" Malina yelled, closing and opening her eyes, praying for sight as she pushed away the stranger.

"You must calm down!" the male said.

"I said let me go!" Malina snapped, and then she felt a surge of megin burst from her.

There was no more restraint, and Malina didn't hesitate. Carefully, she moved to her unsteady feet. *Haiel, what's happening to me?* she wondered. Not expecting an answer, Malina took one step and fell to her knees. She blinked the blurriness from her eyes and frowned. *Everything hurts*, she thought but forced herself to crawl forward. As she neared the door, she was able to see clearly. She looked over to the man she'd shoved away and noticed how limp he was, *I hope he's all right*. Malina thought and clung to the doorframe as she pulled herself to her feet.

"Where am I?" Malina wondered aloud.

"*Serinytas*," Midnight's voice answered as her body grew stronger and warmer.

"I feel better," Malina marveled out loud. "Did you do that?" she asked, looking to her now steady feet.

"*Yes*," Midnight answered matter of factly.

Malina walked into the hallway of the building she was being held in and took in the exotic architecture. The place had tan walls made of clay, tall ceilings, and triangular windows. Malina blinked, confused, and began to walk forward, running her fingers over the roughness of the wall.

"Malina!" a distantly familiar voice said behind her.

Malina turned her head and saw a young girl gazing at her with bloodshot eyes. She ran toward Malina, and Malina pushed off the wall, holding a hand out to the girl, who stopped and held both hands up. Malina's attention shifted from the girl to the gray haze that surrounded her hand. *This is the same hue I saw circulating Jade's hand. Do I have her power now?*

"*No, not exactly,*" Midnight answered.

"Stay back," Malina warned the girl before her.

"*Let's talk about this later?*"

"Malina you should lie down," the girl cautioned.

"Don't call me that!" Malina snapped, "I don't know you," she explained.

"I'm Remilda," the girl offered. "I am Gabriel's friend. We thought you were dead," she said with a frown.

"Well, I'm not," Malina retorted. "Why am I here?"

"You were brought here so that we could save you."

"Well, if you thought I was dead, it must not have worked out," Malina said, glancing behind her to see if anyone else would arrive. "You're an ambassador," Malina commented, "so, where's your vizer?"

Remilda looked to the corner she had just come from, and a burgundy-haired woman stepped into view. "This is Rana. She's only here for my protection. She won't harm you," Remilda explained. "Aren't you tired?"

"I slept long enough," Malina said quickly.

"Of course," Remilda said and lowered her hands. Malina followed suit but refused to lower her mental guard.

"I need to get back to Ekocia. Is Gabriel here?" Malina asked.

"No," Remilda answered, looking away with a frown.

"Why not? Does he know I'm here?" Malina asked, stepping closer.

"I'm not sure?" Remilda said with a frown.

"What aren't you telling me?" Malina asked, stopping an arm's length away.

"I think you should rest," Remilda suggested and reached out to Malina. Malina pulled back to avoid contact, but Remilda's fingertips brushed Malina's arm.

An image of Gabriel flashed in Malina's mind coupled with strong feelings of guilt and worry. *What does she have to feel guilty about when it comes to Gabe?* Malina wondered, squinting her eyes at Remilda, studying her sad face, searching the mahogany eyes that wouldn't meet her own. Malina moved toward her, and Remilda's eyes snapped to her face with a frown, and then Malina was in her mind again. Malina was guided to Remilda's guilt and saw Remilda running away with Khalan, the Pharaoh's surprise, and Remilda pleading her case. The guards taking him away. *Away where?* Malina wondered with dismay.

Remilda looked away and took several steps back. "What did you do?" she demanded.

"Where is he?" Malina shot back.

"You can't—" Remilda began.

"Where the fuck is Khalan?!" Malina yelled, a headache of emotion overwhelming her, causing her to drop to her knees. "Any help, Midnight?" Malina beckoned, but the emotion continued to build.

Remilda dropped to a knee by her side. "Malina?" she asked cautiously.

"Remilda, get away!" Rana yelled but stopped and fell to the floor alongside her.

Just before they fell, Malina felt the pressure in her head release and blanket the chamber in black. Malina crawled toward their crumpled bodies and tentatively reached out to touch them.

"*Don't,*" Midnight warned.

"Are they dead? Did you do this?" Malina asked, watching the rise and fall of Remilda's chest, and calm cooled over her.

"*Yes, I did this,*" Midnight said calmly. "*You will find your answer more easily with them asleep,*" Midnight explained.

Malina frowned with displeasure. *This isn't right*, she thought, but she felt her answers flood her mind. The image of Khalan chained in a dungeon nearby showed in her mind like she was already in front of him. *Where?* Malina asked mentally, and at once, the directions there were known to her. In a daze, Malina walked to a nearby wall and pressed in a brick. There was a release of air as the wall popped apart, and behind it was a hidden staircase that led downward—deep into the darkness.

Malina hesitantly took one step down, using the light behind her until it dimmed as she moved down too far for the light to reach. Pressing her hand to the wall, using the roughness and the sound of a man singing poorly to guide her movements, Malina moved along slowly, eventually coming to a stop.

"*Will you move forward?*" Midnight asked.

"I-I don't know," Malina said, placing her shaking hand on the wall in front of her. When she pushed and the wall gave beneath her force, however, she felt more certain. Calming her nerves, she moved forward and stepped into the dungeon.

In the hall of the dungeon, Khalan's song cut off. *Can he sense me?* Malina pondered and walked toward where she spotted two hands hanging out of a cell. Malina suddenly felt small as she walked to the other side of the hall to see him better.

Khalan wore a serious expression—one of unremorseful anger—that melted into wonder and amusement. He pressed his forehead to the bars, his blood-red eyes watching her approach, and then his head tilted to the side.

"Is that little Malina?" Khalan asked.

Malina's words froze in her throat, and she wasn't sure what to say next. Her vision darkened, and then she felt like she was floating. Her body moved on its own, and with arms crossed, she found herself looking down at the man before her.

"You wish." The voice that sprung from Malina's throat wasn't her own. "She wants answers from you," the voice continued. "She's not ready for those answers just yet."

"Taking over her body is beneath you, don't you think, Jade?" Khalan said.

"I'm not Jade," the voice said, and with a wave of Malina's hand, the metal bars were reduced to dust. "But that doesn't matter. Stop breathing," she demanded as she advanced into his cage.

Khalan dropped to his knees, hands to his throat as choking sounds came from him. Malina watched her body walk around the room and sit atop a small bed, looking upon Khalan's agony with amused pleasure.

Epilogue

A man groaned awake as the sound of footsteps neared his sleeping form. He rolled his head to the side, prepared to deal with the disturbance quickly. Sitting up, he swung his feet to the ground and stood to his full height to face the sister he hadn't seen in two millennia. She had golden-brown hair picked out into an afro. Her golden eyes shone with cool disapproval, and her dark-brown skin shimmered, perfectly complimented by a red dress with black hoops. *She looks good ... healthy*, he thought happily and approached her for an embrace. Yet, his happiness fell the moment his arms passed through her translucent form.

"Oh," he said quietly.

"I'm not truly here, Brother," she said gently. "Have you been sleeping all this time?"

"I'm without family here," he stated. "I have no one to rule with. This is *not* what we wanted!"

"Haiel," she stated gently, "do not lose hope."

"Kami, have you found a way to fix this?" Haiel demanded.

"No," she said with evident regret. Silence built between them. "Haiel, she's back. You must stop her."

"Why?" Haiel demanded.

"Because she will kill you," Kami said.

"After what we did to these people, don't you think we deserve it?"

***

Lunis turned into the warm body beside him, moving his arm into the soft dip of the woman's body. He nestled his nose into the floral fragrance of her curly hair. She breathed out a heavy sigh and interlaced her hand with his. He kissed the crown of her waves and felt himself drift back to sleep.

A gush of frozen air sliced up his spine, tightening his chest and forcing his heart to race. He shot up immediately, breathing in fast, shallow breaths. He shivered with disgust as the recognition of the veil cleared his once foggy mind. He looked around the room he was sleeping in, searching for where the unwelcome guest would be. His eyes landed on wispy blue hair outside on the patio.

Lunis yanked the thin sheet from his half-nude body and walked outside, embracing the early dawn's warmth. The male entity that awoke him stared blankly out to the horizon. His usual warm terra-cotta complexion appeared pale, and his once vibrant blue hair was dull. He wore tan linen clothes that appeared worn and thin in some areas.

"What are you doing here, Haiel?" Lunis said gruffly, leaning his forearms against the railing of the patio.

"She's back," Haiel said simply. He sighed when Lunis didn't respond and turned his head to look at him. "This is bad for you," he insisted. Lunis shrugged, taking in the entity's pale appearance with loathing.

"More for you than me," Lunis admitted, "I killed her, but you and your siblings betrayed her," he elaborated. Haiel broke their eye contact and looked out to the horizon.

"You aren't afraid to die?" Haiel tilted his head and frowned at something Lunis couldn't see.

"My soul has been alive for over two thousand years … I crave the finality you stole from me." Lunis growled.

"It wasn't us that stole that from you," Haiel said calmly, unfazed by Lunis' wrath. "Your all-seeing friend did that. However, I can undo it," Haiel tempted.

"I want nothing from someone I don't trust," Lunis said quickly.

"Kami thought you might say that," Haiel commented and reached into his pocket, pulling out a locket with a protection sigil engraved in the copper metal.

"Where did you find that?" Lunis demanded, recognizing it instantly.

"It holds the soul of your late daughter Kaija," Haiel explained. "Hel does still exist, although we did dispose of the many gods ruling it," he said, clearing his throat and making the locket disappear. "The souls there just burn now."

"Enough," Lunis barked, his hands clenched into fists at his side.

"That's it?" Haiel mused, "I didn't even get to threaten Kaija properly," he pouted.

"I killed *her* before," Lunis said callously, "once she has a body—"

"It needs to happen now."

"I don't know what the host looks like; besides, they're innocent. I don't kill—"

"The host has died before, it's fine, and if you don't, I will toss your daughter's soul into—"

Lunis wrapped his hand around the entity's throat, absorbing his unlimited megin as he squeezed Haiel's throat with all his might. Haiel frowned, wrapped his meaty hand around Lunis' wrist, snapped it, and then placed his hand over Lunis' mouth, pressing his thumb and middle finger into the pressure points on his jaw.

"I hold your daughter's soul in my hands," Haiel reminded, "what you do and don't do will affect the outcome of where it resides. Kill the host, and you have nothing to worry about," Haiel stated, his vibrant blue eyes bore into Lunis' stubborn golden gaze. Haiel threw him to the floor with so much force his body bounced once before settling. When Lunis gained his breath back and he looked up to where Haiel once stood. He saw nothing but empty air.

"Lunis?" a worried sultry voice called.

Lunis did not move from the cement patio that was now indented with his body. The megin he absorbed had already healed him, but inside he was still broken. The godkiller was back, possibly with his siblings. Haiel looked frail and old, but still, Lunis could not do anything to harm him.

Most importantly, he had his eldest daughter's soul; how many others did he have? Lunis felt useless and stunned only two people could help them and neither of them would want to and both are supposed to be dead. An innocent must die soon or Kaija's soul will burn for eternity.

"Gods," Margherita's soft voice whispered as she crouched down beside him. She brought her soft hands near his flesh but pulled away when she was an inch away. "You're leaking bloodlust," she stated with a frown. "Lunis, what happened?" she asked in earnest.

Lunis shook his head and covered his face.

Acknowledgments

This has been the most emotionally draining yet rewarding process I've ever been through. From beginning to end, I want to thank **God** for consistently placing the exact person or situation in front of me to push me through my funk.

I would like to begin my thanks with my loving husband, **Carlos Luckie Jr.** Carlos, my best friend, confidant, sounding board, and inspiration. This book wouldn't exist without you. Your passion is so contagious and electrifying it pushed me through every block I had. Without you … this book would be VERY different, and you know the ending I'm talking about. Thank you for reading all the variations and rough drafts and talking me out of all the wrong ideas. Thank you for the voice inside my head that said, "This is trash; start again."

I'm indebted to my dearest friend **Ameari**. Thank you for lending me an ear to express my displeasure with the various stressors throughout the years and for giving me mental health days. Thank you for our awesome podcast, laughs, and perspectives. Thank you for breaking out of your genre of slice of life and being the first to read my fantasy novel. I swear I will turn you into a "fantasy girly."

To my sister of choice, **Celine**, may good fortune find you as it has me. I would not be who I am if it had not been for you. You are why I write, from random sheets of paper to blue notebooks shared between friends. You unknowingly taught me to keep my imagination flowing even when a random love interest appears from the dead to reclaim his mate. You sparked this fire in me to write, and I could never thank you enough.

I'm incredibly grateful to my **mother** for showing me how beautiful it is to be strong and independent, leading by example, and never wavering under the pressure of the world. Thank you for never pressuring me in any direction to please you and allowing me the room I needed to be my own person. You are an amazing woman and an even better mother. Thank you, I love you.

To my **father**, thank you for reminding me that I was royalty before it became a trend. The confidence you instilled in me has carried me through some dark times. You being a part of my life has taught me not to place my expectations on others and accept people for who they are. This has saved me a lot of headaches and heartaches. Thank you, I love you.

A huge thank you to **Global Book Publishing** for going on this journey with me, and an even bigger shout-out to **Susmita Dutta** for being a patient guide along the way.

Thank you, **Reginald Waller Jr.** for believing in the vision and being a number one supporter. Thank you Jonah Levingston for the artwork that brought the concept of Alethia into focus.

Lastly, I would like to thank myself for not giving up on myself. Thank you Ebony, for growing and taking the criticism, and choosing to adapt and learn instead of throwing your dream away. Thank you for picking up books outside of your taste to learn what makes them great. Thank you for staying curious and having an open mind during tough conversations. Above all else thank you for listening to Syre and developing Lunis.

About the Author

Chellé Luckie was raised in Enterprise, AL and currently resides in Savannah, GA with her husband Carlos Luckie Jr. In her spare time she reads for pleasure and her podcast Book Talk -w- Luckie Jones. When she isn't reading she's gaming or bingeing her favorite true crime show.

 chelle.luckie
 @LuckieAuthor
 chelleluckie@gamil.com

www.ingramcontent.com/pod-product-compliance
Lightning Source LLC
Chambersburg PA
CBHW071157020726
47502CB00002B/450